Dear Miss CUSHMAN

Paula Martinac

Bywater *BOOKS*

2021

Bywater Books

Copyright © 2021 Paula Martinac

Print ISBN: 978-1-61294-215-5

Bywater Books First Edition: December 2021

Printed in the United States of America on acid-free paper.

Cover design by TreeHouse Studio

Bywater Books
PO Box 3671
Ann Arbor MI 48106-3671

www.bywaterbooks.com

The writing of this novel was generously supported by a
2019-20 Creative Renewal Fellowship from the Arts and
Science Council of Charlotte-Mecklenburg.

Culture For All.

For the unabashed theater geeks and nerds.

Chapter 1

New York City, 1852

When the audience began hissing, I knew *Othello* wasn't going to end well. Their response jolted me. We weren't at the Bowery Theatre, where the audience in the pit tossed apples and vegetables onto the stage if a performance didn't please them. The Prince Theatre was one of New York City's finest establishments, catering to the upper ten.

Worse, the actor they hissed at was my father.

I was attending my first theatrical performance ever. Incredible, given that my father was a renowned leading actor, but Mama maintained that theater wasn't a place for young ladies. For my eighteenth birthday, she gave in to my pleading and permitted Uncle James to accompany me to my father's performance of the Moor, one of his most acclaimed roles. Mama insisted I have a new dress, and my sister Maude *oohed* and *aahed* over the sky blue taffeta until I wanted to take it off and give it to her. I myself put little stock in puffy lady things, especially in pastel hues. Plus, the heavy horsehair crinoline the skirt required for shape made beads of sweat trickle down my stomach.

Still, I could abide these discomforts if it meant I got to sit beside my dapper uncle in his lushly adorned box, draped with red and gold silk, and marvel at the glistening gas-jet chandelier that lit the space. Best of all, I got to watch my father tread the boards as I'd imagined him doing, in full costume and makeup for the Moor and sporting his prize sword.

We were barely one act in when Pa dropped a few lines. Then more—even the ones I ran with him that morning "for good measure," as he'd urged. He'd appeared in *Othello* dozens of times, but now the role appeared to baffle him. Although the movement made my stays pinch, I leaned forward, mouthing the words, willing them into his memory.

Taunts rose slowly through the cavernous parquet. Pa squinted toward the footlights in bewilderment, but then the leading gentleman and star in him recovered and soldiered on as if he hadn't missed a cue. The drop came down on Act One, and Uncle James and I both exhaled relieved breaths.

In the second act, Pa missed more lines. The second gentleman playing Cassio attempted to cover the flubs and cue Pa again, but my father fled downstage as if trying to escape. Turning too quickly, he slid first to one knee, then to both, and ended up crouching on all fours staring down at the boards. A shocked "Oh!" rippled through the audience in the parquet seats. Cassio tried to lift my father, improvising a line the Bard never wrote: "Come, on your feet, general!" But the actor couldn't manage it alone, and my father remained hunched like an animal frozen in fear of slaughter until the drop came down again.

"Is that the end?" a lady in the box next to ours said.

"This isn't the way it goes," her gentleman escort complained. "The Moor doesn't die so soon!"

The audience response crescendoed into boos. Uncle James colored crimson. "We're leaving," he announced, spittle collecting at the corners of his lips. He tugged me to my feet. "*Now*, Georgiana."

I badly wanted to stay and support Pa after this debacle, but my youth and sex meant I didn't get a say in the matter. We exited my uncle's box and the theater to his brougham, waiting in a tidy line of carriages on Broadway.

"Bond Street, Louis," my uncle directed his driver.

Pa used to be able to handle the drink and still speak his lines beautifully. He bragged about having a hollow leg, that he never felt the impact of whiskey no matter how much he imbibed. In the past year or two, though, his memory had pickled. When I ran through his prompt books with him to refresh his recall, he sometimes dropped whole pages, skipping ahead without realizing what he'd missed.

Mama didn't speak of Pa's mounting difficulties around me and Maude. For us, she put on a bright face, but it was hard to miss the growing chasm between them, as wide as an orchestra pit, their overheard exchanges sharp and brittle.

Uncle James confronted Pa openly, without caring who heard. As a theater investor, he was a regular at the Prince, and he warned my father, "He'll let you go, Will. Worth was hired to whip the company into shape after Bumby drove it into the ground. Your contract will be worthless paper if you continue to perform badly." He pointed out a clause in the Prince's official rules, instituted by the new manager, stipulating that any actor "unable from the effects of stimulants to perform" would be docked a week's salary on first offense and thereafter subject to discharge.

My father's response had sounded characteristically haughty—that the Prince couldn't afford to lose William Cartwright, who had drawn crowds to match all the luminaries of the day, like Edwin Forrest and Charlotte Cushman. "That theater would collapse without me. Who would play my roles?"

"Worth's a fine leading actor himself," my uncle had noted.

Now, as our carriage clattered toward my home on Bond Street, Uncle James shook his head sadly. "I'm sorry you had to witness that, Georgie."

My stomach twisted this way and that, and not from our jostling over the cobblestones or the stench of horse dung wafting into the carriage. If Mr. Worth sacked my father, how would he earn a living? He'd never done anything but act. Maybe he would get a place at the Bowery or Barnum's—lower rungs on the theater ladder, but at least he'd have an income.

3

On the short trip up Broadway, my emotions ricocheted from anxiety to rage. If the head of our family tumbled, we were doomed to go right along with him.

"What will happen to him?" I asked. What I really meant was, what will happen to *us*?

"I can't say," Uncle James replied. "But you're a smart girl, Georgie. You know the situation isn't good. All we can do is hope Worth gives him another chance." He saw me to our front door but declined to come in when Aggie, our cook and housekeeper, answered with a surprised "Mr. Clifford! Back so early?" I assumed he wanted to dodge telling my mother, his older sister, why he'd brought me home from my special evening two hours too soon.

That unpleasantness fell to me.

The next day, Pa was still not home. The daily papers all head-lined his literal and figurative fall. As it turned out, the theater manager sent out the corps de ballet to quell the crowd's dis-content while he made adjustments to the cast. After a brief *entr'acte*, Mr. Culpepper, the actor who had played Cassio, took over as the Moor. "Unheard of at this fine establishment," claimed the *Herald*.

In the kitchen, Aggie was taking something out on a mound of bread dough. I saw she'd acquired the latest edition of *Broadway Miscellany*, a rag she pored over like the Bible. Aggie's beau took her to the Bowery Theatre many Saturday evenings, and she had become the source of my theater gossip. I sneaked a look at the page the *Miscellany* was open to: "To Be or Not to Be a Laughing-stock," the headline read.

"Wrong play," I muttered.

"He'll get his walking papers for sure," Aggie said as she punched. I understood her fury and fear. Aggie's salary helped support her family back in Ireland, still reeling from the Great Hunger, or famine.

"He'll find a way to keep you on. Don't worry."

She took a right hook to the dough. "I don't know how ever he'll manage to, the soaker."

Aggie was also the source of most of the slang words I knew, so I understood what she meant. Her mouth formed a perfect *O* when she realized she wasn't calling him a drunkard to her beau, but to me, the drunkard's daughter. There weren't five years between us in age, and I spent a lot of time talking to Aggie in the kitchen despite social constraints that said I shouldn't be friendly with the help. Aside from Pa, she was the only one in my immediate circle who shared my interest in theater.

The thought that Pa might be gone for good or dead in an alley in Five Points made a little gasp escape my throat.

"Oh, I should never have said that, Miss Georgie!" Aggie said. "His drinking's not so bad as that. He'll be back before you know it."

At midday, Uncle James descended from his carriage—without Pa. As he talked to Mama, I listened at the drawing-room doorway and heard her sobbing but couldn't make out any of her words.

Uncle James stayed for dinner. Both of my parents' chairs sat empty, and my uncle faced me and Maude across the expanse, tapping his fingers on the white damask. He smiled reassuringly, but the color had drained from his cheeks.

Maude sniffled and wouldn't touch her meal. "May I be excused?" she asked, and my uncle nodded.

I weighed the merits of weeping versus eating and chose the latter. I'd gained an inch in height in each of the past three years, bringing me to a little more than five-six, and I was hungry most of the time. ("So big-boned for a girl!" my mother lamented.) As I chewed slowly and deliberately, savoring the roast's natural juices, I wondered how many fine meals we had left and what we'd eat when we were poor and couldn't afford to keep Aggie on.

My uncle set down his fork and for the first time regarded me like I was an adult and not a girl.

"You're the backbone of this family now, Georgie," he said.

His unexpected statement landed like a cobblestone on my chest. "You understand what I mean?"

"Sir," was all I could say, because my mouth had dried, and Aggie's delicious roast and potatoes had formed a lump in my stomach. I wanted to ask where my father was, if my uncle even knew, but the words wouldn't come.

"There aren't a lot of options," my uncle continued. "The money your mother was saving for the move to Washington Square will go toward household expenses."

Bond Street had been a fashionable neighborhood when I was little, but increasingly the better families were moving uptown. Mama's desire for a more elegant address had deepened the rift between my parents. Pa hated the prospect of traveling a longer distance to work, and I had heard him threaten to move out and let rooms near the theater.

"Of course, I'll help as much as I can," my uncle added.

I couldn't imagine how. Uncle James had what my mother called "a good position" in banking, but he was already giving aid to our widowed Granny Clifford. He also had a fiancée who had been raised among the fine families of Lafayette Place and would undoubtedly expect to continue her elegant life when they married.

"Your mother might have to rent out part of the house. That would be better than the debt collectors hauling furnishings away or the bank changing the locks."

I gulped at the grim picture he painted, right out of a Dickens story.

"As for how we move forward" his gaze dropped to the tablecloth—"your mother will want you to marry while there's still money."

For several years, I had told my family that my aspirations weren't to be a wife and mother. I wanted to be on the stage, like Pa—or more accurately, like my idol, the great actress Charlotte Cushman. I'd devoured every article on her, every review of her performances. Pa had supported my ambition. His family was a theater dynasty, not unlike the Booths; my paternal grandfather and great-grandfather had trod the boards, too. From his travels to perform in England, Pa always brought me back penny plains—cards bearing the likenesses of all the great actors and actresses in their most famous roles. "You'll be on one someday," he had said.

My mother maintained that marriage was the only acceptable path for a young woman of my "station," a word that made me groan. We were solidly middle class, for sure, but our house was modest, with only one live-in servant to run it. There was also a house maid who came three days a week. Pa had never bought a carriage and always relied on hacks. ("A waste of money," Uncle James had said.) When Mama talked about our station in society, she sounded more like Granny Clifford, who bragged about the old New York stock we came from.

Now, faced with my uncle's statement about marriage, my defiance spilled out. "I won't marry," I heard myself say.

Uncle James glanced up and held my eyes with his icy blue ones.

"Pa's always saying, 'You'd make a fine actress, George,'" I continued. "I've read *everything* opposite him, Ophelia and Lady M. to the lads' roles, too, like Mercutio. Why, I know Pa's roles better than he does. I could recite every line he missed the other night. I'm a natural, he says."

My uncle assessed me between sips of claret. "Your father isn't here, Georgie."

I wanted to scream, *I know that! Where is he? Why is he doing this to us?*

Instead, I avoided aggravating the man who now appeared to be in charge of my fate and who looked almost interested in what I was saying.

"You trust his judgment, Uncle. You've said you admire him for knowing raw talent when he sees it. Well, he sees it in me." I refused to use past tense for Pa until I knew what had happened to him.

Uncle James drained his glass and rotated it on the cloth by the stem. A fuzzy smile formed on his lips.

"There will be your mother to deal with," he said slowly.

"And then there's the cost of acting lessons."

Something fluttered in my chest like an exuberant bird. *He's with me,* I thought.

Chapter 2

The prospect of professional acting lessons thrilled me. I'd had little formal education, and all of it had been a waste. From age ten to fourteen, I had suffered through tedious lessons in needlework, watercolors, and table etiquette with Miss Henrietta Haines at her school for girls in Gramercy Park. A woman we simply called *Mademoiselle* tutored us in French.

Mama had hoped the school would garner me and Maude society friends, but I shrank away from girls whose dreams went no further than their wedding gowns, and they in turn looked down their aristocratic noses at "the actor's daughter." Mercifully, when I was fourteen and Maude a year younger, my mother decided to spare the exorbitant tuition and save it for a finer house uptown.

Leaving school had meant I was home while Pa was rehearsing during the day, and I took to listening at his study door as he ran his lines. One day when he caught me lurking in the hallway, he invited me in and asked me to read Cordelia to his Lear. I stumbled a lot and Pa banished me in frustration.

"What did you expect?" I had heard Mama ask him later. "She's just a child."

"You've stopped running lines with me, and I need *someone*."

I had decided to practice on my own so Pa would give me a second chance. When he saw my improvement, he not only brought me back into his study but turned our cueing sessions

9

into instruction, encouraging me to explore my lines, not just spout them to him flatly. He said he wanted our sessions as close to a performance as possible and that he would prepare me for the stage, where I would assume the Cartwright mantle.

"It's about betrayal, George. Ophelia thought Hamlet loved her, but now she sees him for what he really is," might be one of his directions. And another: "The key to Mercutio is his name. He's *mercurial*. That means unpredictable."

Pa was a commanding figure, even though he was compactly built and had but a few inches height on me. His gravitas came from intensely dark eyes that bored into you, a romantic shock of curly brown hair threaded with gray, and a rich baritone voice that he could take down to bass when he needed to. His manner often bordered on crusty, but he sounded softer when he called me George—his pet name for me. There was no ignoring his instructions if I wanted to continue cueing his lines, so I kept a list of them like a private prompt book. Soon, he had made his own scripts available, and I could read the notes he made on his roles.

I cherished those lessons with Pa, which led me to believe I would join him on stage in due time. But then his disappearance dashed my hopes.

Now, my uncle maneuvered to restart my education—this time, in a way that promised to fulfill my dreams. Uncle James managed to convince Mama that acting lessons were a sound investment, given that acting was one of the few ways a woman could make a decent living "if she can't find a husband," to use his words. With his connections in theater, he arranged for me to study with Mrs. Stansbury, a retired leading lady whose very name exuded respectability.

"I told your uncle we'll give it three months," Mama said, counting them off on her fingers for emphasis. "We can't squander any more money than that."

I wanted to object that it wasn't enough time to invest in my training, but I thanked her and kept quiet. I was a quick study, but it was clear I would have to be even quicker.

The drawing room where I awaited Mrs. Stansbury's arrival put my family's residence to shame. There were such a lot of gold things. The velvet curtains cascaded in heavy folds, and the wallpaper appeared to have dragons embossed on it. I couldn't examine it closely for fear of being impertinent, but from where I perched, on a comfortable white-and-gold chair with deep tufts, they did look like dragons. Or snakes.

I'd never been inside a Lafayette Place residence before. The eminent Schermerhorns' manse sat just across the avenue. Once, Aggie had read to me from *Broadway Miscellany* about their costume ball, how they redecorated their public rooms for just one night, at enormous expense, to replicate Versailles Palace. During my years studying with Mademoiselle, I'd learned about the grandeur of "Versa-illies," as Aggie pronounced it.

Mrs. Stansbury's house, with its own lavish French embellishments, seemed like it could compete with her upper-crust neighbors'. I was still puzzling over the wallpaper when I heard a musical voice say, "*Bonjour*, Miss Cartwright! *C'est un plaisir de vous rencontrer.*"

I popped up and gave her a little bow from the waist. I knew it was wrong, but with my gawky height and raw nerves, I worried a curtsey might send me toppling over at her feet. "*Enchantée, Madame,*" I replied. Her eyes widened in disapproval, but she didn't rebuke me for choosing a man's greeting over a woman's.

I owned a penny plain of Mrs. Stansbury in her prime, performing Cleopatra in full Egyptian garb, but she was now many years past that, a square, gray-haired woman maybe as old as fifty. Still, her voice never faltered and the hand I took in greeting was as smooth as a velvet curtain.

I hoped she didn't intend to conduct my lessons in French, because I'd reached the limit of what I could recall from the exchanges at school. Happily, Mrs. Stansbury reverted to English.

"You have the height of Miss Cushman," she said, scanning from my crown to my slippers. She was a full head shorter than I. "Your strong bones *could* be an asset."

"I take after my father," I replied too quickly, then bit my lip as I recalled Uncle James's advice: *Whatever you do, I wouldn't bring up your Pa.*

"Don't bite your lips like that, young lady, or lick them, for that matter. They're delicate tissues, prone to cracking. An actress must take great care with her mouth."

She lowered herself onto a chair in a graceful sideways motion, and I consciously followed her example instead of plopping into mine, as was my custom. When we were facing each other, Mrs. Stansbury continued to assess me for a good long minute before speaking again.

"Your uncle tells me you've a great talent," she said.

My neck heated at the compliment. "Thank you, Mrs. Stansbury."

"He said it, not I. And I haven't known your uncle to have studied the craft of acting. I imagine he's merely repeating your father's words." The phrase *your father's* came out with a whiff of disdain. "I will make my own determinations over the course of our weeks together. Now—please watch your posture, Georgiana."

What had I gotten myself into—deportment lessons? This was not what I had in mind when my uncle arranged the private instruction. It felt like I was listening to Mama pressing me at dinner to remove my elbows from the table and stop slouching.

"Acting requires control of your posture at all times. An actress must be at one with her spine."

I'd never thought much about my spine and didn't particularly want to. But I'd no sooner straightened up than my new teacher moved on.

"Tell me, Miss Cartwright, what do you want to accomplish?"

Her question took me aback. "Here?"

"Yes, but also in your life."

No one had ever asked what I wanted for my life.

"I want to be a successful actress," I said without hesitation. "I want to be self-sufficient, as wealthy as Miss Cushman or Mrs. Kemble or the Bateman sisters." This time, I remembered not to say anything about my father and how he had left my family treading rough waters.

Mrs. Stansbury's brow creased at my reference to the Batemans, young performers P.T. Barnum promoted. "There are other paths to wealth. You could train to sing opera."

Mama favored opera and had allowed us to hear Jenny Lind when she toured the country. I chuckled at Mrs. Stansbury's suggestion. "My sister could do that, but I sound more like *Mr.* Lind than Miss."

That made the great lady smile, something I wasn't sure she did often. "You come from an old family on your mother's side. You could marry well—"

My father's voice in my head chided me, *Think harder, George. Why the stage?*

Why? Because I liked the idea of playing someone else, taking on new personas. I wasn't thrilled with my own persona, mostly because I didn't know who I was. Pa seemed to like me as me—his George. He didn't know that sometimes when I was alone in the house and his study wasn't locked, I slipped on his costumes and strutted in front of the mirror, imagining myself as Miss Cushman in a breeches role playing Romeo or Hamlet. I didn't fancy being a boy, but male clothing represented freedom and suited me so much better than the uncomfortable stays and crinolines I had to wear.

But I couldn't say any of *that* to Mrs. Stansbury.

Think, George. Pa had expressed a noble reason for acting, so maybe it could be mine, too. "Since I first discovered the beauty of the Bard's poetry," I found myself saying, "I have wanted the stage and nothing else."

Mrs. Stansbury blinked quickly. Had I gone too far? Did it not sound reasonable? Or had she, like me, heard Pa say it?

But then she nodded as if my answer pleased her. She reached over, rang a tiny gold bell positioned on the table

13

beside her chair, and the butler appeared.

"The book, Parker," she said, and he retreated obediently. Then, to me: "Now, let us begin."

Chapter 3

Mrs. Stansbury's lessons didn't mesh with my expectations. Having enjoyed her prime thirty years back, she favored an outmoded, declamatory style of performance, with the actress (me) facing the audience (her) while reciting some dramatic monologue or other. If I followed my instincts to move around or address an imaginary actor to my left or right, she corrected me with a verbal smack.

"Stop flapping like a fledgling, Georgiana! A lady might incline her hand *subtly* toward a gentleman, but aside from that, arms at your sides, please."

Her direction discouraged me. My mother was investing in my potential and expected me to garner a position in a good theater posthaste. Aggie had told me that the performers she and her beau most enjoyed at the Bowery Theatre portrayed characters in a realistic way.

"You should have been there!" Aggie had said after attending one melodrama. "Didn't Miss Morris's character have heart failure in the final act, right on stage! Two doctors in the pit thought it was real and rushed to her aid!"

I'd watched Pa put enormous effort into the physical aspects of his acting. In his prompt books, his scribbled directions to himself included everything from leaping and striding to crawling and staggering. After a rehearsing session in which he'd expended so much energy that sweat dripped from his brow, he warned me, "Anyone not accustomed to rigorous exertion shouldn't go into acting, George."

But with Mrs. Stansbury, I was to stand still in one place and speak . . . beautifully.

Truth be told, I did pick up stronger elocution and projection skills from my teacher, and quickly. After two weeks of daily lessons, I'd acquired the confidence to fill a two-thousand-seat venue like the Prince Theatre with my voice. My gestures, however, when Mrs. Stansbury allowed me any at all, were stilted.

"Are you sure I shouldn't move, say, in this direction as Lady Macbeth speaks?" I ventured one day. "I haven't seen Miss Cushman perform the role myself, but I've heard that she gives each character . . ."

When I fumbled for a noun, my teacher rushed in with one that hadn't occurred to me. "Masculinity," she said with a frown. "Even the female roles. Her stance alone is far too male."

"What I heard was that she gives each character unique physical traits," I said. "Maybe Romeo jumps back and forth during the balcony scene, or Lady Macbeth shudders and droops a little when she says, 'Had he not resembled / My father as he slept, I had done't.'" Aware that I was correcting my teacher, I added quickly, "But as I said, I haven't seen her perform."

"Jumping and shuddering and drooping on stage are quite uncalled for," Mrs. Stansbury replied. "I thought you were here to learn the classical craft of speaking words so precisely they become part of your being."

I nodded but was thinking, *if this were 1822, that would be more than enough.*

Clearly, I couldn't push Mrs. Stansbury any further on the matter of physical movement; she was too firmly entrenched in the past. I had to content myself with what she could offer me about elocution. For other aspects of acting so necessary to success in the present day, I approached my uncle about expanding my instruction.

Through Aggie's papers, I learned that Miss Cushman had a three-week engagement in New York at The Broadway Theatre, playing everything from her signature role of Romeo to Lady Macbeth and Rosalind. When my uncle approached my mother about escorting me to a performance, he stretched the truth, saying Mrs. Stansbury had recommended it.

"For Georgie's education, Sister," he explained while I eavesdropped from the hall. Maude came up behind me with a click of her tongue. I shooed her away, but she stayed to listen in.

"Georgie can't become a proper actress without seeing others perform," Uncle James continued. "And she's only been in a theater, well . . . that one time."

"But an actress . . . playing a *man*," my mother said, the distaste heavy in her voice. "Breeches roles are unnatural, James. Perverse."

"It *is* kind of odd," Maude agreed in a whisper.

I shushed her.

"Miss Cushman plays Romeo opposite her sister," my uncle added, although this was another stretch of the facts. Also an actress, Susan Cushman had played Juliet to Charlotte's Romeo many times, but she'd retired from the stage, and I knew my uncle was counting on my mother not knowing the latest theater news. "It's all very chaste and proper, and Miss Cushman is unsullied in her personal life. She's never had even a whiff of scandal."

"I don't know—"

"If you prefer, she's playing Viola later in the week."

I groaned inwardly when my uncle gave in so quickly to my mother's objection. Viola pretending to be a boy in *Twelfth Night* was simply not as interesting as watching a woman play a bona fide breeches role, one written for a man. Transforming into another sex struck me as the ultimate display of acting ability.

17

"But," my uncle added, "the *Romeo and Juliet* performance will be a very special one. And they're doing it from the original text." This was something all the great actors, including my father, insisted on and took enormous pride in—not using the scripts the Bowdlers had shortened, but working from the Bard's folios. Uncle James knew what would appeal to my mother, who had shared my father's love of Shakespeare's original words. Pa said it was one of the things that had brought them together. I could still remember times when I was young and the two of them read aloud together from the tragedies after our evening meal.

"You always wear me down, James," Mama said with a tired-sounding laugh. "I'm trusting you know what you're doing with the girl."

Maude sneezed at that inopportune moment, loud enough to disclose our presence as spies.

"Maude! Georgiana! Get in here!"

I scowled at my sister, thrust out my chest, and entered the drawing room first.

"How many times do I have to tell you it's bad manners to listen at doorways?"

From experience, I knew it was best to "Yes, ma'am" my way out of a lecture. After all, I'd gotten what I wanted—the chance to see Charlotte Cushman perform.

To say Charlotte Cushman was my idol would be an understatement. I had read and reread stories about her in Aggie's papers and clipped them for my theater scrapbook. My collection of penny plains included two of the great actress: one as Romeo and another as Hamlet. The day before my eighteenth birthday, Pa had presented me with a Staffordshire figurine of the Cushman sisters as Romeo and Juliet, and it now held the place of honor on my bedroom mantel.

Originally from Boston, Miss Cushman had launched her career at about my age, but in opera. When her singing voice failed her during a performance, a mentor suggested theater instead. A lucky connection brought her to the Bowery Theatre and later to the more prestigious Park Theatre. She made her name in startlingly realistic performances. To play Nancy in *Oliver Twist*, she had exchanged clothes with a fallen woman in the alleyways of Five Points. Her breeches roles, though, were what secured her fame, transfixing critics and audiences in London and across America.

What intrigued me even more was her independence—or what I could glean about it from the papers. Other actresses became Mrs. Who's-It or Mrs. What's-His-Name in short order, leaving the stage and settling into bearing baby after baby. Miss Cushman appeared to have eschewed marriage, as I intended to do.

"Sad kind of life," Aggie concluded about Miss Cushman's choice. She sliced bread as I read aloud from the *Miscellany* about the actress's national tour, which she asserted would be her farewell to the stage. According to the story, the English poetess Matilda Hayes would accompany her cross-country.

"She's got to be nigh on forty years," Aggie added. "It must get awful lonesome."

Could no one see the beauty of it but me? The acting, the travel, the companionship of another intelligent woman! It all sounded like heaven. Given Aggie's reaction, though, I knew to keep the thought to myself.

My uncle didn't have a box at The Broadway, which meant he and I sat in the parquet in seats so near the stage I could see the actors' spittle fly. *Romeo and Juliet* was among my least favorite of the Bard's plays; the idea that love would make you want to kill yourself struck me as odd, but then I'd never been in love. Miss Cushman was the sole attraction for me, and that night all the other characters evaporated as she *became* Romeo, moving with confidence and ease. I forgot who was wearing the tunic and tights, although it wasn't a bit like she was mimicking a man. Her Romeo was a magical mix of masculine and feminine traits, adventure and tenderness, passion and shyness, and I wanted to *be* him—or maybe to be *her* being

19

him—in possession of some of each sex.

When it was over and the two lovers were collapsed in a heap, I hopped from my seat, erupting in applause along with the rest of the audience. I wished I had camellias to throw onto the stage like many in attendance.

In my uncle's carriage, I dried my eyes and blew an unladylike honk into my handkerchief to recover from tears of emotion.

"I take it you found it memorable," Uncle James said.

"Oh, Uncle! That's exactly what I want to do as an actress, make the audience *feel* like they're right there with the characters, experiencing their pain."

"I'm happy you learned something. I'm stacking up quite a few chits with your mother on your behalf." His tone bordered on amusement.

"I won't disappoint you. It will be worth it when I'm on the stage." I didn't know how far I could press him to help me make that happen, but since we were on the subject anyway, I pushed onward. "You know, for my education it would be helpful to see Miss Cushman's *full* range, don't you think? Maybe Lady Macbeth or Rosalind? Before she leaves the city on her tour and then retires?"

The next day, I put pen to paper to gush out my feelings for my idol.

Dear Miss Cushman,

I had the pleasure of accompanying my uncle to The Broadway last night to see your performance of Romeo. All I can say is thank you, thank you, thank you! I want to be on the stage, too!

My letter didn't shimmer on paper the way I'd imagined it in my head. Although reciting other people's words presented no problem for me, my ability to come up with my own fell short. I crumbled the sheet and tried again, but my second effort was no stronger than the first. With all the thank-you's and exclamation points, my letter suggested I was a gushing girl when I wanted to look like a serious, aspiring actress whom Miss Cushman might respond to with counsel or encouragement.

I asked for Aggie's help, because I knew she wrote lengthy letters to her mother in Ireland, but her effort on my behalf, sprinkled with phrases like "a wee bit of advice," sounded like I'd just hopped off the boat from Galway. I thanked her but didn't mail it and put the idea of writing to Miss Cushman to the back of my mind.

Chapter 4

I progressed so well and so quickly at my private lessons with Mrs. Stansbury that by the end of July, she cast me in a parlor theatrical designed to showcase the talents of her students. She held these programs at her home each month, pairing off actors and actresses for brief scenes from classic plays. The audience consisted primarily of her friends and neighbors, but sometimes theater managers attended, too. It excited me not only to have a real audience, but to meet other students who shared my interests.

My portion of the program was short but substantive and came toward the end of the evening like a digestif. "You will perform from *Hamlet*, Act IV, Scene Five," my teacher announced.

Ophelia's mad scene! I whooped like a boy and began reciting the lines aloud: "'There's rosemary, that's for remembrance. Pray you, love, remember. And there is pansies, that's for thoughts.'"

Mrs. Stansbury cut me off with a low growl. "You will rehearse in good time. Mr. Murtagh will play opposite you as Laertes. Now please try to remember you're a young lady!"

Although our teacher thrust us together, Ned Murtagh and I became fast friends. Something about him felt familiar, as if I'd known him before and we were just picking up again after a pause. He was two years my senior and had already performed in several farces at the Bowery Theatre. With his red-blond forelock and chiseled cheekbones, he seemed destined for leading gentleman parts, but he said he needed Mrs. Stansbury's imprimatur to take his career to the next level.

"Right now, I'm relegated to playing the Irish fool," he explained. Although he'd been born in New York, the way he said *fool*, long and drawn out, reminded me of Aggie.

His aspiration, like mine, was to tread the boards at a grand theater like the Prince—and to be independent of his father, who wanted Ned to join him in his booming daguerreotype business.

"At least you'd have a job. You'd be out in the world meeting people," I said of the photography studio. "If acting doesn't work out for me, I'll be someone's chattel."

Confusion clouded Ned's face. "What do you mean?"

"*You* know. I'll be forced to marry."

"Marriage isn't *slavery*. Slavery is an evil institution. There's no comparison between being married and being literally in chains and not in command of your own life."

I bristled. "When women can move about on the streets freely without being seen as harlots and when they can sign contracts and control their own property and when they can be their children's legal guardians . . ." My list veered on becoming a rant, so I drew it to a close. "Well, then maybe you'll convince me."

He backed down. "We've known each other a day and you've already managed to poke holes in my argument," he said with a little bow. "Brava, Miss Cartwright."

In my limited experience with the opposite sex, mostly at school cotillions, boys dismissed me with a look that said I wasn't worthy of their time. Ned, however, assessed me like a peer and colleague.

He was the first person I told of the new plan I'd been concocting. "I'm taking a stage name," I announced. "What do you think of Georgiana Clifford? It's my mother's maiden name. I could use it for Mrs. Stansbury's theatrical."

Given my uncle's support, taking his last name seemed

like an apt choice. In addition, I'd keep my same initials—
the ones Miss Haines had taught me to embroider on all my
handkerchiefs—while avoiding the embarrassment and shame
now heaped on "Cartwright."

"Downright musical." Ned stroked his chin. "Maybe I
should change mine, too!"

My uncle didn't warn me in advance, but he'd invited a special guest to Mrs. Stansbury's parlor theatrical. If I'd known, I
might have tripped over my lines or my feet. Being blissfully
ignorant, I performed my scene with Ned without a hitch.
When I reached the line where Ophelia says, "There's a daisy.
I would give you some violets, but they wither'd all when my
father died. They say he made a good end," I heard tiny sobs
from women in the parlor. Even Ophelia's singing didn't get
the better of me. My voice wobbled as I tried to take it higher,
but that made perfect sense in a scene about a girl's madness.

Ned got his moment in the limelight, too, in a plum
scene—Mercutio's exchange with Benvolio about Romeo.
Unfortunately, he stuttered on the key line "O, he is the cou-
rageous captain of compliments," and came back into the second drawing room looking undone.

"Nerves," I reasoned. "Completely understandable."

Ned shook his head ruefully. "But you! Next stop for you,
the Prince!" He added in a whisper, "The manager's in the
audience."

Thomas Worth was the young mastermind who had
recently assumed the role of managing the Prince Theatre. He
replaced Mr. Bumby, a friend of Pa's with a knack for choosing actors but apparently a poor head for business. A story
in *Broadway Miscellany* claimed Worth had spared the Prince
from "imminent financial ruin." A talented actor himself,
Worth got his start in his teens at the prestigious Park Theatre
as a walking gentleman, or supporting player. Now in his late
twenties, he was building a stock company to rival that of the

Park, which had burned to the ground a few years earlier.

He was also the man who had sacked Pa.

"I recognized him," Ned continued. "He sat for his daguerreotype a few years back, and Da has it hanging in the gallery. I bet your performance caught his attention."

To my relief, Mrs. Stansbury had approved of me listing my name as Clifford in the program, so my connection to Pa was hidden. My chest fluttered at the possibilities ahead of me, but Ned looked downcast.

"I'm sure Mr. Worth will be looking at you, too," I said to cover my glee.

"I rather doubt it. I made a mess of those *c's*."

After, there were refreshments, a lovely fruit and cheese plate, apple compote, and sponge cake. Ned and I dipped into the punch, which was disappointingly spirit-free.

"Not a drop of rum to be found," said a deep voice behind us. For a split-second, I mistook it for Pa's.

The voice belonged to a young man with wavy mahogany-colored hair and deep-set blue eyes, who looked charmingly disheveled in his evening clothes. Uncle James rushed over to introduce us.

"Tom, this is my niece, Miss Georgiana Clifford," he said. I had cautioned my uncle in advance about my stage name, and the choice had flattered him. "Georgiana, this is Mr. Thomas Worth of the Prince Theatre."

"Miss Clifford," Worth said with a forceful kiss to my hand. "Or perhaps I should call you Mistress Ophelia?"

I introduced both men to Ned, but Worth's eyes latched onto me in an unsettling way, as if I were a prize to win.

Worth coaxed me aside and confided in a backstage whisper, "I don't attend these parlor entertainments as a rule. I respect Mrs. Stansbury, don't get me wrong, but I came tonight at your uncle's insistence. He knows I'm on the prowl for new company members, and he assured me I wouldn't be wasting my time." The word *prowl* stood out as an unusual choice. "Miss Clifford, I wonder if you'd deign to join us at the Prince."

"You want . . . me?" I stammered, bringing a curled smile to his lips.

"I do indeed," Worth replied. "I just lost a walking lady. She went and got herself . . . Well, I can't speak of her predicament in polite company. You would do quite nicely as her replacement."

My cheeks went hot at the veiled suggestion that the supporting actress had left because she was in the family way. Between that and his offer, I couldn't form words, and Worth's head tilted like he was rethinking the whole thing.

"It isn't an easy job, you know. You'll get your own small roles, of course, but you might be called to replace a second leading lady on short notice. A walking lady is always at her part."

"Oh, Mr. Worth, I would be honored!"

"Twenty dollars a week to start, but there's the chance of a yearly increase if you perform well. I'm sure you'll advance quickly when you pick up more experience."

The amount he offered was four times what I might earn as a shop girl. In fact, theater provided women with the best opportunity for independence. Even walking ladies and ballet girls, the workhorses of the company, earned a decent living, and leading ladies could grow wealthy. A smile exploded across my face. "This is my dream!"

That's when I turned and saw Ned staring at us with his mouth slightly agape. Had he overheard? It would be so much more fun to have a friend at the theater.

I took a deep breath. "Do you need a walking gentleman, too?" I asked. "You must have noticed that Mr. Murtagh was a formidable Mercutio."

Worth shot a glance toward Ned, who averted his eyes to the cheese plate as if he sensed we were discussing him.

"A good-looking chap. Hard to secure actors for the younger roles. I wouldn't call his Mercutio formidable, what with that stammer in the middle, but it was workable." Worth's facial muscles clenched. "Your beau?"

"Oh, no, sir! My aim is to be married to the theater."

Worth loosened up again and smiled in the slightly lascivious way that I'd soon recognize as his trademark. "Good, good. It's fine to catch some romance on the sly, all of us do, but you'll have no time for a proper beau, what with learning your parts and fashioning your costumes."

I knew actors and actresses supplied their own costumes, and my skills with a needle were limited. Mama had sewn Pa's costumes in the early days of their marriage, but when Pa secured the leading gentleman spot at the Prince, he had engaged a seamstress and tailor. I hoped I could coax Mama into helping.

"I'll think on young Mr. Murtagh," Worth added.

I grabbed another chance before it evaporated. "Perhaps not too long. He is awfully nice-looking, as you noticed. Why, the ladies in the audience will swoon."

Worth regarded Ned again. As if on cue, three fawning matrons surrounded my friend.

"I *would* like to attract more ladies to the theater," Worth said, thinking aloud. "Matinees help bring them in, but a handsome young man—"

"And he told me just today that The Broadway has expressed interest"—an outright lie, but I didn't specify what they'd expressed interest *in*.

"Is that so?"

Within the week, Ned and I were both ensconced at the Prince Theatre.

Chapter 5

My mother met the announcement of my new position with an explosion of delight. "Oh, Georgie! Oh, my girl!"

The "I can stop looking for your husband" I hoped to hear didn't follow. Instead, she added, as if counting our money aloud, "It's not near what your father brought in, but it's so much more than we have now. We won't have to take in boarders!"

"Mr. Worth thinks I will move up quickly," I said. "Why, I could be a second leading lady in the new year. We could buy that new house you wanted!"

"'Count not thy chickens that unhatched be,'" she said, quoting from some poet or another. "The theater profession pays handsomely, but it's volatile." She gave me a sideways glance.

"Won't be in my case," I mumbled.

"What did you say, Georgie?"

"I said, yes, of course, Mama, I see your point completely—just in case."

She looked unconvinced; my response didn't come close to the same number of syllables as what I'd uttered under my breath. But she simply repeated, "Yes, just in case."

Uncle James sent his carriage to transport me to the theater, but on my first day I had a surplus of nervous energy and wanted to walk. Mama didn't approve; young ladies didn't go about on their own, even for a few blocks. As Louis the driver helped me into the brougham, I asked him to stop at Houston Street so I could walk that last long block to the Prince.

"Your uncle'd have my hide, miss," Louis said.

"Then it will be our secret."

We compromised, and Louis slowed midway between Houston and Prince, then halted and hopped down from his seat. His brow was furrowed with concern, but he said nothing as I alit.

"I promise you, Louis, this never happened"—an assurance that brought a smile to his broad face.

I would have arrived at the theater on time, but I couldn't locate the actors' entrance. I assumed I'd go in the way Uncle James and I had on the evening we saw *Othello*, between the stately columns that faced Broadway, diagonal to Niblo's Garden, the theater where my parents had met all those years back. The Prince's ponderous front doors didn't budge, though, and I scrambled to the Prince Street side to find another way in, sidestepping rotting garbage and horse dung.

"Not that one." The voice belonged to a bespectacled young woman with chestnut hair, carrying a flat package tied up with twine like fabric from the dry goods store. "You don't look like a harlot to me. You look quite respectable." She smiled as she approached the second of two doors and nodded to it.

"Public women have their own door?" I whispered as I followed her through the entrance.

"When the theater was built, yes, and there was an assignation house right next door. Theaters have pretty much gotten rid of the whiskey and the whores, and that door's locked most of the time." I must have flinched at the vulgarity of *whores* because she added, "Sorry. My mother would slap me for using that word."

I wondered if she, too, were an actress. With her round frame and specs, she didn't resemble an ingenue. Then again, with my height and jaw, neither did I. I thought it would be nice to have another friend in addition to Ned. I didn't get a chance to ask her, because just inside the stage door, she bolted down a narrow hallway after motioning to me with her free hand toward the stage.

In the wings, an older gentleman with eyebrows like fuzzy black caterpillars handed out scripts. Actors and actresses queued up, grabbing their pages and either groaning or gasping delightedly. When it was my turn, the prompter, whose name was Harry Pendergast, presented my script and said, "Rehearsal Wednesday morning for the eight o'clock performance, Miss Clifford."

I choked on my question. "*This* Wednesday?"

"You get more time 'cause you're new," Harry said with a smirk. "Mostly, you've just a day to learn your lines. Wednesday you'll get your Friday role. Best to stay on your toes, missy."

As I turned away, my eyes found Ned, who'd been cast in the same play. "You could have warned me about the pace," I said.

"You're William Cartwright's daughter. How could you not know?"

I shushed him so my identity wouldn't be uncovered. In a whisper, I explained that, as leading gentleman, Pa enjoyed a repertory he'd been performing for longer than I'd been alive. Although new roles occasionally slipped into his rotation, his preparation mostly meant refreshing his memory of familiar lines.

Now I understood what Worth had alluded to when he told me, "A walking lady is always at her part." He simply didn't specify how many parts that might add up to.

The play for Wednesday was *London Assurance*, one of the many British comedies of error that had become as popular in American theater as melodramas, designed to bring in more ladies as ticket-buyers. The starring role of Grace went to an accomplished leading lady; and I was cast as her maid, with the comical name of Pert. Ned got the meatier role of the valet, Cool, with Worth banking on his looks as a draw to the ladies. The plum role of Lady Gay Spanker, a part I knew

30

Miss Cushman had commanded on other stages, went to the Prince's senior-most leading lady, Mrs. Reynolds.

To my disappointment, my prompt book from Harry was slim. Pert had just one scene in Act Two.

Harry must have read the chagrin on my face. "Don't dwell on how many lines you got. Less to learn, think on it that way. Trick is, make Pert your own." And that was the sum of the direction I got.

Since I was adept at memorizing, my biggest concern proved to be my costume. I thought of approaching Aggie about borrowing a frock, which would certainly have been authentic, but such a request to a servant in our household seemed inappropriate. Instead, I begged Mama for help. From an attic trunk, my mother unpacked an out-of-date black frock she'd worn to a relative's funeral. Because of Mama's petite size, the dress was snug at my waist, so she let out some gathers and installed a makeshift panel that allowed me to breathe. When she removed the lace pelerine from the shoulders and tacked some spare black cloth onto the hem to accommodate my height ("No one will notice from a distance that it's a different fabric," she assured me), the frock passed for a maid's uniform. I adorned it with a plain white apron purchased at a dry goods store.

My costume didn't settle all my problems, though. During Wednesday morning's rehearsal of my scene, I experienced a flash of vertigo as I entered stage left. The downward slope of the boards from upstage took me by surprise, and I clung to a chair on set to steady myself. As I stood paralyzed under the lights, a bead of sweat dripped from my nose.

Worth, who was portraying the romantic lead but didn't appear in my scene, watched from the wings, and I noticed the lady playing Grace shoot him a frustrated look, as if she couldn't believe she had to work with someone so green.

What proved worse was my "performance" of Pert, which consisted of reciting my lines stiffly while employing random eye blinks. In my anxiety about my first role, I'd forgotten what Pa taught me about inhabiting a character and instead fell back on Mrs. Stansbury's instructions.

Worth didn't appear to notice. As I exited the stage, I saw him checking his pocket watch and yawning. The prompter stopped and took me gently by the elbow.

"You'll get used to the raking," he said, referring to the stage's slope. "Feels like being on a ship, right?"

"It does," I agreed, although I'd never been on a ship. I was just grateful for his kindly tone.

"Picture it flat. That'll help."

"Thanks for the tip, Mr. Pendergast."

"You learn lines fast," Harry added. "Didn't miss a word."

I blushed at the praise, but it was short-lived.

"Here's something struck me funny, though. Your Pert's a bit twitchy. When she's not hugging that chair, she looks a bundle of nerves. Was that *your* nerves or the way you're playing her?"

"I'm sorry, Mr. Pendergast, I'm not sure."

When his eyebrows lifted, it was like they sprang to life. "Well, you'll sort it out by tonight."

Rehearsal proceeded while I descended to the walking ladies' dressing room below the stage, deflated as a toy balloon. Darkness cloaked the narrow staircase, and a blast of hot, stale air greeted me. I stumbled on the bottom step as something skittered in front of me.

"Watch your step, miss," a voice said. A hand reached out of the void and grabbed my arm to stop me from falling. "The mice've made a nest under the stairs."

As my eyes adjusted to the dim lights, I stood facing a servant girl about my age, wearing a brown calico dress a shade darker than her skin and a wrinkled apron. Her hair was hidden by a head wrap, but one crinkled wisp poked out from the side as if in defiance. In her muscular right arm, she balanced a pile of women's costumes.

"Thank you for the warning. The last thing I need is to

literally break a leg on the day of my debut."

"There's a mouser you'll see around, a big orange tabby name of Falstaff, but he's gotten too fat to catch 'em all." The girl withdrew her hand from my forearm. "You the new supe?" I'd heard Pa use the slang word "supe," short for superlative, but I preferred the more official term of "walking lady."

"Yes. Georgie Clifford."

Her head inclined to the left as she regarded me. "You got a boy's name, miss."

Some would have taken issue with her familiar tone, but I found it comforting. "Short for Georgiana. What's more, my father calls me George."

That brought out her deep dimples, as if God had chiseled perfect half-moons in her cheeks.

"And you're—?"

"Sallie, miss. Sallie Meeks."

"The maid."

My assumption straightened Sallie's back. "I keep things clean, but I'm a trained seamstress. I'll help put together your costume for twenty cents."

The charge for sewing seemed low, and I made a mental note of it.

"I also help the supes dress."

As leading gentleman, Pa had a private dresser, but I didn't know if Pa or the theater had employed him. "Does being my dresser cost extra, too?" I figured I would probably need the assistance later as I tried to shimmy into Mama's frock in the flickering gaslight.

"No, miss," Sallie said, "that's included." She glanced around, assessing if we were still alone. "But you want cues on the side, that's twenty cents. Sometimes I run lines with Miss Angelina. I mean, *ran* lines." I assumed Miss Angelina was the unfortunate actress I'd replaced.

"Don't tell Mr. Worth, though," Sallie continued. "I figure, I got these skills, so why not use them?"

"It's between us," I said. "Now could you point me to the walking ladies' dressing room? I need to practice my delivery

33

in front of a mirror."

"Oh, there ain't no mirror for you, miss."

No mirror? How was I to apply my makeup? What if a role required a wig? And how could I correct the twitching Harry had brought to my attention?

"Is a mirror . . . extra?"

"Only the leading ladies and the seconds get them provided. The supes and ballet girls got to bring their own. I keep them safe so nobody steals them." She smiled. "Just a nickel a month."

I was beginning to wish for a menu of Sallie Meeks's useful services. Any girl who devised such a list must be sharp as a blade. "Sallie, could I pay you to be my mirror today?"

It was an odd way to put it, and Sallie stared at me like I was one of Barnum's oddities. I fumbled for the pocket I had sewn into the folds of my dress—one remnant of my sewing lessons I had deemed useful. Mama preferred a reticule, but they were impractical for me because I was always leaving my little bag someplace.

My pocket turned up a ten-cent piece and some pennies. "I've only got this much on me today. But I don't require prompting. Memorizing and cues aren't a problem. I need to know"—I searched for words someone who wasn't an actress would understand "—what I *look* like as I'm saying them."

"You mean, if you got the character figured out?"

"Exactly. You must have worked here a long time to know that."

"I come from theater, miss," Sallie explained. "My daddy played at the African Grove when he was not much older than me. I reckon I know more than most." I said I'd never heard of the African Grove, so she explained it was an all-Negro theater that was now defunct.

"What happened to it?"

"White folks got it shut down. Said it was too rowdy." Her lips pressed into a tight line.

I was still holding onto the coins, which had gotten slick in my hand. I thrust them out to Sallie, and she counted them

34

carefully before speaking again.

"This looks about right for playing a mirror," she decided.

Chapter 6

With Sallie's assistance, I adapted my interpretation of Pert so the character better matched her name and became cleverly impertinent. During the evening's performance, the tilt of the raked stage still bothered me, but I followed Harry's advice and imagined it as flat as any other floor.

For my pains, I got a passing, positive mention in the review in *Spirit of the Times*—right before the reviewer complimented the realism of the set, complete with working doorknobs.

"In the role of Pert the maid, Miss Georgiana Clifford lent a minor character a saucy edge that rendered her memorable," Aggie read aloud. She grinned at me over the top of the page. "'Saucy edge.' I like that."

"You were my inspiration."

I reached for the paper to reread the line about me. Several times. In the paragraph above, the notice for Ned wasn't as positive: "more vexed than one would expect of a valet named 'Cool,'" the reviewer griped.

Ned despaired, even as we rushed to learn our next roles. In the Scottish play, he would appear as Malcolm, and I as Lady Macduff. For a second time, Ned had secured the heftier role, but he was convinced his fortunes would soon reverse.

"He's just casting me for my looks," Ned said, pushing back his forelock, a shade of red-gold I envied. "Thank God

I've got that in my favor, or I'd be playing *valets* forever."

Ned's comment pinched. I worried that my appearance might relegate me to minor roles—the character with just one scene. My height, but nothing else, was notable: hair and eyes the color of some indistinct wood, a jaw too square and strong for a girl. In contrast, Mrs. Reynolds, the leading lady of the company, was a petite, raven-haired beauty with a heart-shaped face and jade eyes. Pa had sometimes mentioned her looks in an admiring way that made me uncomfortable.

Reviews for my acting continued to glow, however. My Lady Macduff, said the *Herald*, "skillfully evoked a wife's fury blended with a mother's fierce attachment to her child." Thanks to Mama, some clever makeup and padding around my hips aged me, so the reviewer didn't comment on my youth. For motivation, I drew on my mixed feelings about Pa, how he'd supported my ambitions but then deserted me.

After a week of additional small parts—another saucy maid, then Audrey in *As You Like It*—the *Herald* pronounced, "This reviewer will be watching to see what Miss Clifford accomplishes next." It sounded like a gauntlet, as if the writer were waiting as anxiously as I for a larger role.

And indeed, the next time Harry parceled out our prompt books, mine had more than doubled in size from the first ones I received.

"This'll give you the meat you deserve, Georgie," Harry whispered as he placed it in my hands. "And you've got three whole days to learn it."

Worth was pacing backstage, gesticulating at the young woman who had pointed me toward the stage door on my first day. When he saw me with Harry, he advanced toward us, waving for the woman to follow him.

"Miss Clifford," he said with an exaggerated bow. We hadn't exchanged more than a few polite words since the night he hired me at Mrs. Stansbury's parlor theatrical. "It seems the *Herald* is *watching*, to see what you're about next."

My cheeks warmed.

"This is your Abigail," he said to the young woman. "What

do you think?"

The woman pushed her wire spectacles up her nose, all the while holding my gaze. I had no idea who she was or why I would be hers.

"Wonderful!" she pronounced, her hand darting out toward me. "Miss Clifford, we haven't properly met, but I saw you on your first day. I'm Clementine Scarborough. I wrote *All My Sisters*." A glance down at the title page of my book confirmed her as the play's authoress.

"Clementine is something of a prodigy," Worth said. "A regular girl genius."

The playwright reddened. "*Genius* is a strong word," she said, although she didn't object to *prodigy*.

Just then, an elegant woman about Mama's age swept into the wings in a shimmery, blue-green frock, calling out for "Tom," and Worth's eyes and attention swiveled to her. Without a bow or a good-bye, he took his leave to join her, and Miss Scarborough and I stood facing each other, awkward strangers.

"I hope you like the part," she said. "I know the three older sisters have more lines, but Abigail's my favorite of the four. I wrote her to have gumption." Her face colored again, emphasizing a scattering of freckles that fanned out from her nose in almost perfect formation.

"Gumption is something I can handle." We took a few steps deeper into the wings, and I whispered, "I can't believe anyone so young wrote a whole play!"

"It's my third. No, sorry, fourth. There was one I tossed in the bin. Thinly veiled revenge at an old love." Her laughter rippled at the private joke.

"Fourth? How old *are* you?"

"Twenty in November. I've been writing as long as I can remember. Novels, plays, poems, stories, essays. I've published some, but this is my first piece to be presented on stage. Mr. Worth's been scouting for what he calls homegrown talent, and I guess I qualify since I grew up on Long Island."

I sucked in my jealousy. She wasn't quite two years older

than I and already so accomplished. Plus, she hadn't bothered to ask me a single question about myself. *A bit self-centered*, was my initial assessment.

Still, to get ahead, I knew I should flatter everyone I met at the Prince. "Miss Scarborough, as I prepare for my part, might I ask you questions? I could use your expert advice. We're left pretty much on our own."

"I'd love that! I'd feel like so much more a part of everything." The wistful admission softened her tone and exposed her vulnerability. "But no more formality, OK? I'm just Clem."

I agreed and offered my own boyish name in return. There wasn't much time to learn my role, so I pressed, "Are you free tomorrow, Clem?"

Her mouth flew open. "Bloody hell! Tomorrow's Sunday and then I work all day Monday."

I must have looked baffled because she explained, "I work for a milliner. Horrible trade, all those feathers up my nose, but it pays the room and board and it's cleaner than a factory job."

I'd pictured female writers as women of leisure who scratched out poems in their spare time and then reclined on divans eating bonbons. Instead, Clem explained she had earned an independent living since she was sixteen, rooming in a ladies' boardinghouse during the week and taking the ferry most weekends to Williamsburg in Brooklyn, where her family now lived.

"My family isn't much for church," I said. "We're practically heathens. If you like, you could come to dinner tomorrow, and after we could discuss the role."

The offer spilled out even though I knew Mama would be suspicious of a girl who peppered her speech with "OK" and "bloody hell" and lived on her own at just nineteen.

Clem blinked quickly, as if navigating a waterfall of thoughts. "They expect me," she said, "and I do like to see my sisters and brother. Truth is, though, my family isn't much for church either. It's really *just* about dinner, and it's an awfully long way to go for a stew."

39

"We're right on Bond Street. Our cook fixes a roast or chicken on Sundays."

"You've got a cook?"

"We do." I paused for the finale. "And she often makes a cream cake for dessert."

Her eyes lit up at the mention of cake. Somehow, I'd guessed that sweets were Clem's weak spot, as they were mine. "I'll be there," she said.

As expected, Mama treated Clem with caution, lobbing questions at her throughout Sunday dinner—so many that by the time Aggie cleared the table for cake and coffee, Clem had barely had a chance to touch her meal. She watched her plate disappear into the kitchen with a forlorn look.

I regretted subjecting my new friend to the parental torrent: Why didn't she live at home? Did her parents approve of her move to Manhattan? Did they support her financially? What kind of magazines had published her writing? What sort of education had she received?

Mama eyed her with skepticism while Clem delivered polite responses. Her father was a schoolmaster, a perfectly respectable profession, and he and her mother had encouraged her desire to write. They did often pass her spare coins when she went home to visit.

Her reply to the question about her schooling drew Mama's attention. Clem had enjoyed a first-rate education at the Bellport Academy for Classical Studies on Long Island. She was much better educated than I, having studied not only French, handwriting, and English grammar, but literature, Greek, Latin, mathematics, history, and philosophy—alongside boys.

"I've heard of that academy," Mama said with a respectful nod. "Neighbors of my mother in Brooklyn Heights sent their boys there."

I smiled into my cake, in awe of how Clem handled herself

under pressure. "Your education sounds so thorough," I said—one of the only comments I made during the meal.

"You actually went to school with boys?" Maude asked. "Wasn't that distracting?"

"Only when they got higher grades," Clem said with a sly smile. "But I surprised everyone when I took the prize in mathematics my final term."

After a nibble of cake, my mother asked, "And what will you do with mathematics, dear?"

"I'll need it when I start my own magazine," Clem replied without missing a beat. "That is, someday in the future." She refrained from elaborating and took a few big bites of her own slice.

Mama nodded slowly. I knew she had managed the money in our house. "We'd be penniless if it weren't for me," was a complaint I'd heard her lob at my father for hiring hacks and buying expensive accessories for his costumes.

After dinner, Clem and I retreated to my bedroom, our hands clasped over our mouths to hold in the explosion of giggles. We perched on the bed, so close our arms and legs pressed against each other. Neither of us moved away.

"I am *so* sorry!" I whispered after we'd calmed down. "You didn't even get a proper meal out of it."

"I wasn't very ladylike about the cake. I was afraid Aggie would snatch it away!"

"I had no idea it would be that grueling. Mama—" I broke off, unable to complete the thought.

"—was just being a mother," Clem finished. "Although at times it felt like I was being interviewed as your suitor."

That made us both shy and quiet for a moment, although I wasn't sure why.

"Pa would have shown more respect for your achievements. He wanted a son, but Mama delivered three boys too soon and none of them survived. Maybe that's why he called me George."

Clem cast her eyes down, assuming the worst from my use of past tense. "I'm so sorry. When did your father pass away?"

41

My memory flitted to the evening I witnessed his disgrace, the days and days in which I waited for him to come home.

"We lost him in June," I said, massaging the truth. I didn't know how close Clem was to Worth, who could never know about my connection to Pa.

"Was it sudden?"

"Yes, very. A fall." Technically true. Thoughts tumbled in my head as I searched for a fall befitting a tragedian. "From a . . . high place."

"How terrible!" Clem slid an arm around my shoulder and squeezed. "I'm lucky to have a boring schoolmaster for a dad, who's never got his nose out of a book."

I'd missed the experience of having a normal, boring father, but I would never regret learning from Pa, soaking up what he knew about acting. The regret was that he wasn't in the wings now as I performed, saying "Brava, George!" as I exited stage left. My eyes welled up at the memory of his rich voice.

Clem's free hand dabbed a tear from my cheek, her finger resting there for a second. "I'd love to hear more about him."

The tender gesture produced a rippling in my stomach that I didn't understand and dismissed as a spot of dyspepsia. I wriggled away from her arm, her finger, and all thoughts of Pa. "I can't," I said.

Clem's hand retreated to her lap. "OK, I understand," she said.

I sprang off the bed. I'd been gruff with someone who was just trying to help. "Oh, golly! I didn't mean to snap. You're here doing me a favor! Let's look at my prompt book, shall we?"

Chapter 7

Ned's prompt books were still fatter than mine, although he was not garnering the best notices from reviewers. *Spirit of the Times* deemed his interpretation of Casca in *Julius Caesar*—a role he stepped into when the second gentleman came down with a fever—"serviceable." I'd spent valuable time running lines with him, time I needed for my own preparation, but he still struggled with the role.

"I just can't get the hang of the tragedies," he complained. "And I so want to!"

When Ned read the Casca review, he bent over and choked back tears. I'd never seen a boy or man cry openly.

"You did get the pages late," I consoled him.

Yet, even after groaning about his inadequacy as an actor, how he'd never be a leading man, Ned recovered quickly and basked in the attention he got at the stage door, where women of all ages crowded to catch a glimpse of the handsome Mr. Murtagh. He feigned surprise at their flattery, brushing back his curly hair with an affected gesture.

"I might hate him if I weren't so darn fond of him," I confided to Clem when she found me rehearsing with Sallie in the green room. Although Clem and I hadn't been friends long, I had already picked up words like *darn* and *bloody* from her that I had to remember not to repeat at home.

Clem openly disapproved of the way I "coddled" Ned, to

use her word.

"I find him insufferable. I don't know why you fuss over him. What do you think, Sallie?"

The dresser clicked her tongue. "I think Mr. Ned'd make a pretty good infant."

The two exchanged a laugh over that, but Clem buttoned it up quickly. "We shouldn't make sport of him if Georgie likes him *so much.*"

Her emphasis made me flinch. "I'm not interested in Ned like that." If compelled to put my finger on what appealed to me about him, I would have said he brought out my protective instincts, like he was one of the brothers I'd lost. "The thing is, I'd cry, too, if I got such a review. See here, Clem, suppose a reviewer calls *All My Sisters* 'serviceable' as drama?"

"Don't say that!" Clem hissed. She rapped on the top rail of Sallie's chair. I had thought only actors were superstitious, but dramatists apparently were, too.

Sallie collected her twenty cents and left to press costumes.

"You know, I'd run lines with you, and you wouldn't have to pay me," Clem said.

"I don't mind paying Sallie," I said. My voice fell to a whisper. "She lives here, under the stage. Can you imagine? I went exploring in the back hallway of the cellar, and there was this tiny room right near the alley door with a straw mat and a quilt and costumes stacked everywhere. Such a cramped space, and she has to share it with a cat."

"Oh!" Clem said. "Where's her family?"

Sallie had mentioned her actor-father and made a passing reference to an older sister who taught her to sew, but I had no idea where they lived or why she had taken up residence at the theater.

"I . . . you know, I didn't think to ask." I fumbled for a more intelligent response. "Well, don't most Negroes live down in the 5th Ward or up in Seneca Village? Maybe travel was of concern."

Clem eyed me curiously, nodding in a halting way. I

didn't want her to think me the least inquisitive girl ever, so I changed the subject.

"Looks like I'm finished for the day," I said. "How about a little adventure? Maybe an ice cream at Taylor's?"

Clem fished for an excuse, possibly because of the awkwardness about Sallie but more likely because she didn't have money to spare on frivolities.

"My treat," I added so she'd agree.

As I pulled the dressing-room door closed behind us, a low rumble gathered force and swelled into deep, resonant thunder, followed by the rattle of a hailstorm.

"Oh, just our luck," I said. "We'll be drenched."

"No, we won't. Harry said they're trying out the new thunder roll," Clem explained. The sound effect—accomplished with cannonballs released down a chute above the stage—grew louder as we moved to the wings, where Ned, in a frock coat and topper, looked to be in a hurry to leave.

"Where are you off to? We're going for ice cream. Want to come?"

Clem sighed loudly.

"I need something stronger than ice cream," Ned replied. "I'm headed to Groff's."

The name of the beer cellar that had been Pa's second home sent a chill down my spine. I harbored a vague hope that Pa was alive, just too ashamed to come home. Might he be living above the saloon in the room he occasionally let there?

Clem perked up, seeming to forget her objections to Ned. "Groff's, Georgie! Now there's an adventure. That's where all the Bohemians go. Mind if we tag along, Ned?"

"Come along, then," he replied. "Hurry up, though!"

I heard my Granny Clifford's voice coming out of my mouth: "A lady can't go to a saloon."

"You most certainly *can* go to Groff's," Ned said. "Our own Mrs. Reynolds was there just last week. She's nothing if not a lady."

"We're too young, aren't we?" I persisted, even as excitement rippled through me.

45

"No one'll care how old you are. Herr Groff will just wink and look the other way."

Clem was already following Ned toward the stage door, but then she hung back, waiting for me. Ned's expression was turning to impatience.

"Georgie, you coming or not?"

Groff's sat diagonally across from the Prince's stage door, which explained its appeal for Pa and other members of the company. Its proximity, Ned said, was the reason for the clause in our contracts that had undone my poor father: "Any member of the Company unable from the effects of stimulants to perform, or to appear at rehearsal, shall forfeit a week's salary on first offense, and thereafter shall be liable to discharge." Pa had obviously progressed past his first offense.

Because it was tucked into the cellar of a hotel with no street sign, I'd passed Groff's many times, completely unaware of its existence. As we descended the flight of stairs to the entrance, "Restaurant and Lager Bier Saloon" came into view over the oak door.

"Please try to act like you've been here before," Ned cautioned. "And don't gawk at people and embarrass me."

The interior was exactly what the imagination might conjure up for a below-ground saloon: stone walls and arched ceilings; a thick layer of sawdust on the floor; scarred wooden tables and benches; a scattering of gaslights; and absolutely everywhere you looked, smoke—enough so that Clem and I choked upon entry.

Ned greeted the proprietor, Mr. Groff, a portly gray-haired gentleman who looked as if he drank a lot of his own lager. He pointed us to the only available seats at a table wedged at the end of the narrow room. Even at five o'clock in the afternoon, customers packed the space like pickles in a barrel, lifting sweating pewter steins to their lips. A few women mingled with the mostly male crowd, shadows dancing across their faces and forms. In the distorted lighting, Ned's face became elongated, and Clem's body appeared stouter.

"They have lager, of course, but there's food, too, reasonably priced," Ned said when we were situated. "I've taken meals here after a play. The coffee's lovely and a bargain at three cents."

"You pay to take your meals out?" Clem said. She had told me she roomed on Pearl Street where her board included two meals a day. "How can you afford it?"

"Well, I live with Ma and Da, so I've no room and board. There's costumes and hacks to pay for, but if I'm careful twenty-five dollars a week lasts a while."

A clamor of voices echoed off the walls, and I wasn't sure I'd heard him correctly. "Did you say twenty-*five* dollars?" I asked.

Ned acted oblivious, but then it *was* noisy. Besides that, his attention had darted to the far end of our table and a young man with romantically long lashes over hooded eyes. I watched the two of them exchange nods of recognition.

I fumed silently over Ned's salary. Not only was he getting juicier parts than I was, but he earned five dollars more a week—and with less favorable reviews than mine.

I ordered a cup of coffee, but it tasted bitter and I left most of it untouched. Close to my right ear, Clem explained the term *Bohemian*, how it originated with the Romani people of Central Europe and migrated to Paris and then this country, but I only half-listened. My eyes struggled to adjust to the odd light in case Pa was there somewhere, and my ears were tuned for his distinctive timbre.

After a half hour, the smoke continued to burn my lungs and eyes. As an excuse for leaving, I said I was worried about protecting my voice for the matinee, but more than that, I feared what Mama would say about my frock and hair reeking of smoke. Clem looked as if she wanted to stay, but we both knew a girl couldn't leave alone, so she made her farewell at the same time. Ned stood and gave us a half bow, then slid his stein toward the other end of the table and the mysterious young man.

As Clem and I wove through the throng to the exit, a dark figure caught my attention, an older man hunched near the front of the bar and contemplating the drink in his hand as if it were the most important thing in the world. Pa had perfected such a bent posture when I helped him rehearse for *Richard III*. I inched closer, steeling myself to gaze into my father's face. But when the man raised his head from his lager, he wasn't Pa at all, just a dodgy fellow whose mouth opened like he might take a bite out of me. Clem grabbed my arm and pulled me toward the door.

"What was that about?" she asked when we were safely on the street.

"The lighting played a trick on me. I thought I saw a ghost."

Thanks to Worth's efforts, ladies overflowed the parquet for the matinee of *All My Sisters*. In a flash of promotional brilliance, my employer had championed the play with advertisements geared to women in the *Herald* and ladies' magazines: "moral drama," "perfect for groups of ladies," and "close to Taylor's." Respectable women could attend the theater together, without male escorts, then stop for cake or ice cream on the way home—an enticing full afternoon's entertainment.

The mostly female audience loved us, and our reviews glistened. In particular, the *Herald* reviewer who had been "watching" me bubbled over: "As youngest sister Abigail, Miss Georgiana Clifford exceeded all our expectations. Her character possessed a range of realistic emotions, and her lines were perfectly delivered and timed. Miss Clifford improves with each performance. Although still new to the boards, will this young actress soon capture the leading role she deserves?"

With so much enthusiasm for the play, Worth announced we would run it every Wednesday afternoon through October. Almost unheard of—theaters changed their bills every day and didn't repeat themselves for months, keeping ticket-holders' interest piqued and the company hopping. Frances Muller, another walking lady, was often so exhausted by the pace, I'd found her dozing off in the dressing room.

Within the week, Worth engaged Clem to write a second melodrama as fast as her fingers would allow. "Something the same but different, he said," Clem told me. "Preferably with *sisters* in the title."

"*Most of My Sisters?*" I suggested. "*All of My Sisters Return?* Or maybe *My Youngest Sister*—starring Abigail, of course."

I was joking, but Clem's eyes sparkled with interest. "Not bad."

Armed with my stellar clipping from the *Herald*, I decided to approach Worth about my salary. The manager's office doubled as his dressing room. Sallie caught me standing in front of the closed door, poised to tap on it, and coaxed me to follow her down the hallway.

"You don't want to go in there alone, miss," she advised in a whisper. "Not if you don't have to. He's got some hands on him."

The way she phrased it made me laugh, but Sallie's eyes were steely, and her cheeks didn't show her dimples. "I'm serious, miss. He's famous for handling ladies. Some like it, some don't. I reckon you might not."

"He grabs them?"

"Sometimes more. Miss Angelina got—" Sallie's lips closed over the sentence. Worth had implied something unsavory about my predecessor, that she'd mysteriously gotten herself with child, but now Sallie was hinting he'd played a critical role.

"I need to talk to him, though, and there's no way to do that but in person."

"Well, you been warned. Just know Miss Angelina weren't the only one."

I considered postponing my encounter with Worth, but only for the half-minute it took to thank Sallie and walk back down the hall to the door marked "Manager." I wanted five dollars more a week and I wanted the bigger roles Ned was getting. When I glanced toward Sallie, she shook her head at me and disappeared into another dressing room with her broom and dustbin.

After several raps, Worth said sternly, "Enter."

In the dim light, the first thing I saw were the soles of Worth's boots resting on his massive desk. Falstaff nestled in his lap. The tabby gave me a quick once-over before closing his sleepy eyes again.

Worth was in shirt sleeves, turning the pages of a script—probably *King Lear*, his next role. He was decades too young for the part, but makeup would age him well enough to trick the audience, and his performances all exuded a certain gravity anyway. *Lear* required the thunder and rain machines—effects guaranteed to bring gasps from the parquet and boxes. The papers had praised Worth for his use of spectacle, so he continued to favor plays that required lavish effects.

"My dear Miss Clifford," he said, setting his script aside. His voice dripped with honey as he stroked the cat's head. "What a delightful surprise." He waved me toward him, and, remembering Sallie's warning, I was careful to leave the office door ajar.

"You continue to woo our friends, the critics," he observed before I had a chance to speak. Worth liked to woo the critics in a different way—with a private spread of cheeses, cakes, and ale before a performance so they'd puff it in the papers. "They appreciate the subtlety you bring to your characters, I can tell. It's like you're giving us the layers underneath them. All the best actors do that. The worst just repeat their lines." He scowled but didn't name names.

His eyes traveled from my now-warm face down my bodice before resting at my waist. Nervously, I glanced down, too, but my dress was in fine order. With Sallie's words still in my thoughts, I considered turning back toward the door.

"What can I do for you?" he asked, his eyes catching mine with something like concern.

"It's come to my attention—" My voice wavered, and

Worth leaned forward. "Mr. Worth, I'm paid less than a walking gentleman!"

He sat back and guffawed. The sudden movement disturbed the tabby, who hopped from his lap and scurried out the open door. "Is that all? For a moment, I feared you'd been stolen away by another company. Of course you're paid less. You're a girl."

Worth's focus returned to his book, as if that settled the matter of my pay.

But I pressed on, summoning up the gumption Clem had written into my character in *All My Sisters*. "I'm getting stronger notices than Ned, yet I'm paid less and my roles aren't as important," I said in a rush. "I think the *Herald* reviewer is right. I'm still new, but I've proven my value to the company and it's time to give me more to work with."

Worth's face was unreadable. It wasn't just the darkness of the space; his impassive look was odd for an actor and it confused me. He might say anything next, from "You're absolutely right" to "Pack up your costumes and be gone."

What he actually said was more enigmatic. "Hmm." He paused. "Well, Georgie—that's what they call you, isn't it?"

"Yes," I answered. A rivulet of sweat dribbled between my bosoms.

His second pause was a tease—like prodding Falstaff with a feather, as Ned was wont to do.

At last he said, "Miss Burton has to travel to Troy next week to visit her family—an illness or death or some such inconvenience. Mrs. Reynolds is a shade too old to be a convincing Juliet to my Romeo, but don't tell her I said that, or she'll be taking off for another house. That rascal at The Broadway is always trying to spirit away my best people." He rambled on, thinking aloud. "I can't afford to bring in someone from outside. The audience'll start to expect it. How old are you again?"

"Eighteen." My breath got shallow as I waited for his next words.

"Perfect. You'll play Juliet a week from Wednesday," he

said. "Miss Muller isn't ready for it, but you might be."

My heart danced in my chest, even though it wasn't a role I'd pick for myself. Worth seemed to think it might be a dodgy choice, too. "You'll have to pretty yourself up. See if you can fit into Miss Burton's costumes. And for God's sake, do something about your hair. Would a few curls hurt you?"

My hand rose to the tidy braid across my head, which I considered the smartest look for my features. No one had ever called me pretty; but still, Worth's assessment left the imprint of a slap.

"The audience needs to believe I'd actually be attracted to you."

Tears pricked at the corners of my eyes, but I blinked them back.

"Now go. Tell Harry to give you the prompt book."

I struggled to regain the confidence he'd ripped to shreds. "Thank you, sir," I managed. "I know the part well. I recently saw Miss Anderton perform it opposite Miss Cushman."

He smirked. "You know the part from seeing it once?"

I'd tripped up, forgetting that the reason I knew it was from reading Pa's scripts.

"I've read it many times," I said as cover. "My parents brought me and my sister up on Shakespeare. You won't regret casting me."

"Yes, I'd rather not," he said. "And you'll still have the *Sisters* matinee, you know. Two performances in one day will be a lot for someone just eighteen."

I spotted a way to regain my footing and dignity. "I heard you started young, too, didn't you, sir?"

Approval lit his face. I'd gambled that he liked some sass in a girl and won. "You've got a way about you, don't you, Georgie?"

I shrugged, coy as could be, but his next statement made me regret giving him anything to like about me.

"You and I will rehearse together. Friday afternoon. Here. Without the book, or you'll forfeit a dollar." That clause was in our contracts, too.

52

My thoughts raced as I mulled over the unhappy prospect of rehearsing with him alone. In his private space. And for such a romantic role. Could I handle a handler? In my eighteen years, no boy or man had given me cause to learn.

All I said was, "I haven't forfeited a single dollar yet, sir."

Mama would never assent to my having a private rehearsal with Worth. She wasn't even keen on my rehearsing with Ned, who was more like my brother than an actual man. I worried she might put a stop to my first leading role.

Unless I omitted some of the details when I announced the new part at home.

Worth's focus turned back to his prompt book, but before I left, I wanted to remind him of the other reason I'd come to his office.

"Sir, one last thing. If I do well as Juliet, could we discuss my pay again?"

A skeptical eyebrow shot up, and I wasn't sure if he'd answer or ignore me.

"It's possible," he replied. "Now, off with you before I change my mind and give the role to Miss Muller."

Chapter 8

"I'm playing Juliet!" The words popped out the minute Clem appeared in the doorway to the dressing room.

Her smile faded, and her eyes darted to the opposite end of the room, where Frances Muller was emoting into a mirror, running lines with her reflection. As a consolation for not playing Juliet even though she had seniority over me, Worth had given Frances the juicy part of Lady Sneerwell in *The School for Scandal*.

"You're Juliet?" Clem said, turning her attention back to me. "Well, isn't that a stunner?"

Her words wounded my pride, and I snapped back, "You know I'm plenty good enough."

"Oh, I know! Sorry, George." She had recently started calling me George, and though it was Pa's special name for me, I found I didn't mind. "It's just there's a flock of ladies ahead of you, Mary Louise and Mrs. Reynolds and—" She jerked her head toward Frances.

"Mary Louise will be out of town, and Mrs. Reynolds is too old. But you didn't hear that from me." I couldn't comment on Frances's shortcomings in her presence, even if she seemed oblivious to our conversation.

"Good for you, then," Clem said. Her tone was flat, with none of the enthusiasm I'd expected. "Congratulations."

I pouted. "I thought you'd be happy! Friends are supposed

to be happy for friends. It's my first lead!"

Clem held out the stack of pages she was carrying. The top sheet read in her neat handwriting, *My Youngest Sister, A Melodrama*. I'd flippantly suggested the title, and Clem had run with it. She was writing the play Worth commissioned with *my* character as the lead role.

Clem lowered her voice. "I thought this would be your first lead. Worth would have to cast you after the smash you made in *All My Sisters*. I mean, reviewers would expect it, wouldn't they? And you're the one who gave me the idea. I know you were kidding, but I thought it was brilliant."

She sniffed and tucked the pages back under her arm, her tone changing from sad to defiant in an instant. "That's what I thought, anyway. But if you'd rather play the *insipid* Juliet, go right ahead."

"Insipid" had been my own assessment of Juliet, which she was now using against me. On a Sunday afternoon when Clem didn't go home to Williamsburg, she and I had finally gone to Taylor's. She had never been to the restaurant; and she spent a good deal of time before we ordered, pivoting her head from the vaulted ceilings to the gilt-frame mirrors to the marble counters.

Over a dish of strawberry ice cream—Clem insisted on sharing because of the extravagance, and because I was paying—we had agreed that Shakespeare reserved his strongest roles for men. We then compiled two lists of his female characters: the most thrilling and the most grating.

"Who would you play in a heartbeat?" she'd asked to start us off, our heads almost knocking over our treat.

Lady M. landed at the top of our list, along with Beatrice in *As You Like It*. I also offered Emilia in *Othello*, to which Clem shouted an enthusiastic "Yes!" that caused some ladies enjoying tea and sandwiches to glance in our direction. "'Let husbands know their wives have sense like them,'" Clem recited before I could get the words out.

At the top of our choices for the most grating was fair Juliet.

"Juliet is insipid," I'd stated.

"So true. She's nothing without her Romeo." Clem had rolled her eyes at the hero's name.

Now it stung when Clem reminded me of my own drubbing of Juliet.

"See here, Clem, Worth didn't *ask* me," I rushed to say in my defense. Frances had suddenly gone quiet and cocked an ear in our direction, so I chose my words with care. "It's in my contract that I have to accept any role I'm assigned. Besides, it's a great honor to be picked for Juliet."

Clem nodded with reluctance. "It'll get you more notice for sure," she allowed. A smile creased her face. "I just hope your feelings about poor, *insipid* Juliet don't get in the way of her passion for Romeo."

From the corner, Frances coughed, reminding us of her presence, and I shifted topics quickly.

"Tell me about your play," I said. "I want to hear the whole plot, start to finish. Don't leave out a single tiny detail." I imagined that would get rid of Frances, and I was right. Only a few sentences into Clem's lengthy summary, Frances yawned daintily and left the dressing room, making it easier for us to talk freely.

"I think it's a good play, but who knows what the man in charge will say," Clem said. "Worth can be unpredictable. Will you read it first, George? Please?"

Perspiration trickled down my neck. "I wouldn't know what to say. I'm not a writer."

"But you're my best friend."

My cheeks warmed, thrilled to merit the place of Clem's best friend. Still, I had to admit to my inadequacy as a critic. "Look, Clem, you should know that writing wasn't my strong suit in school. I don't feel like I could say anything helpful. Once, I tried to write a letter to Charlotte Cushman and couldn't even do that! A simple letter, Clem, and it came out sounding so stupid, I didn't send it."

Her face lit with interest. "I can write a letter for you, George," she said. "Why were you writing to her, anyway?"

Part of the problem, beyond my own clumsiness with words, was the letter's lack of purpose. I had wanted to compliment Miss Cushman's portrayal of Romeo first of all, and I also wanted to introduce myself as an aspiring actress. But it went even deeper than that. I wanted Charlotte Cushman to *see* me.

"I wanted her to write back," I said.

"Tell you what. If you read my first act, I'll write your letter. It'll be the best letter Miss Cushman ever received, guaranteed."

Clem positioned herself next to me. She always carried a pen and a capped inkwell in her satchel, and she used the back of the title page of her manuscript for the letter. In addition to the scratched-out words, her handwriting was at first difficult to make out. Although she'd studied penmanship at school, she hadn't put much store in the subject, and her words slanted severely.

"What's this word?" I asked.

"Aspiring," she said. "You'll copy it over on your own stationery, of course. Don't judge the handwriting, just focus on the content."

Dear Miss Cushman,

First, please allow me to introduce myself so it will be clear why I, an utter stranger, am writing to you. My name is Georgiana Clifford, and I am both a great admirer of yours and an aspiring actress. I have been following your progress as an actress for four years, since I first recognized my calling to a life in the theater.

Like you, I started in the acting profession young, at eighteen. After private lessons with the great Mrs. Stansbury, I secured a position as a walking lady at the Prince Theatre, where I have played everything from Pert in "London Assurance" to Abigail in a new melodrama, "All My

Sisters," by the rising young playwright, Clem-
entine Scarborough.

That made me laugh out loud. "You're promoting yourself
in *my* letter!"
"Is it too much?"
"No, I like it."

> *Next week, I will step in to portray Juliet in*
> *my first leading role, opposite Mr. Thomas Worth*
> *as Romeo. I am writing in hopes you might offer*
> *advice to a young actress who has taken such*
> *great inspiration from your work.*
> *I had the pleasure of accompanying my uncle*
> *to The Broadway to see your magnificent perfor-*
> *mance of Romeo in Mr. Shakespeare's great trag-*
> *edy. I was fairly sobbing at your portrayal of the*
> *young hero. It was as if you <u>became</u> Romeo and*
> *the audience forgot you were a woman. Trust me,*
> *<u>I</u> never forgot! You brought both masculine and*
> *feminine aspects to your portrayal. How were*
> *you able to accomplish that?*

I looked up from the page with wonder. "You put what I
felt into words! You're a genius."
She shrugged but her smile suggested she agreed with me.

> *I wish I had the means to send you a bouquet*
> *as a thank-you. I am in your debt for the foot-*
> *prints you have left on the boards for actresses like*
> *me to tread. If you have suggestions for success on*
> *the stage, I would dearly love to hear them. I also*
> *take inspiration from your noble pursuit of an*
> *independent life as an unmarried lady.*
> *I wish you safe travels with Miss Hays and*
> *a successful and profitable national tour! If you*
> *find a moment in your busy schedule to reply to a*

young actress's admiring note, I would be deeply honored.

Yours humbly,
Georgiana Clifford

I took a deep breath as I finished reading. The letter was more than I had hoped for. If I ever received such a letter as an actress, I'd reply immediately.

Clem hovered over me. "I can change anything you like. Maybe 'Yours humbly' is too much? Or I could add a poem—"

I stood and hugged her, the gesture taking her by surprise. Although stiff at first, she relaxed into it and let her arms go around my back.

"It's perfection," I said.

Her face colored a pretty pink.

"And I'd actually prefer it be in your handwriting. Mine looks like a schoolgirl's and yours is so much more . . . mature," I said.

"I don't have any paper fine enough."

"I do." My grandmother had gifted me with a box of vellum stationery on my birthday, as if eighteen were the age of needing to write to people. "And would you address it to The Broadway Theatre and post it, too? Miss Cushman's left on tour, and I don't know where she's gone. Maybe write 'Please Forward' on the envelope?" It was a lot to ask, but I *had* agreed to read her play in exchange. I fished in my pocket and added, "Here's a nickel for the stamp."

"That's too much."

"I know, but when she writes back, we'll be prepared!"

Chapter 9

"I have a surprise for you," Ned said with a bashful smile. He often escorted me home after an evening performance, but it was a surprise to find him waiting at the stage door in broad daylight following a matinee. He still had traces of makeup on his cheeks, and I dabbed at them with my handkerchief before we left the building.

"You bought me my own private carriage?" I said as a tease. A dream we shared in common was to earn enough money to purchase a fine brougham like my uncle's, with a driver who would wait patiently at the stage door to whisk us home. I never understood why Pa hadn't made the investment.

"I'm still saving up for that," he said. "You'll like this, too, though, I promise."

Ned never stooped to taking omnibuses or walking, so he engaged a hack at Broadway, mumbled something to the driver, and off we went—where, he wouldn't say.

"Is the surprise edible?" I asked, but then Taylor's passed out of sight.

"No, better."

The hack reduced speed at Barnum's museum, and my mood sank. The last thing I wanted after a day of work was to sit through someone else's performance or to tour the oddities at Barnum's. The waxworks and the Feejee Mermaid had thrilled me as a little girl, but such attractions now bored me.

But it was just a spot of traffic that held us up, and we continued past St. Paul's Church. The hack slowed again in front of Mathew Brady's portrait studios, two side-by-side buildings that were a fixture on Broadway.

"You're taking me for a sitting at Brady's? How extravagant and exciting!"

Ned's cheeks flamed as the driver kept going past Brady's and turned onto Fulton. "Right here will do," Ned called out the window.

As Ned helped me from the hack, I finally understood our destination. The lettering painted between the third and fourth stories of the narrow building read "MURTAGH & SON DAGUERREOTYPES."

"It's not Brady's, but my da runs a class establishment," Ned said. "And today he's agreed to do *your* sitting for free. I told him you're to play Juliet."

It was my turn to be embarrassed. "Oh, how lovely, Ned! I can't wait."

With that, he grinned and showed me into the building.

"Is there another '& Son,' a brother you haven't mentioned, or is your father still hoping you'll change your mind?"

"Shh," he said as we entered a long waiting room, lined with daguerreotypes. Ned led me down the rows of portraits. Some I recognized as minor politicians, now out of office; here and there was an actor or actress before they reached fame. A few likenesses Ned said were local tradesmen, but the majority appeared to be ordinary citizens who wanted a record of themselves.

"Here's Worth," Ned pointed out. I recalled that was how he had recognized the manager at Mrs. Stansbury's theatrical, the night we were both hired. In the likeness, Worth looked much younger; but even as a less prominent personage, his chin lifted a few inches in disdain as if rebuking anyone having the audacity to look into his eyes. "He was probably saving money by not going to Brady's."

"Or maybe he heard of your father's excellent work," I said, still trying to put my mistake behind us.

61

Ned chuckled as if he knew what I was about. "Da's not trying to compete with the top tier," he said. "He chose this location for a reason. He picks up customers who decide it's not worth the wait or the extra dollar across the street, and everyone leaves happy. I'm proud that he's offering this service to regular folks."

An older woman with ginger hair appeared through the curtain at the back of the hall, dressed in the stark black bombazine I associated with mourning. Ned hadn't mentioned any family tragedy, though, and she seemed jolly enough, so I assumed it was just her style.

"My boy!" Mrs. Murtagh said, grabbing him for a quick kiss on both cheeks, as if she hadn't seen him in years when, in fact, he lived at home.

"Ma, this is Miss Clifford," he said. "The young lady I told you about? She's here for her sitting."

A look passed between them that I didn't understand.

"Dear Miss Clifford," his mother said. "What a pleasure to finally meet you!" How much had Ned said about me, and what? But then, I talked about him at home, too, as one of my best friends.

"Thank you, Mrs. Murtagh. This is an honor, to have my portrait done. It's a surprise, though. If Ned had told me, I'd have worn a better dress."

I glanced down self-consciously at my day frock, which I wore often because it didn't pinch or itch. Its rich midnight blue color would probably show up well in the print, but it had a pattern of fainter blue dots I wasn't sure about. Also, I had tied the ribbons at the neckline haphazardly when I changed at the theater.

To get a better look at my frock, Mrs. Murtagh took my hands and fanned them out to the side. Her face registered sheer delight.

"You look beautiful, dear. That dress never came from a rack, did it? And Ned, shame on you. You might have warned her." Then, with a wink toward me: "So like a man, isn't it?"

Her voice held the faintest lilt; she'd come from Ireland as a child, Ned had told me, and met Mr. Murtagh, a more recent immigrant, at church.

Mrs. Murtagh led us up two long flights of stairs to the uppermost level, which housed the studio. She was winded at the top, and Ned patted her back reassuringly.

"I'm fine, I'm fine." She leaned toward me to explain. "I assisted when Mr. Murtagh first opened, but he's had hired help for years now, and I'm rarely here. Today is special, though, isn't it? I didn't want to miss the chance to meet *you*!" She exchanged another secret look with Ned, and I had a flash of worry that he'd misrepresented me as his sweetheart.

Our voices echoed in the cavernous studio where the portrait work occurred. The only furnishings were the camera on its tripod, a faux pillar, a movable reflector, and an upholstered armchair positioned in front of a bluish-gray screen. Natural light from two skylights flooded and warmed the space. Off to the side, an assortment of iron stands with sinister-looking prongs converged as if in a meeting.

"Don't tell me! This must be Miss Clifford!"

Mr. Murtagh's appearance was so starkly different from his son's it stunned me. He stood a head taller than Ned, with the dark hair, complexion, and eyes of the Black Irish. He, too, expressed enthusiasm at making my acquaintance.

"She's a pretty one, Ned," he said, as if assessing a visage in a daguerreotype.

For this "special occasion," as Mr. Murtagh called it, he would perform his own camera work, relying on his assistants for the setup of the plate and then the polishing and sealing.

Mrs. Murtagh adjusted my neck ribbons and got me seated in the chair. "Bring the smaller rest, Ned," his father instructed.

Ned lugged over one of the iron stands, which his father said was designed to keep the neck and head straight during the process. When he first started the business, he explained, customers had to sit still for three whole minutes, but now it was under thirty seconds.

My eyes must have widened because Mr. Murtagh hastened to add, "It's not a clamp, mind you. The seconds go by quick, but you might like to rest your head." I leaned back onto the prongs, which were rounded and happily didn't bite.

What we were aiming for, Mr. Murtagh continued, was a half-smile. "You don't want to grin, now do you, and you don't want to frown or look too stiff neither."

"Just look at Ned and that'll give you the sweetest smile," Mrs. Murtagh suggested.

That bit of coaching must have brought a crease to my brow, because Ned called out, "Better yet, think of your favorite ice cream at Taylor's!"

An actress knows how to summon up her best look, so my thoughts turned not to ice cream but to Clem and the splendid letter she'd written to Miss Cushman. The muscles in my forehead and jaws loosened.

"Lovely. Now look at the peg just below the camera." Mr. Murtagh pointed to the spot.

When he was satisfied that my facial expression had relaxed sufficiently, Ned's father removed the shutter and reached into his vest for his pocket watch. What he assured me would be about twenty seconds felt like four or five times that as I struggled to keep my face still but not clenched, my hands immobilized in my lap where Mrs. Murtagh had neatly arranged them.

"And . . . you're free to move!"—more welcome words I'd never heard. "I think we'll all be pleased with that one."

It would be about an hour, Mr. Murtagh said, before the daguerreotype would be finished in the mechanical department and fitted into its presentation box.

"We'll enjoy ourselves in the parlor," Mrs. Murtagh suggested. The family didn't live in the building, although when the studio first opened, they had done so. "Crammed in like steerage! Now, I keep some rooms on the first floor for special guests like yourself."

My throat dried to dust as we descended to the aforementioned parlor, where a table was set with a flowered porcelain tea service. Almost immediately, Mrs. Murtagh excused herself to fetch the apple cake she'd forgotten to lay out, adding with a mischievous smile, "Behave yourselves now!"

When she disappeared, I poked Ned hard in the ribs and hissed, "What in the world did you *tell* them?"

He cast his eyes down, so I poked him again until he was forced to look at my anger head-on. "I, well, I may have given the impression you were my girl."

"Ned!"

"I didn't say it outright, Georgie. It was just a bit of a hint. Kind of, there's this *special* girl I'd like you to meet, blah blah blah."

"'Blah blah blah'? Why would you do that? You know it isn't true!"

"Well, you *are* special, Georgie. That's the truth."

"Oh, please!" My thoughts raced to the worst case in this scenario. "Please say you didn't tell them we planned to marry."

His silence suggested the worst.

"Blast it, Ned!"

"I didn't, Georgie, I swear," he said. "They may have assumed so, but I never, ever said it outright."

I flopped onto the settee. "You lured me into a trap."

Ned sat next to me and took my hand, as if assuming the role of suitor. I yanked it back into my lap.

"I don't feel that way about you," I said. "And honestly, I know you don't feel that way about me. I've never gotten the slightest amorous feelings from you. Good Lord, we could be brother and sister. Why this charade?"

"I can't tell you here," he said. "Please just go along with it, would you? It wasn't meant to hurt you. It was selfishly meant to protect me. I promise I'll tell all soon."

His eyes clouded over, and deep lines formed across his forehead. I didn't know what could cause him such pain, whether it had something to do with the "& Son" hopes his father still harbored, but I didn't want to contribute to it. As I reached over to take his hand back, Mrs. Murtagh returned.

"Now that's a darling scene to come upon, isn't it?" she said, setting down slices of cake that exuded the tantalizing aroma of cider. "Cream and sugar, dear?"

Chapter 10

Worth answered his dressing room door wearing everyday breeches and a wrinkled shirt unbuttoned halfway down his chest. A mat of dark hair protruded from the gap. He often looked disheveled, even on stage, but now he seemed to have just awakened, and I flushed with embarrassment.

"We'll begin with Act Two, Scene Two," he said without any greeting.

The balcony scene. I gulped.

Although Worth wasn't in costume, I had determined to come to rehearsal dressed for my part. Mary Louise Burton had kindly lent me two of her frocks—gauzy, billowing affairs that required squeezing into. "Being a little gaspy is probably good for the role," Mary Louise had reasoned, pulling so vigorously at my stays it took my breath away.

Maude and I had both inherited straight hair from our mother, but only my sister considered it a burden. I was quite content to pull my hair back in a bun or twist it into a braid and be done with it. Worth had requested at least a few curls, though, and Maude worked hard to force them into my hair. That night, I flipped from side to back in my bed as I tried to adjust to a headful of knotted curling rags.

In the morning, Maude admired the locks framing my face, calling them "springy." I found the style repellent. I kept seeing the curls bob up and down from the corner of my eye, like they had minds of their own. But when my mother pronounced my hair "feminine," I knew Worth would approve. Because the unseasonably warm weather threatened to undo Maude's work, I engaged a hack to take me to the theater, reducing the chance my curls would succumb to the humidity.

After all my efforts, Worth didn't deign to comment on whether or not I met his standards for Juliet. Instead, he launched directly into "But, soft! what light through yonder window breaks? It is the east, and Juliet is the sun," as if I weren't in the room. When he got to the final line of his soliloquy, "O, that I were a glove upon that hand, that I might touch that cheek!" he directed his attention to me with softened eyes.

That part of the balcony scene required the young lovers to conduct their conversation at a chaste distance. In Worth's office, we didn't have the option of a balcony for him to scale, and he spoke the rest of his lines just inches from my face, so close I could smell the spicy orange fragrance he wore.

When he arrived at the line, "With love's light wings did I o'er-perch these walls, For stony limits cannot hold love out," Worth reached out and seized my waist. The unexpected gesture made me recoil.

"Georgie, she *wants* to be with him. Do you understand? She's *aching* for him. Feel her lines, girl! Think of where she says, 'What satisfaction canst thou have to-night?' What does that mean to you?"

"Maybe she's confused about what he expects from her?"

"No, no, *no*! She's flirting, Georgie; she's leading him along. She *wants* him. She wouldn't flinch at her lover's touch; she'd lean into it."

"Sorry"—a word I said more than once during that rehearsal.

We proceeded, but the second time Worth took me by the waist I fared no better. I leaned out of the embrace instead of into it, and he huffed in exasperation. Then, as if struck by a bolt of recognition, he stepped back and squinted at me.

"Oh, I see," he said. "You've never been in love!"

I reddened to my scalp.

67

"I'm *right*."

"I'm just eighteen, Mr. Worth," but the excuse sounded weak even in my ears. Plenty of girls were already married at eighteen; both my mother and grandmother had been my age at the altar.

Worth shook his head. "Have you never danced with a fella, Georgie? Had the thrill of him pulling you in so close you smell his musk?" My mind traveled to Miss Haines's cotillions, where I always stood at the periphery of the room unchosen, though not unhappily so.

"For God's sake, girl, have you never been kissed?"

I cast my eyes down. The truth would only get me into further trouble with him, and the rehearsal had already taken such an uncomfortable turn.

"There's a remedy for that."

Worth yanked me into his chest and forced his lips against mine. They were as plump and wet as eels, and his chest hairs tickled my throat. His tongue pried my startled lips apart and explored the depths of my mouth, while his free hand traveled to my breast and rested there. Had this happened to my predecessor, too? I prayed it would be over before I was ruined, but when he forced his tongue in deeper and deeper, I used all my strength to push away from him and out of his unwanted grip.

As we faced each other, both panting, the back of my hand flew up to my lips, as if to wipe away the memory of his. It wasn't the smartest response to the attentions of someone who fancied himself a living Romeo taking pity on an undesirable girl, and Worth stared at me in disbelief.

"This is what men and women *do*, Miss Clifford," he said, almost spitting out the words. "And much, *much* more. Has your mother taught you nothing? She's done you a great disservice then. Someday soon you should learn to like it—or at least tolerate it. You don't want to find yourself a dour old maid like Charlotte Cushman, only good for breeches roles."

Please, God, I thought.

"Get out," he said, his tone approaching disgust.

Bile rose in my throat, and I groveled to save my first leading role. "Sir, please don't replace me with Frances! She won't be able to learn the part so quickly, I've seen her struggling with lines, and I can do better, I know I can. You just startled me, is all. You're right, I'm . . . inexperienced." I swallowed the thought, *and disgusted by you,* and forced down whatever pride I had left. "I have so much to learn from you, I'm sure."

He tucked in a shirt tail that had worked itself loose and ran a hand through his messy hair.

"Go on now. Think about your role," he instructed, now much less belligerent. "Be on stage at ten sharp tomorrow to rehearse with the company."

My first kiss left me shaking, and not in a good way. I was pretty sure my shakes were supposed to feel more like swooning.

My inclination was to seek advice from someone at the theater. Because Worth was everyone's boss, confiding in one of the other actors or actresses made little sense, and Sallie would just say she told me so. My best option was solid, dependable Harry, who could be gruff at rehearsals when too many players called out "Word!" for their line, but who'd never shown me anything but kindness. At times, he reminded me more of a father than my own pa—or what I supposed a father should be.

I caught the prompter alone near the green room just before the full-company rehearsal of *Romeo and Juliet.*

"May I speak to you, Mr. Pendergast?" I asked.

"You're already speaking."

"By ourselves." I nodded toward the space that I knew would be empty until rehearsal started and Act One players began filing in.

Harry's bushy eyebrows knitted into one continuous line, and I considered withdrawing before it was too late. But he opened the door to the green room and gestured for me to step inside.

"Georgie, don't even tell me you're not off-book," he said. "You know I can't make exceptions for anybody. I'll dock you a dollar sure as look at you."

"It isn't that. You know I've always got my lines."

"You do indeed. You've the talent for it, that's what I told Tom the first week." Harry and Mrs. Reynolds were the only ones in the company who called Worth by his first name. "So, then—what?"

"I've a question. A hypothetical is all."

He shook his head emphatically. "I try to stay away from what-ifs. It's what actually happens in life that matters."

"Oh, absolutely. But I was just wondering—" I searched for a good choice of words. "Suppose you found out somebody in the company—an actor, say—had done something—"

As I faltered, Harry rubbed the stubble on his chin. Although the hair on top of his head was still primarily black, his wiry beard was flecked with white.

"*Done* something? What're you getting at, Georgie?" We both glanced toward sudden commotion in the hallway as the company convened for rehearsal.

"You talking something serious?" he said, shifting his attention back to me. "Robbery? Arson? Assault?" The felonies flew easily off his lips, as if he'd dealt with all of them.

I blinked hard. Being forcibly kissed by the theater manager didn't rank among the crimes Harry recognized, not even assault. It wasn't a crime at all, as far as anyone knew. It just didn't seem . . . right.

Harry cracked his knuckles, anxious to get to his post in the wings. In addition to being the prompter, Harry functioned as the eyes and ears of the company, as Sallie did downstairs, and I was willing to bet he knew everything. His final words that day suggested he already sensed what I wanted to say.

"You learn to get on in the company, Georgie, however you can. That's the rule of thumb."

He paused as Worth strode by the door, laughing with Julius, a second gentleman. Both of us followed Worth with our eyes, and then Harry shifted his attention back to me.

"What happens between men and women, well, that's just what happens."

Chapter 11

At rehearsal, the balcony creaked beneath me and the stage-hands rushed to repair it on the spot so it wouldn't collapse. Luckily, that glitch presented a greater problem for me than did Worth. With the entire company watching, the manager touched me respectfully, like a gentleman steering a lady through a waltz, and his kiss was dry and perfunctory.

For my part, I devised a trick to persuade the audience that Juliet was enamored of her beau. What if I imagined Miss Cushman playing Romeo instead of Worth? If I cast my eyes down dreamily while Worth's arm encircled my waist, I could conjure up Miss Cushman's gallant, irreproachable figure as I'd seen her onstage. The idea of it sent an unexpected chill of pleasure through me.

It was an unconventional tactic, to be sure, and one I knew better than to share with anyone. A woman just couldn't think about embracing another woman romantically—even if the other woman dressed as a man.

And it worked. Behind my closed lids, I pictured Miss Cushman in clinging tights and red tunic instead of Worth and had no trouble leaning in.

At the close of rehearsal, members of the company rushed to congratulate me. Mrs. Reynolds, who'd been passed over for Juliet to play her mother instead, offered a double-edged compliment. "With your height and your strong features, I doubted you could ever carry off Juliet," she said. "But my dear, you are cut from leading lady cloth." She didn't know how true a statement that was for William Cartwright's daughter.

Ned wasn't aware of the depth of my disgust for Worth, but his teasing hit the mark. "You were wonderful, Georgie!" He winked at me. "I thought you actually *fancied* him."

For my big night, Uncle James planned to accompany Mama and Maude to the performance. The prospect unnerved Mama, who hadn't been to the theater in twenty years. One challenging pregnancy after another had kept her at home, often in bed, and then later she was too busy raising Maude and me to attend Pa's performances.

"Those days, the theater was as bad as a racetrack or saloon," she said over dinner with my uncle and sister. I gulped at the word *saloon*, glad I hadn't divulged my excursion to Groff's.

"Things have changed a lot since then, Mama," I pointed out. "Isn't that true, Uncle?"

"It is. The last time you were there, Sister, they served whiskey and allowed gambling" —he lowered his voice— "and public women. There's none of that now. And they've got comfortable chairs instead of benches, and people actually pay attention to the play. On the whole."

"And there are many more ladies like yourself," I added.

Mama put down her fork with a sigh. "The theater is tempting and sneaky, Georgie. It was your father's undoing."

"But that's where you two met!" During the stretches of time when she and Pa were getting along well, my father liked to reminisce about those early days, and "the pretty girl at the stage door" of Niblo's Garden with her friends, waiting for William Cartwright to emerge.

"He drank so little back then," Mama explained. "After a performance, he might sit with me for hours talking and talking with one glass of claret or ale. And he always came home from the theater sober as a judge. It was when he got on at the Prince, when he started going to Groff's and not coming home . . ." Her voice trembled, and she shot a worried look at me and Maude, as if she'd said too much. Sympathy for her welled up in me.

My uncle corrected her gently. "The drink was Will's undoing, not the theater. He couldn't handle it. There are plenty of actors who socialize with their peers and get along just fine. Edwin Forrest is a model."

Mama's temper flared. "I don't want to hear about other actors! I only care about one."

With all the talk about Pa, Maude broke into tears, but I remained dry-eyed. I was intrigued by my mother's use of *care* instead of *cared* for my father.

"This is inappropriate dinner conversation," Mama said, regaining her composure. "It's upset Maude. Girls, you're excused."

Maude fled the table, but I lingered. "I'm not upset," I said. "And we've not had dessert."

"You're better off without dessert," my mother said. "There are Juliet's dresses to fit into, and they're snug on you as it is."

Her rebuke stung, and I blinked back tears. Mama must have suspected I'd listen at the door, because she engaged in nothing but small talk with my uncle about his impending marriage until I was so bored I retreated to my room.

After dinner with my family, I wanted to rid my mind of Pa and his decline, and I decided to venture downtown to Clem's boardinghouse to surprise her. I'd never been to her residence although I knew its location.

Having tea with Clem on Sunday afternoons was one of my favorite pastimes, but it was an extravagance she couldn't often indulge in. When she traveled home to Brooklyn, her father slipped her a dollar to see her through the week, but she'd been so busy taking in extra trim work from Mrs. Tassie's shop and hurrying to finish *My Youngest Sister* that she hadn't been to Williamsburg in weeks. Her coin purse was light, she told me, and I'd noticed her blue and white day dress fraying at the cuffs.

I concocted a plan for an alternate tea, asking Aggie to wrap up two pieces of her pound cake in a square of muslin. I'd finished reading Clem's first act and had so few comments that I thought maybe a piece of cake would distract her from my inadequacy as a reader.

I should have engaged a hack, but I decided to have a bigger adventure and board an omnibus—something I'd never done alone and that would make Mama gasp if she found out. The sight of a young woman boarding a bus on her own turned quite a few heads, including two ladies seated across from me who whispered back and forth to each other.

I didn't care. There was so much else to pay attention to. Broadway buzzed with families and couples: mothers showing off their marriageable daughters, hoop skirts swishing from side to side, and gents in their high silk toppers. I was more interested in the gleaming marble buildings that a slow bus ride gave me a grand view of—everything from the Winter Garden Theatre to the dry goods emporium, the Marble Palace, stocked to the rafters with just about everything one could want to buy, including ladies' frocks that were sewn and ready to wear.

The farther south we rode, the more Negroes appeared on the streets. At one stop, two young Negro women burdened with packages asked if they could board, but the conductor told them loudly to wait for the "colored bus."

It seemed silly and unfair. I wondered if the young women were hurrying to an appointment and how long they'd wait until a bus for Negroes came along.

The ladies across from me placed the blame on the young women and not on the transportation system. "Imagine," one of them said with a sniff. "Those girls should know better!"

The bus carried on down the avenue, and when it pulled up in front of the New York Hospital, I knew we'd reached the closest stop to Clem's boardinghouse. "Have a nice day," I

75

chirped to the ladies, just to be contrary and give them something else to gossip about.

Attempting to cross Broadway on my own, with the avenue's noisy crush of carriages and pedestrians, was akin to having a death wish. As I was considering when and where to step out, I glanced across the wide expanse at the massive facade of The Broadway Theatre, where my uncle had taken me to see Miss Cushman perform. At that moment, I spotted a commanding figure wearing a stovepipe hat atop wavy hair, hovering outside the theater's entrance. Although I couldn't make out his face, my pulse picked up speed. All I could think of was getting from where I was to where he was.

"Pa!" The gentleman moved away from the entrance and joined another fellow. Panicked at not being able to reach them, I watched as the two strode toward a side street. I cried out in my loudest voice, one I hoped would project through the clatter of street activity, "Pa, wait!"

I leapt forward into oncoming traffic, holding up my right arm like a shield—as if that could stop any carriage from flattening me. The wheels of a hansom cab squealed to a halt just inches from me, so close the startled horse whinnied in my face.

As the coachman lobbed harsh words at me for getting in his path, a strong hand reached out and pulled me from harm's way. The sudden jerking motion made my package of lemon cake slip onto the cobblestones, but the hand that had saved me scooped it up before it could come undone and be trampled into crumbs.

My savior proved to be the tallest woman I'd ever seen. She had a gentleman's umbrella tucked under her arm, which she used to deliver a series of sharp raps to the side of the cab. "How dare you use such language with a lady!" she scolded the coachman in a sonorous voice. "On your way, scoundrel!"

As the cab clattered off, the lady fixed her full attention on me. She towered above me, straight as a pole, with two floppy gray curls on either side of her face that matched the color of her dress. Her unnaturally cherry-red cheeks shone. Facing her, I wasn't sure where to rest my eyes, which fell at the height of her bosom.

"I hope you're all right, dear. My, that was close, wasn't it? These cabs are so reckless! You take your life into your hands when you cross Broadway. The city needs to build a bridge here." She handed me the muslin package, but not before she sniffed curiously in its direction. I couldn't blame her. All the way down on the bus, the cake's lemony fragrance had tantalized me, too.

"Thank you so much!" I said. "I got distracted and wasn't thinking." My eyes darted back toward The Broadway Theatre, but the figure I'd imagined was Pa had disappeared.

"My advice is to always cross in pairs or trios or even quartets, if there's one handy," the lady said. "Safety in numbers, and all that. I live nearby and have had many scrapes just trying to get home."

The near miss with the cab had disoriented me. "Since you live around here, ma'am, could you do me one more favor and point me in the direction of Pearl Street? I've gotten all twisted around."

"Why, that's where I'm going! You're still shaken, I can see it. Let me take you myself."

As luck would have it, we soon discovered we were heading to the exact same address. The kind woman turned out to be Miss Bottoms, who ran Clem's boardinghouse.

"I'm so happy Clementine has a friend," the lady said. "She works so hard, poor thing, it puts me to shame."

Clem had told me she'd chosen her residence primarily because it was advertised as "genteel apartments within a moment's walk of Broadway"—absolutely necessary for her, since she had to rely on her own two feet for transport. From Clem's block of Pearl Street, both Mrs. Tassie's millinery shop and the Prince Theatre were easily walkable.

"Plus, who could resist a landlady named Miss Bottoms?" Clem had said with a giggle.

The boardinghouse was wedged between a chemist and a Presbyterian church. The frame structure bore sagging green shutters and flaking grayish-white paint. The boards of the front steps groaned like they might snap under my weight. Miss Bottoms had livened up the stoop with a pot of happy marigolds that showed no signs of going to seed, even in early October.

In the foyer, a squat, toffee-colored spaniel lumbered toward us and began pawing anxiously at Miss Bottoms's skirt. If this was its habit, the excited little thing would eventually shred all her hems to ribbons. Miss Bottoms didn't scold the creature and bent to rub its graying muzzle before depositing her bonnet on the hall table.

"This is Bella," she said as a kind of introduction.

The scent of the fresh lemon Aggie infused in her pound cake wafted through the stuffy air. The spaniel pounced onto my skirt next, sniffing toward the package.

"Bella, down! You can do that to me but not to guests. I'm so sorry, dear. She does love treats." She nodded toward the package of cake.

I'd pictured Clem and me enjoying the slices together, but my mother's warning about fitting into my costume for Tuesday suddenly echoed in my head.

"It might be the worse for wear, but I'd love to offer you a slice, miss. It's the most delicious pound cake, made fresh today by our cook. You could enjoy it with your tea. It's the least I can do for you saving me."

"Why, aren't you a thoughtful girl!"

She fetched a plate and accepted the slice, which had split into two equal pieces in its fall. "I'll give Bella a few bites, too," she added.

Miss Bottoms pointed me to the staircase. "You'll want to see Clementine now. Go up to the second floor and turn left. Front room, nicest in the house. The girl must be busy with her scribbling because she didn't come down to dinner."

The banister trembled under my grip, and at the top of the stairs I almost tripped on the edge of a worn carpet. According to Clem, the establishment had catered to single young women for more than twenty years, and the place showed its age. Still, it appeared to be clean; my glove came away from the railing without a speck of dust.

Across from Clem's room, I thought I heard a raspy male cough from behind a door, which confused me. The ladies in residence all worked in shops and factories in the area, Clem said, and no men were permitted above the first level. That feature had so appealed to her parents they'd paid her first month's rent.

I tapped on Clem's door twice before she called out, "A minute, please, Miss B!"

I'd never seen my friend so disheveled. Busy and preoccupied, yes, but not unkempt. Although it was mid-afternoon, she was outfitted in a thin cotton dressing gown, which she gripped tightly over her bosom. She had pushed the gown's sleeves to her elbows. Her chestnut hair tumbled to her shoulders in a messy cloud, and her glasses had slipped halfway down her nose. As I peered in, I spied a rumpled room furnished only with a narrow bed, a scarred chest of drawers, and a rickety-looking desk and chair. There was a carpet between the bed and the desk, as worn as the one in the hall; it looked like it had once been blue and red. "Nicest in the house" wasn't saying much of this room, not even as cozy-looking as Aggie's attic quarters on Bond Street. An array of loose satin bows in rainbow hues lay strewn across the bed's ivory quilt like a patchwork design, adding the only hint of color.

"George!" Clem said with a look of horror. "What are *you* doing here?"

"Hello to you, too, Clem," I said. "Do you greet all your visitors this way?"

Her right hand traveled to her rat's nest of hair and made an attempt to smooth it. The index and middle finger were stained black with ink.

"Oh, God, George, I'm sorry! I don't *get* visitors! I look a fright. I haven't washed or eaten since yesterday and the place is—" She glanced over her shoulder toward the room. "Well, you aren't blind. There were all these damn ribbons to make by tomorrow for Mrs. Tassie, and I think I stayed up all night writing. What time is it, anyway?"

"Past three," I said.

She greeted the time with a low moan. "Ugh. No wonder I'm so hungry. I missed dinner! Well, it was only turnip pie." When I grimaced, she explained, "Miss Bottoms is a vegetarian. I've gotten used to the menu."

"No meat at all?"

"She makes an exception for oysters, which we have *way* too often."

Although Clem's befuddled state had initially bothered me, now I found it kind of charming. She stepped aside and gallantly swept her arm to invite me into the room.

I held out the muslin toward her. "Lucky for you, I come bearing cake. When I got out of the bus, it fell into the street and was almost flattened by a horse on Broadway, but I think it's still edible." I omitted the story of Miss Bottoms saving me, for fear of having to explain my vision of Pa.

Clem accepted the cake with a snort. "How tantalizing you make it sound." Then her voice softened. "I can't believe you came all the way down here to bring it to me."

"I knew you'd like it," I said, overtaken with shyness I didn't understand. It was just Clem, after all.

"And you took a bus by yourself? I'm proud of you, George."

"My mother wouldn't be, so you must never mention it," I said. "And gosh, I had to talk to *someone*. I'm a bundle of nerves about my debut. If only we had a quicker way to communicate, like a personal telegraph or something."

"That would be something." Clem's smile vanished. "Ned wasn't available, I take it."

"Oh, bother! I didn't mean to sound so rude. I wanted to talk to *you* specifically. I read your first act."

She perked up and rushed to gather the bows from the bed. "Sit, sit! The desk chair wobbles, and this is the only comfy spot."

Comfy was probably not the right word choice. The bed sagged under my weight and I felt the imprint of the ropes on my behind.

"What'd you think?"

I had a few small quibbles with lines, but I led with praise. "I loved it," I said. "It's going to be grand."

Clem cocked an eyebrow. "*Going* to be? It isn't now?"

I swallowed hard, not wanting to anger her. A prickly writer, even if she was a cherished friend, might reduce my part or give the better lines to another character. "Oh, no, Clem, it's wonderful *now*. I just meant that I can imagine how great it will be when it's finished. You've just got the one act, and—"

With a tremble of excitement, she broke in, "George, it *is* finished! I stayed up all night because I was so close to the end and the lines came pouring out of me. I was literally writing *END OF PLAY* at the bottom of the page when you knocked on my door. It's ready for a reading with the company."

There was no point in my mentioning the changes I'd planned to suggest. Maybe in the reading or rehearsal I could bring them up. Right now, she looked wild with happiness.

"You should eat your cake. You must be famished."

Clem unwrapped the muslin. The tart aroma reached our noses as she inspected her slice, which was amazingly unharmed by its tumble. Then Clem did something I'd never seen a girl or woman do before—she didn't bother looking for a fork or spoon, but broke off a small piece with her ink-stained fingers and dropped it onto her tongue.

She said something unintelligible while covering her full mouth. After she swallowed, Clem sighed. "Sheer heaven!"

I must have been side-eyeing her cake because she added, "You had some, didn't you, George?"

I shook my head and found myself repeating Mama's line about having to fit into my costume.

"That's just sad," Clem said and broke off another piece. "You're on your way to being the most important actress of your generation. Before long you'll have costumes special-made for you." She flew the morsel toward my mouth like it was a sparrow on the wing.

I opened my lips. It *was* heaven. We smiled through our bites and polished off the slice together.

Chapter 12

Based on dress rehearsal, no one could have predicted the fiasco that was Tuesday's performance.

The day started out well enough. Maude set my hair again, and that morning my curls bounced like they were living creatures. To ensure my hair wouldn't get in my way on stage, my sister bundled the ringlets at each side of my face with satin ribbons.

"I hardly know it's you, Georgie!" she said.

I rolled my eyes. "Thanks, I guess."

My sister hurried to soften the statement. "I mean, you're prettier than any Juliet *ever*." She'd never been to the theater, but I accepted the compliment anyway and gave her a grateful smile.

At my request, Aggie prepared the lightest of all breakfasts, just a slice of bread. "Not even jam?" she asked, accustomed to serving me a more substantial meal of soft-boiled egg with two slices of bread, fresh fruit, butter, and jam. "You ill, Miss Georgie?"

She grew more concerned when I refrained from eating for the rest of the day. An empty stomach, I told her, would calm my nerves. What I was really thinking was that it would help me slip more easily into Mary Louise's frocks.

Sure enough, when Mama cinched in my waist that afternoon, I sucked in my breath and didn't groan once.

"I'm so proud of you," my mother said. She leaned in and kissed both my cheeks. "Imagine, my own Georgie playing Juliet!"

As a talisman, I brought my penny plain of Miss Cushman in full Romeo regalia to the theater, where I displayed it on the dressing-room vanity to boost my confidence as I applied dots of rouge to my cheeks. Sallie remarked on it as she helped me into my costume.

"That Mr. Forrest?" she asked, referring to one of the greatest living Shakespearean actors. Not even Pa had approached him, according to the critics.

"Oh, no, it's Miss Charlotte Cushman. She's world-famous for playing Romeo. I take my inspiration from her."

Frances overheard us and said with an unladylike snort, "That would be incredibly useful *if* you were playing Romeo."

Her comment didn't faze me, though. It was Worth himself who got the better of me—again.

Although he'd behaved well during rehearsal, performing before an audience made him cockier and more aggressive. The first time his piercing eyes fastened on mine, I read a weird kind of possession in them and my stomach jiggled. There was no food in it, I reminded myself, so I was in no danger of vomiting all over his tunic.

Miss Cushman, Miss Cushman, I repeated in my mind, summoning up the card in my dressing room.

When Worth's hand first played about my waist, I breathed through it. But as his arm dropped to his side with the words, "Oh, wilt thou leave me so unsatisfied?" Worth's hand found my right buttock.

And fondled it.

And slipped lower still.

The stone balcony obscured Worth's lewd gesture from the audience and from the company in the wings, but for me there was no mistaking what he'd done. Mary Louise's dress was a diaphanous thing, and in an attempt to be somewhat true to the historical period, didn't require a hoop. There was scant little between Worth's hand and my private parts.

84

I shuddered as I began my line, "What s-satisfaction canst not . . . c-canst thou . . ." I peered toward the footlights, hoping in vain to catch a glimpse of Clem's face, but the lights blinded me and I stopped cold.

A confused look passed over Worth's face, and he covered for me. "What satisfaction canst I have? The exchange of thy love's faithful vow for mine."

He waited a moment while I remained frozen in place, then he jumped forward in the text. "Wouldst thou withdraw it? For what purpose, love?"

At that spot in the text, Juliet should have made a pretty speech professing her deep, boundless love, but Miss Cushman's image had faded away from me, and I couldn't dredge up more than the opening phrase, "But to be frank—"

I heard nervous rustling from Harry in the wings, and I glanced in that direction to avoid the fury in Worth's eyes.

"I hear some noise within; dear love, adieu!" My hand darted out toward Harry in a gesture that must have looked stilted. "Anon, good nurse! . . . Sweet Montague, be true. A thousand times good-night!"

The many lines I'd dropped were the heart of a critical plot point, when Juliet entreats her lover to send word the next day about the time and place of their marriage. Without that, the play couldn't continue without confounding the audience. Worth grabbed at my hand to keep me from exiting, as my words called for, and he scrambled to condense some of Juliet's lines as if they were his own.

"My bent of love be honourable, my purpose marriage. I'll send thee word to-morrow, where and what time we wilt perform the rite."

"Madam!" Frances as the Nurse called from the wings.

Sudden, sharp awareness hit me that the company, the audience, my uncle, my mother, Maude, Clem—I'd bought her ticket myself—*everyone* was witnessing my hideous performance. With that thought, an image of my father flashed into my mind—not on hands and knees in his own moment of disgrace, but tall, upright, and powerful.

Get to your line, George, Pa's voice said in my head, snapping me back to my place in the script.

"I come, anon," I began, sweat trickling down my neck. My voice quavered but then grew stronger as I forced myself to finish the scene.

Ned was waiting in the wings for his entrance as Mercutio. "What just happened?" he whispered. My shoulders shook, and he laced an arm around them to steady me. "Bad case of nerves? You know I've gotten them myself, Georgie. And it *is* a big part."

I couldn't tell him the truth. *What happens between men and women, that's just what happens.*

Worth stormed toward me, a human cyclone. Luckily, Romeo was to appear in Scene Three following a soliloquy by Friar Laurence, so he couldn't linger. "This company has not been so humiliated since Cartwright's fall," he said through tight lips. He took me roughly by the arm and yanked me away from Ned's comfort.

"Ow," I complained, which made him give my arm an extra twist before dropping it.

"I should sack you. You're lucky Clifford's your uncle, or you'd be gone tonight."

From the stage, the friar said, "Within the infant rind of this small flower, poison hath residence and medicine power." Worth straightened his spine, composed his face as if nothing had transpired between us, and reentered the set on cue.

Tears blurred my vision. I had been completely at my part and would have sailed through the scene if only Worth had not made free with my body and thrown me off.

Reason told me I should have ignored his mischief and moved on. Likely, other actresses before me had done just that. Why else would Harry have warned me, *You learn to get on in the company, Georgie, however you can.*

But also ricocheting through my head was the question of why Worth had done such a thing during a crucial scene. After what happened in his office, was he looking to humiliate me and bring me down with a solid reason for dismissal?

As I slinked toward the stairs to the dressing rooms, I caught Harry's eye. The prompter's face registered kindness and not a sliver of anger. In fact, Harry mouthed something that looked like, *It's OK, Georgie.* He might have said something else, but that was what I decided to believe. At any rate, as I passed him, Harry reached out and patted my back before taking his place again for Scene Three—one that, happily, Juliet wasn't in.

I hurried back to the dressing room to drink water and collect myself. It wouldn't hurt either, I thought, to have a glimpse of Miss Cushman's penny plain on my dressing table. There was no water in my pitcher, and I grumbled under my breath that Sallie hadn't thought to refill it. I hastened through the maze of hallways to her door, rapping once, forcefully, then again with less vigor. There was no need to take it out on Sallie, who had warned me about Worth.

I heard shuffling within, but Sallie didn't answer. "Sallie?" I called out. "The dressing room needs water, and I need help with my change."

Still no reply, but I thought I heard a groan from behind the door. The knob turned slowly in my hand, and Falstaff darted out past my feet. I peered into the dark room, squinting so my eyes could adjust. As I did, I saw not Sallie, but a young Negro man, not much older than I, lying on Sallie's mat, his eyes wide with terror.

"Who are *you?*" I asked, but my mind went to the worst scenario: Sallie was hiding a beau in her room, where they did *things* on her mat.

He didn't answer but raised himself up on his elbows. His face was scratched and dirty, and he was wearing a shirt that looked suspiciously similar to one of Worth's.

"Where is Sallie?"

"Don't know, miss," he said in a thick voice.

"Well, if you see her, tell her Miss Georgie needs her." I closed the door and hurried back to my dressing room. Sallie being unavailable for costume changes was unacceptable, and I would have to speak to her.

87

As it turned out, she was already in my dressing room. "There you are, miss. You ready for your change?" She had withdrawn my second costume from the wardrobe and smoothed the skirt with appreciation. "Miss Mary Louise's gowns're so silky. Someday I'll buy me a gown like this."

"Sallie, where were you just now? I had to go looking for you."

"Miss Muller needed me," she said, still staring at the gown and not me. "Said Scene Two didn't go so good and she was feeling faint."

I straightened my spine, and my next words exuded a confidence I didn't feel. "I'm the one who had a bad time in the scene, Sallie, not Miss Muller! *I'm* the star of this play, and she doesn't even have a single costume change! You should be here for *me*. I need water, I need . . . things."

"Yes, miss." Sallie's face remained impassive. "Something bad happen on stage?"

"Just get me out of this thing."

She nodded and undid the lacing at the back of my gown. I imagined the imprint of Worth's hand seared onto the skirt.

As she worked, I caught Sallie's eyes in the mirror. "I went to your room to find you," I said.

"When was that, miss?"

"A few minutes ago. Imagine my shock."

She lifted her chin in defiance. "You can tell Mr. Harry, don't matter," she said. "He knows what's what. But don't go saying nothing to the others." She must have realized how far she'd stepped out of line because she added, "Please, miss."

Harry knew she had a man in her room and didn't care? And Sallie—that really surprised me. She presented as levelheaded, determined to support herself by making the most of her many talents. Even now, she was planning to own a beautiful dress. Surely the last thing she needed was to get with child.

But I didn't have time for a discussion like that or to worry about Sallie's future. My stomach fluttered, the memory of Worth's hand still lingering, as the time to go back out on stage drew closer.

"There's no reason for me to tell anyone," I said to Sallie, and her face in the mirror relaxed—until my next words. "Just please don't shirk your duties again."

Her lips tightened, and she gave my laces a final, aggressive tug. "You're all ready now, miss."

When I was dressed and back upstairs, I paced the green room, ticking off the remaining scenes I had to play with Worth and steeling myself to get through them. Luckily, the wedding scene would be brief, and then Romeo and Juliet had only one more extended time together while they were both alive.

The second balcony scene required a kiss, however. On stage, my heart picked up speed when I cued Romeo, "Then, window, let day in, and let life out," and Worth replied, "Farewell, farewell! One kiss, and I'll descend." I pressed my eyes shut and braced for an assault. To my surprise, Worth kept the kiss brief and professional and without any slimy tongue—just like at the full-company rehearsal.

And then that was it. We'd reached the scene where Juliet was not on stage with Romeo again until after he had drunk his deadly potion. Seeing Worth laid out motionless, I imagined my tormentor truly dead, and a bubble of relief burst in my chest.

The applause was robust, as if the audience had already forgotten or forgiven the travesty of the second act. Worth took my hand during our company's curtain call and bowed gallantly in my direction. After, he disappeared quickly without speaking to me.

At the stage door, my family was waiting to whisk me home in my uncle's carriage. There was no sign of Clem.

Mama's expression when she saw me was a puzzle. She'd known the play well at one time, but maybe she'd missed the confusion of Act Two. If she was embarrassed for me or vexed, she held it back, muttering something about a fine performance. My sister smiled shyly and complimented my appearance.

My uncle offered me a bouquet of yellow chrysanthemums. "Proud of you, Georgie." I wondered if he meant in general or because I pulled myself together and recovered in Act Three so my family wasn't disgraced a second time.

At home, Aggie waited with an expectant look. When she saw my grim face, she said, "Sorry, Miss Georgie," with downcast eyes.

"You'll see the reviews tomorrow, I expect," I whispered back.

The next morning, Mama and Maude left after breakfast for a visit to Granny Clifford in Brooklyn. I would have welcomed the exhilarating ferry ride and the chance to forget the previous evening, but I had to appear at the theater by noon to pick up my next prompt book and perform in the matinee of *All My Sisters*. Although I woke up starving, I skipped breakfast and allowed myself an extra hour to wallow in self-pity in bed until the housemaid arrived to make up the room. I wasn't sure how to face my mother, Maude, or anyone at the Prince, especially Clem.

A couple of dailies were lying out when I staggered downstairs to the kitchen. Aggie hurried to hide them, but I assured her it wasn't necessary. The company, especially Frances, would let me know soon enough how bad the notices were.

"You must be hungry by now," Aggie said. "We've ham and—"

"I'll just have coffee. My stomach's not quite right."

But Aggie was already slicing bread, laying out an egg cup, and pouring my coffee.

"Eat what you can," Aggie said. "You got another long day ahead. You don't want to faint away on stage."

"That might be an improvement over my performing," I said.

My fingers brushed the papers gingerly, but I didn't pick them up.

"The *Herald's* not so bad. They said you looked 'radiant.'"
Aggie paused. "You'll want to skip the *Spirit*, though."

With that, I dug the *Herald* out of the pile, my eyes traveling to the paragraphs about me.

"'Miss Georgiana Clifford, in her first starring vehicle as Juliet, looked radiant and comported herself nicely.'" I smiled at Aggie, then continued, "'She enunciated clearly and projected even to the tiers, as she has done in smaller roles.'"

So far, so good.

"'However—'" The rest I read silently.

> In a most unfortunate turn of events in Act II, Miss Clifford appeared overwhelmed with nervousness, and skipped over much of the crucial balcony scene. Imagine this reviewer's surprise when Mr. Worth stepped in and recited many of Juliet's lines until Miss Clifford could find her place in the script! After a break of several scenes, Miss Clifford returned in Act III and seemed to recover the poise she displayed in Act I. Perchance she is too untried for such major roles and should step back into supporting roles to see if she matures in her craft.

I didn't venture a look at the other paper because the review Aggie called "not so bad" used the dreaded word *if.* Since starting at the Prince, I had worried that my plain appearance would be the sole hindrance to my progress, that a player had to be as comely as Ned to advance. To think it might actually be a lack of ability that held me back was more than I could bear to take in.

Aggie placed a thick slice of bread and a pot of blackberry jam in front of me. I picked at the bread and managed only a mouthful of soft-boiled egg. I was imagining what the critic Aggie suggested I skip had written—*no talent, woefully miscast, the Bard has turned in his grave*—and what would happen when I reported to the Prince.

Chapter 13

At the theater, it was Harry, not Worth, who asked to speak to me in private. I'd been expecting that Worth wasn't finished with my lashing, that he would relish the opportunity to bring me down a few more pegs, but at noon he wasn't backstage or downstairs. I sighed, relieved for a moment. The talk with Harry was likely to be uncomfortable, but he'd never yelled at me.

Harry didn't have an office, so we huddled at a backstage table stacked with scripts and the occasional odd prop that a stagehand had dropped there out of laziness. I peered across the table expectantly, but Harry didn't have a book for me.

My voice shook. "I'm sacked?" Worth had said he would dismiss me if not for Uncle James, but I didn't think he really would.

Harry blew out a loud breath. "He's docking you two weeks' pay, and there's no role for you this week or next."

"*Two* weeks! It's my first offense! Even if someone drinks before a performance, they only lose a week's pay! I've read the rules."

"We've not had something exactly like this before, but Tom's looking at it as clause number seven . . ." Harry fished the rules from the messy pile on the table and flipped the pages. "'A performer introducing his own language into a script or improper gestures shall forfeit two weeks' salary and be suspended from other roles during that time.'"

"It wasn't my own language," I said.

"Well, to repeat, we've not had this exact situation before, dropping most of the scene like that."

"As for improper gestures, well, that's rich! Let me tell *you*—" Anger frothed on my lips.

"Let you tell me what, Georgie?" Harry's dark eyes pierced mine. He was too smart not to suspect what was what, but he had made his position clear that day in the green room. Clueing him in that Worth had touched me lewdly wouldn't change a thing.

"Nothing. Never mind." *What happens between men and women, well, that's just what happens.* "So, I play Abigail for the matinees, but no new roles for two weeks?"

Harry's lips twitched. "Miss Lafarge will take over Abigail."

That bit of news made me break into sobs so fierce I couldn't catch my breath. Harry rapped on my back in alarm.

"Now, come on, Georgie, it's not so bad as that," he said, handing me a big, square handkerchief from his pocket. It appeared to be clean and freshly pressed, so I blew into it fiercely. "You'll be back at it in no time. It's almost like having a little rest after all the hard work you've been doing."

A rest that would make my family forty dollars poorer. And after this, Worth would likely never discuss the extra five dollars a week.

"Just keep telling yourself, I didn't get the boot," Harry said. But with that, the prompter did, essentially, boot me out. He turned toward other members of the company who had begun approaching him and handed out their books.

Ned was among them, looking scruffier than usual, with the shadow of a ginger-colored beard.

"I heard," he said.

"How? *I* just heard."

He shrugged, then glanced around. "Want to meet up later? There's something I wanted to tell you." I wondered if his news related to why he looked unkempt.

I feared Mama's reaction when she got home from Brooklyn and learned of my suspension, so it seemed wise to be out of the house for as long as I could. I agreed to meet Ned at the stage door so he could take his lunch at Groff's before the evening performance.

With time on my hands before I met Ned, I took myself to the only place where a girl could disappear for hours on her own—Stewart's Marble Palace. I had only enough money for the bus ride home and couldn't afford to buy anything, but I knew from trips to the emporium with my mother that ladies could meander from floor to floor with no pressure to make a purchase.

The thing I liked best about Stewart's was the building itself. The crisp marble exterior made me think I'd traveled to Italy or Greece, but I'd never been further from home than Brooklyn. Past the uniformed doormen, Stewart's atrium boasted a domed skylight, and the balcony gallery offered a place for a leisurely stroll, a way to see and be seen. Aisles and aisles of low mahogany counters tempted customers to touch and admire all the latest goods from Europe. You felt rich just being there. I imagined Miss Cushman shopping at Stewart's regularly.

I ambled through the glove department, fixing a look of mild interest on my face, casually brushing a hand across a counter, while really thinking about how I was going to break the news of my suspension to Mama. A young man's voice cut through my thoughts. It had the slight trace of an accent, like he was either British or pretending to be.

"The French kid would look stunning with your frock. Soft as butter."

My eyes focused on the gloves in question, which were in fact very attractive. The lace at the cuffs was too fussy for me, but Maude would drool over them as a Christmas present—*if* I had money by then.

"Would you like to try them?"

I fingered the leather and the pearly buttons and finally met the clerk's gaze. I'd seen those long lashes before—at Groff's. He was the same young man Ned had exchanged furtive glances with and then joined after Clem and I got up to leave. The emporium hired only the most handsome young men, and this one fit the bill.

I must have looked startled because he asked, "Have we met?"

"I don't think so." I withdrew my hand from the counter. "They *are* lovely. My sister's taste, though, not mine. Maybe I'll come back with her."

"I'd be happy to help you any time. Ask for Mr. Pomeroy."

I moved down the long counter toward the evening-wear gloves, but when I glanced back over my shoulder, the clerk's eyes had followed me. Had he pieced together that Ned and I were friends? I could have just acknowledged seeing him at Groff's. That would have been a friendly thing to do, but it felt strangely intimate.

Mr. Pomeroy smiled and nodded, and I did the same.

To take up more time, I wandered back and forth across all of Stewart's floors, through fabric and lace up to tea sets and desk accessories. The only item that caught my serious attention was a small traveling inkwell covered in fine leather, which I knew Clem would love. Her own travel well had a tendency to leak, but this one had a tight-fitting brass cap etched with swirls and flourishes.

I will have money again someday, I thought. *Enough to buy anything I want, even a handsome inkwell for Clem.* I fantasized about having enough to buy the Prince Theatre and sack Worth.

Till then, I would practice economy, sparing even the bus fare. Even though it would make Mama faint if she saw me, I walked back to the Prince on my own to meet Ned.

When I joined him at the stage door, my friend had shaved off his shadowy beard, and he smelled like cloves.

"I thought maybe you'd given up shaving for a role."

"I was in a hurry leaving the house this morning. That's what I wanted to talk about." In characteristic form, Ned seemed to have forgotten that I'd come inches from being dismissed and might have a greater need to talk to someone.

Seated at Groff's, within seconds of ordering two pickled eggs and coffee, Ned burst out, "Oh, Georgie, I'm in such hot water!"

Anger rose in me. "*You're* in hot water? For God's sake, Ned, I'm unemployed!"

He stared at me as if confused that I'd elevated my problem above his.

"Just temporarily," he pointed out. He reached into a trouser pocket and brought out a gold eagle and some smaller coins. How he could walk around carrying so much money was baffling. With the theater not that far from Five Points, I'd be worried about thieves.

"Here," he said, "let me spot you an eagle till you're back."

His kindness overwhelmed me. I broke into fat tears that I whisked away with a napkin. I stuffed the coin into my own pocket before he could change his mind and realize he needed the money.

"You're a good friend, Ned," I said. "So go on, tell me what's wrong. Your hot water."

He sucked in a deep breath. "Mama knows the truth about you and me. She kept pressing me about when we might set the date, and I told her you'd ended it."

I winced. "That's your idea of the truth?"

"I know, I stretched it. But I had to. She wanted to meet your *mother*. She was going to invite her to dinner!"

"Golly. Well, glad you nipped that in the bud. But so sorry I broke your heart." His predicament was more amusing than I thought it would be, a pleasant distraction from my own.

"Yes, that's all fine for now. Unfortunately, that's not the worst of it," Ned continued, after Mr. Groff refilled his coffee cup.

I waited, nursing my free tumbler of water. I didn't want to break my eagle on Groff's muddy coffee.

"Here's the thing. Ma's lined up someone else for me. One of Da's best clients has a marriageable daughter—Irish Catholic to boot. Ma's through the roof with excitement."

"And why's that a problem? You're just not ready, or something worse?" I ran through the possible issues he might have with the colleen in question. "You've seen her and she's . . . unattractive? She's two heads taller than you? Ten years older?"

"The why of it is—"

The "why" caught in Ned's throat, and we sat for a few awkward moments in silence. When he found his voice again, it was barely a whisper. "I don't know as I can say outright, you being a girl and all." A tear slipped onto the table, and Ned rubbed it into the wood.

"Just say it, Ned. Look at me—I'm not so much of a girl, after all."

As he spoke, his finger circled the spot where his tear had landed. "It's, well—I fancy someone else, you see."

I sighed. Ned's troubles paled next to mine, but the gold eagle he'd lent me made me ever so patient with him. "Can't you just tell your Ma that? Unless you've given your heart to a lady of the evening, it's hard to imagine your mother would care."

Ned inhaled dramatically, then released the breath.

"Oh, no, that's it, isn't it? You love a . . . harlot?"

He shook his head fiercely and leaned toward me to whisper into my ear, but the ribbon securing my bonnet got in the way. I removed the whole contraption and set it in my lap.

His hot breath tickled my ear. In the din of the room, I barely heard him say, "The one I fancy's a fella."

My mouth flopped open.

"You understand what I mean?"

My head jerked up and down. Since working as an actress, I'd come to understand very well. One afternoon, I'd been standing in the wings when Worth stormed offstage, muttering "damn sodomite" under his breath. He'd been rehearsing a scene with Mrs. Reynolds and Mr. Culpepper, a bachelor nearly as old as Pa who after decades in the theater had never progressed past second leading gentleman. Both Ned and I overheard Worth's outburst, and my friend blushed and lowered his eyes. Somehow, I instinctively knew not to ask Ned about the word.

Instead, I had asked Harry. The prompter reddened, too, and stammered, "It's not . . . it's not polite to talk about . . . least, not with a young lady."

"I'm not that delicate," I insisted. "If it's so important it sent Mr. Worth into a frenzy, I think I should know."

Harry had mumbled an explanation. "A sodomite's a man likes other men." When my face scrunched in confusion, he added, "In the way men are supposed to like *women*."

Now, here was one of my dearest friends, sharing his intimate secret. Ned continued to sniffle, but in the crowded atmosphere of Groff's, no one paid him any mind but me.

"Oh, Georgie, I'm going straight to hell. Father McAfee told us choirboys years ago about all sorts of sins. There's a long list. This one's near the top."

I didn't believe in sin. And even if there was such a thing as sin, how could it be wrong to love someone?

I placed my hand over Ned's on the table. Anyone who didn't know us might have mistaken us for sweethearts.

"I bet Father McAfee's got some sins of his own." When Ned looked shocked at the suggestion, I leaned closer and whispered, "Who's the fella?"

His face lit, and the tears shone on his cheeks. "Richard Pomeroy. He's a clerk at Stewart's, and he's the most comely—"

"I met him!" I blurted out. A few nearby heads turned our way, so I lowered my voice. "Today, before I came here. I was dilly-dallying, just filling time, and he waited on me at the glove counter. He's handsome, for sure."

"Isn't he just?" Ned's smile faded, and he twirled his coffee cup between his hands. "But what am I to do about Ma? She's set up a meeting for me and Miss O'Fallon."

From out of nowhere, I pulled the only reasonable solution. "Tell her I've taken you back," I said. "But you'll have to clarify that it's all very tentative, so no meeting my mother or anything like that."

"Brilliant!"

"And you could say Mama is against my marrying before I'm at least twenty-one. That gives you three years to stall."

His red-gold lashes fluttered. "You might have to come 'round again in those three years."

I huffed, but I wasn't seriously annoyed. "Oh, all right. But I've heard that serious suitors bring very nice presents."

The inkwell I'd eyed at Stewart's for Clem sprang suddenly to mind. I didn't know what women could feel for each other, if there was a female version of sodomite, but I did know my attachment to Clem seemed stronger than friendship. It was the perfect time to ask Ned, but the mere idea made heat rise in my cheeks and I couldn't form the words.

Instead, I dismissed the thought by continuing to tease Ned. "Anyway, isn't it time you left the nest? Maybe move out and get your own place" —my voice dropped— "with Richard."

Ned rubbed his chin. "Can't afford it now. I'd have to make second gentleman."

With that, I remembered the theater and my own misfortune. I could no longer avoid that I had to go home and tell my mother.

Chapter 14

When she heard about my suspension, all Mama said for a long time was, "Oh, Georgie." Her head wagged back and forth. It was hard to face her disappointment.

"We'll tighten our belts," she said finally, as if convincing herself. "We've done it before. That means no amusements or extravagances whatsoever."

No Taylor's, no hacks—

"And I think it would be better if you didn't see your friends for the time being."

My eyes clouded at the punishment for something I hadn't done.

"That isn't fair!"

"Honestly, Georgie, you won't die. This will give you a chance to spend more time with Maude and me. You'll come along on our errands and hopefully learn some things."

"Learn some things" in Mama's language meant she was losing confidence in my ability to make a life on the stage. The plan to marry me off was about to resurface, I was sure.

I came close to blurting out what really happened with Worth, but I feared Mama would make me leave the Prince—and acting—for good. It was just two weeks, I told myself. Better to weather the small indignities she meted out.

I could live without seeing Ned for a few weeks, but what worried me was I hadn't talked to Clem since the Juliet debacle. Would she think less of me now, that I was unworthy to star in her play? Unworthy of her respect and friendship? It took me several tries to write her a brief note.

Dear Clem,

How are you? I think about you and Ned all the time, I'm in a sort of prison for two weeks. (That means, Mama is keeping me close.) You must think me an awful failure, you were SO right about Juliet! The only good to come of this is, I'll have plenty of time to read your play. I can't wait to return to my friends!

Affectionately,
George

I suspected I'd gotten the commas all wrong, but Clem would overlook my grammar. Plus, because I'd written only a few letters in my life, mostly to my grandmother—and not including the failed draft to Miss Cushman—I wasn't sure if "Affectionately" was a good closing for a friend. And why had I inserted Ned in there?

Imperfect as it was, the note would serve the purpose of letting Clem know why I couldn't see her. The trick would be getting it to her. Aggie was my best bet.

"How would I know where to take it?" she asked as she tallied a delivery from the grocer's. "I've never been inside that place. Too fancy for the likes of me."

"I can draw a map of the backstage area." My drawing was about as good as my writing, but I figured I could scratch something onto paper. "If Clem's not there, you could get the note to Sallie, the maid."

"And how will I know her?"

"She's the only Black girl in the place."

She finished her task without agreeing to the plan, so I took it a step further.

"I could do something for you in return," I offered.

Aggie snickered but didn't state the obvious—I wasn't good at anything she had to do.

"I'll get you a ticket to any show you like at the Prince." Harry was notoriously stingy with free tickets, so I'd have to buy it myself.

Aggie's eyes widened. "I'd love to see one you're in sometime."

"Absolutely!"

"Two tickets, not one," she said. "I can't be going by myself."

I agreed reluctantly. At a dollar apiece, two tickets were hardly a fair trade for her simply transporting my note.

"There's just one more thing," I added.

Aggie frowned at the catch.

"There might be a reply. From Clem. She'll send it here, and I need to make sure Mama and Maude don't see it."

"Mrs. Cartwright never takes in the mail."

"But sometimes Maude does when she's bored."

Maude was sympathetic to my plight, but I preferred she not know I got a letter from the Prince Theatre, just in case she accidentally leaked the news to Mama.

"It's a deal," Aggie said.

In the weeks I'd been employed as a walking lady, Mama had stepped up Maude's education in household matters, and my sister now accompanied Mama on her rounds of shopping. No surprise that during my two-week internment, I was forced to join them.

"The mistress of the house must know how to purchase groceries," my mother said on my first outing with them.

I was willing to wager a week's salary—when I *had* a week's salary again—that Miss Cushman paid someone to buy her groceries. Or better yet, that she took her meals at Delmonico's and didn't give groceries a second thought.

"You want a relationship with your purveyors," Mama said as we walked to our first stop. "Mr. Van Dusen reserves the finest produce for his regular customers. We're fortunate to have his shop right in the neighborhood. That is something to consider when your husband is purchasing your home."

I stifled a groan.

The quantities at the grocer's overwhelmed me—dairy, vegetables, fruits, and dry provisions like flour and sugar—but Mama traversed the aisles efficiently and with ease, ordering as she went.

"How do you know how much to order?" Maude asked at one point, after Mama took at first five pounds of potatoes then amended the amount to three pounds.

Mama looked at her younger daughter proudly. "Such a good question, Maude! There's a trick to it, that's for sure. I made many mistakes when I was first married. As you girls grew up, the amounts had to be adjusted again."

"Because Georgie eats so much," Maude said with a smirk, and I poked her in the ribs.

After the grocer, we traveled a block to Honeycutt, the butcher, where the potent smell of raw meat and animal blood made me gag as we entered.

"You get used to it," Maude assured me, but I'd been happier not thinking about where our delicious roasts and chickens came from. Maybe Clem's landlady, Miss Bottoms, had had a similar experience that turned her to vegetarianism.

Our stay at the butcher shop was brief, and there was no stop at the ice creamery, to my disappointment. As Maude and I stared wistfully into the front window, Mama said, "The weather's turning cool." In fact, fall hadn't arrived in full force, and we wore only light capes in the evenings. My guess was Mama wanted to spare the expense while I was on furlough from the theater. I noticed she'd reduced the amount of her other purchases, too, like the potatoes. When the butcher asked if she'd have her usual order, she replied, "Not this week," and took only chicken and some stewing beef, no veal or roast.

Clearly, we wouldn't be eating as well or as much until I went back to work.

Shopping with Mama was boring, but not the worst way to spend a morning.

The nightmare for me came with the Saturday promenade. The excursion required me to dress in my best bonnet and frock for fall, a striped blue silk Mama had chosen "because you need something womanly." The dress required gasp-inducing stays, so I thought of it more as an instrument of torture than a passage into adulthood. I could barely shuffle in the thing, yet I was expected to parade down Broadway with my mother, sister, Uncle James, and his fiancée, Miss Lillian Templeton, along with the rest of New York society and those who aspired to be in it.

The promenade was something all the fine families did. Mama had spared me the ritual because I worked at the theater on Saturdays, but my sister had told me all about it.

"It's really grand, Georgie," Maude said as she fussed with my hair. "Everyone looks so colorful! You see all the latest fashions. I'm dying for a bonnet with a cherry-colored lining. I saw one a few weeks back, and it made the girl's cheeks bloom."

I knew the promenade was not just about who was wearing what that season. Families used it as a way to show off marriageable daughters. Maude had apparently caught the eye of one of Miss Templeton's cousins, and Mama expected the gentleman to pursue a courtship any day. Now I was to join my sister on display, like a choice cut of meat at the butcher's.

"The Templetons are a distinguished family," Maude said of her potential suitor, but her tone lacked excitement. "It would be . . . a solid match."

Her hesitation suggested some flaw in the Templeton cousin, maybe bad skin or an overbite. I snorted. "What's wrong with him?"

Maude gave my curls a satisfied pat and ignored the question.

"Tell, Maude."

"He's not *ugly*. Though his nose is a bit fat, and his laugh is more of a honk. On the plus side, he's got plenty of thick blond hair like Miss Templeton, and he's several heads taller than I am." She paused in her physical assessment.

"But?"

"He's *old*, Georgie. Maybe thirty? Why isn't he married? It can't just be his fat nose."

Mr. Templeton's nose had gone from "a bit" to straight-out "fat," and the shift made me smile.

"I keep wondering if there's some problem that's not visible." Maude's face showed her complete misery.

"Well, Uncle James is still a bachelor and he'll be thirty-five by the time he and Miss Templeton marry," I pointed out. "Does Mr. Templeton have a widowed mother he's taking care of?"

She shook her head.

"A career that's kept him busy?"

"He does some kind of banking thing. Uncle James knows him and says he's got a reputation for hard work."

"That's it, then."

Still, my words gave Maude no relief. "What if he works so hard he's got no time for a wife or a family? What if banking is all he can talk about and I'm bored silly by him?"

"You know, Maudie," I said, slowly, "you don't *have* to marry. You could choose a career, like me. I could see about getting you on at the Prince. Maybe not as a walking lady at first, but—"

I stopped when she drew back from me as if disgusted.

"I can't believe you still think girls like us have much choice about our lives," she said. "The sooner you let go of the idea you can be independent, the better. And don't underestimate Mama. She's trotting you down Broadway same as me, isn't she? She'll have us *both* married in the new year, maybe to fat-nosed brothers."

The accuracy of my younger sister's words hit me like a blow.

105

On our promenade, I walked alongside Uncle James and Miss Templeton—a tight fit on the sidewalk. Miss Templeton clung to my uncle's arm, which allowed more space for me.

Whenever we met up with a person or family Mama wanted to engage with, she urged me forward first, pushing me ahead of Maude. "You remember my eldest daughter, Georgiana," became her refrain. "She's eighteen now." Nothing about what I was doing with my life, just the number that indicated I could marry and bear children. My stomach, full of chicken and peas from our midday meal and bound by my corset, felt like someone's hands were squeezing it.

The mating ritual disgusted me, and my face must have shown it. Miss Templeton, who encouraged me to call her Lily, whispered at one point, "We'll likely stop for tea and cake at the end. That'll make up for the rest." I appreciated her warmth and kindness and could see why my uncle had been drawn to her. Actually, I was sure her emerald eyes, blond curls, and wealthy family hadn't hurt.

As much as Mama tried to showcase me, most young gentlemen gave me no more than a passing glance. It must have been the dour look Lily picked up on, or maybe the squareness of my jaw scared them off. As a result, I didn't even bother giggling or batting my eyelashes like Maude did.

Near Stewart's emporium, Lily's cousins, Samuel and Barnaby Templeton, approached us. Both of them had bulbous noses and looked to be at least thirty, so I couldn't tell which was Maude's potential beau until I noticed Maude fluttering her eyes at Barnaby.

When Mama introduced us, Samuel proved to be the first gentleman who showed interest in me—but not for the reasons Mama hoped.

"I've seen you before," he said.

"I don't recall meeting, sir."

"No, no, I've *seen* you. You're an actress, aren't you? At the Bowery?"

I flinched at being mistaken for someone who'd perform at the lower-class Bowery Theatre, but I didn't correct him. Mama pinched my arm as if to say, *Don't speak.*

"No, I remember now. It was at the Prince! You were Juliet. My younger sister begged to go, so I escorted her. Not keen on plays myself, but the ladies do favor them."

My eyes fell to the sidewalk, where I focused on the toes of my black boots. Our housemaid had polished them for our excursion, and they shone.

"You weren't half bad," Samuel said. At another time, I would have taken offense at his dismissive comment, but in an odd way his review actually worked in my favor. It indicated he wasn't even slightly familiar with the play so he couldn't have known how badly I'd botched it.

"I didn't know you were a Cartwright," he added.

Mama rushed to end the conversation. "Georgiana had a brief stint as an actress. If you're ever blessed with daughters, Mr. Templeton, you'll understand having to indulge their whims! That's all behind us now. Georgiana's ready to settle into a more traditional life."

My hands clenched into fists. I didn't know if Mama really believed what she said or if she was acting herself.

"Well, that's for the better, isn't it?" Samuel said. "Don't want anyone to get the wrong idea about such a fine young lady." His leer reminded me of Worth's, and my stomach roiled anew.

Mama took his words as her cue to invite the two men along with us for tea at Taylor's.

"That would be most enjoyable," Barnaby said with a knowing smile toward my sister. "I've never been. I assumed it was just for ladies."

"A lady has to accompany us," Uncle James explained with a wink toward his future cousins-in-law. "And we've plenty of those to go around."

"See?' Lily murmured, leaning toward me. "I told you there would be cake."

The prospect of cake should have felt like a reward for

this awful outing, but that was the precise moment that my dinner rose in my throat. I clasped a hand across my mouth to avoid throwing up my meal on Lily's leaf-colored dress. Panic crossed her face as my cheeks ballooned with bile.

"Georgie seems to be unwell," she announced to our party. "She's gone quite pale."

My mother approached me, assessing my loss of color, but she was careful not to get too close. "Oh, I'm sure it's nothing. We'll get you some chamomile tea." She turned a tight smile toward the Templeton brothers. "This is Georgiana's first promenade, and she's overly excited."

"Quite the dramatic little thing, isn't she?" Samuel said with another leer.

And that was when I spewed my dinner onto the sidewalk. Right there, on Broadway, in front of everyone—my family, the Templetons, and passersby who gasped at the show and dodged out of the way. I don't know which was worse: the projectile of peas or the retching noise that came out of me, monstrous and animal.

Luckily, I avoided hitting anyone in our company. My nicely polished boots bore the brunt of my sickness and came away coated with green chunks. Lily fished into her drawstring bag for a handkerchief so I could wipe my mouth, and its scent of lavender water calmed my stomach.

"I am so sorry," I said to no one and everyone.

In a fog of humiliation, I heard my mother apologize to the Templetons and tell them we would have to cut our outing short.

"Yes, perhaps another time," Barnaby agreed, sounding eager to leave.

"Oh, no!" Maude said with a little catch in her voice. "Can't we—" When I managed to look over at her, my sister's face displayed a tangle of emotions, embarrassment and disappointment with a dash of anger at me for spoiling everything.

"There will be other times, Maude," my mother said.

"I think it would be a shame to postpone," Lily said, facing her cousins. "Barnaby, you and Samuel should escort Mrs.

Cartwright and Maude to Taylor's as planned. It's a beautiful afternoon, and you'll have a lovely time. James, you and I will see Georgie home. I've been to Taylor's many times and missing this once won't hurt."

If any of our company objected, Lily's commanding tone didn't give them room to do so openly.

Chapter 15

Despite Lily's efforts to salvage the afternoon, Barnaby didn't ask to call on Maude. No amount of tea and ice cream could erase the memory of my dinner spurting out of my mouth. I wondered if the Templetons added up my illness with my career and came up with a vulgar sum: the eldest Cartwright girl must be expecting. Not a family to marry into.

Maude burst into my room when she and Mama arrived home from Taylor's. "What a mess you made of everything! It's over with Mr. Templeton before it ever got started. I'll die an old maid, thanks to you!"

I wanted to laugh at her dramatic turn, but instead pointed out that she was only seventeen and much prettier than I. "Clever, too," I said, although I doubted that held any attraction for a man looking for a young wife to bear his children. "You'll have other chances. Besides, you were right about Mr. Templeton. He *does* have a fat nose."

Maude snarled. That's the only word to describe it, like some feral beast. I guessed she hadn't confided her feelings about his looks to Mama, who had also come into my room and now chimed in to end the exchange.

"Noses aside, Mr. Templeton was a good match for Maude," she said. "He came approved by your uncle and Miss Templeton, and Granny Clifford was thrilled. Now we will all have to start from scratch." For the first time, I realized how many people had been involved in the matchmaking.

As she turned to me, Mama's eyes narrowed to slits. "And with your performance today . . . well, let's hope the Prince takes you back, because I'll never find a husband for you now."

My heart skipped in my chest. No husband for me! I smiled, and Maude must have misread that as making light of her misfortune. With her eyes darting around furiously, she grabbed the thing she knew I cherished most: the Staffordshire figurine of Charlotte and Susan Cushman that was the last present Pa had given me.

"No!" I screamed, popping off the bed where I'd been resting.

"Maude, put that—" but Mama's admonition wasn't in time. Maude flung the statue to the floorboards in front of the mantel.

On my hands and knees, I picked through the pieces trying to see if the figurine was salvageable. Miss Cushman's head had come off in a clean break, but Susan's had split down the middle and the bodies had shattered to bits. Tears streamed down my face until everything looked out of focus. I cradled Miss Cushman's head in my hand, thinking I might never speak to my sister again.

"Georgie, please get up off the floor," my mother said. "This is not the end of the world."

It was the housemaid's day off, so Aggie would be tasked with cleaning up the mess. I wished Maude would be made to do it, but my sister got off with a simple rebuke. "That was beneath you, Maude, no matter how hurt you feel," Mama chastised her as she swept out of the room.

Maude followed her, storming out in a huff. I continued to stare at the head, such a clear likeness of Miss Cushman as Romeo. A sharp edge nicked my palm so it bled, but I ignored my wound and finally set the china head on the mantel by itself.

For days after, Aggie was the only one in the household who spoke to me. I spent as much time as possible in my room or in the kitchen, taking most of my meals there. Whenever I appeared in the dining room, my mother and sister talked around me, as if I were wearing a cloak that made me invisible.

The high point of those lonely days was the arrival of a return note from Clem. Aggie slipped it to me while I was reading *My Youngest Sister* in my room.

"Came for you earlier. It's a heavy thing!"

"Clem likes to write," I said eagerly.

A fatter-than-average envelope promised all the latest gossip from the Prince, but Clem's missive outlined only mundane details of her life outside the theater. She'd gotten deathly sick on one of Miss Bottoms's oyster pies and had missed going to visit her family.

> *My brother and sister surprised me by arriving at my boardinghouse unannounced! I was in no shape to have visitors, but John fetched me some ginger beer, which calmed my stomach. I have since recovered nicely.*

In addition, Mrs. Tassie had advanced her from making silk bows and flowers to cutting bonnet linings from paper patterns.

> *I made mistakes right out of the gate, forgetting to cut it on the straight-way, but now I have the hang of it. Tedious work, but Mrs. Tassie promises me a salary increase by the end of the year!*

I turned the pages over, hoping for news about the company or when the rehearsals for her play would commence.

112

The only hint about the theater was a curt line:

> *I haven't seen Ned, so I can't tell you any-thing about him.*

I knew I should have taken out that mention of Ned from my letter.

> *I've enclosed an envelope that came for you and I'm sure will lighten your spirits, judging from the return. Sallie didn't know how to get it to you. You'll be back at work in a flash and can tell me all about it.*
>
> *Your friend,*
> *Clem*

The envelope she mentioned was heavy cream vellum, similar to the stationery we had used for Miss Cushman's letter. My hands trembled as I read the front, addressed to *Miss Georgiana Clifford* in care of the Prince Theatre. In the left-hand corner was the inscription, *Miss C. S. Cushman, c/o The Broadway.*

Charlotte Cushman had written to me!

My inclination was to rip into it, but instead I eased the envelope open ever so gently to preserve it.

> *Dear Miss Clifford,*
>
> *The Broadway Theatre kindly forwarded your charming note to me on my travels. What a delight it was to read! I love to hear from audience members who have been moved by my performances, but it means even more when the praise comes from another actress. Your own accomplishments in the profession at such a ten-der age are impressive, and you deserve to be*

proud of them.

I draw on my own feelings and emotions to play any part, with Romeo no exception. Portraying him has been one of the great challenges of my career—how does a woman disappear into a male role? I imagined what it is like to be so in love that the heart aches and one can no longer go on without the beloved. Love, as you know, is neither exclusively masculine nor feminine, but a sentiment that speaks to the human condition. If my Romeo "possesses some of each sex," as you so eloquently phrased it, I'm grateful. It is because his ache and longing for his beloved are universal.

My advice to you as you move forward in your career is to hold tight to those universal sentiments. Juliet was not a role suited to me, so I have no particular tips to offer on that score. (And I fear that by the time you receive this, your performance may have already occurred.)

I will say that my career benefited enormously when I began to pursue breeches roles. The opportunity to portray Romeo, Hamlet, and others allowed me the freedom to express all the different parts of myself and to spread my acting wings. I recommend it to you, if Mr. Worth would consider the possibility. Perhaps he will let you try a smaller role to start. He has not been keen on breeches roles to date, but he is a businessman first and foremost and may see the benefit of the novelty to his ticket sales.

With all good wishes for your continued success.

Fondly,
C. Cushman

Charlotte Cushman had not only written to me, but she had offered sage advice and signed herself "fondly." I carried the letter in my pocket and drew it out to reread as the days went on. By the end of the week, my folding and refolding had worn the paper thin, and the ink blurred where a couple of happy tears splatted onto the page.

Breeches roles! Would Worth ever let me try one?

Would Mama?

Temporarily shunned by my family, I spent more time with Aggie in the kitchen, reading her newspapers from top to bottom and front to back. They reported rapid changes taking place at the Prince Theater, and I worried what my place would be by the time I returned.

"Ned Murtagh has been promoted to second leading gentleman," I read from the *Broadway Miscellany*.

"That's the lad who's your friend? Isn't that a fine bit of news?"

The advance would likely double Ned's salary—enough to board at a higher-end rooming house or rent a small house of his own if he wanted to leave his parents.

"The girls'll be running after him for sure," Aggie said.

I smirked. "They won't get anywhere," I muttered, so low Aggie didn't hear it.

"'Mr. Ernest Culpepper has taken his leave from the company to go West,'" I continued to read. "Oh, that's sad! Such a sweet man. I enjoyed the times I spent on stage with him, and I'll never forget how he tried to help Pa during that final performance." Had Worth finally forced the "sodomite" out, or did Mr. Culpepper depart of his own accord? "To go West" might be code for something else.

The bigger shock, though, occurred further down in the story. Frances Muller had also advanced in the company. "N-o-o!" I wailed, tossing the paper onto the floor. "Not *Frances*!"

Aggie didn't take her eyes off the stew she was stirring. "Well, who's the green-eyed monster in my kitchen?"

"It isn't jealousy, Aggie. This is about fairness. Worth's

done this on purpose, promoted her while I'm away. It's spite, I'm telling you. Frances Muller's not half the actress I am."

Aggie clucked over her pot. "Maybe what you need instead of tonight's stew is a big slice of humble pie."

I ignored the quip, picked up the paper again, and read on.

The much-anticipated new melodrama by Clementine Scarborough, *My Youngest Sister,* would open at the Prince at the end of the month. Sooner than expected, but I had finished reading the play and had already commenced memorizing the lines. Even with the other roles I would have to learn when I returned to work, the schedule shouldn't be a problem.

But wait—

Miss Muller will play the lead of Abigail, a role originated by Miss Georgiana Clifford in All My Sisters.

That brought on a choking fit, and Aggie hurried to the table to pound on my back fiercely.

"Now see what you've done! You're getting yourself all worked up over a bit of jealousy."

"But she got my role, Aggie! *My* role! It was written for *me*! I deserve it!"

Was this why Clem never mentioned the theater—or the play—in her letter?

Aggie returned to the stew. "When you figure out how to get all you deserve from life, well, I hope you'll let me in on that little secret."

There was still a day remaining on my official suspension, and I wasn't supposed to show up at the theater before then. Still, I defied the restriction and stormed down to the Prince.

I had no spare coins, so I had to use my own two feet for transport instead of a hack or bus. My bonnet sat askew and my face was flushed by the time I reached the theater.

A rehearsal was underway, and I couldn't tell which play at first. It didn't take long to figure out. I'd already committed most of Act One of *My Youngest Sister* to memory. Plus, Clem stood in the wings next to Harry, mouthing words Frances stumbled over.

"You're not supposed to be here yet, Georgie," Harry said,

but he looked embarrassed, not angry.

Hearing my name, Clem turned, her face crumbling. "Oh, George!" she whispered. She tugged me away from the stage. The motion was so frantic and unexpected, I almost tripped.

"Nice welcome back," I said when we were out of Harry's earshot. "I had to read about it in the paper. Imagine how that felt."

"I wanted to tell you myself, I did, but I didn't know how." Two perfect rivulets of tears coursed down her cheeks.

I softened instantly. "It's OK, Clem. I know it wasn't up to you. This is all *him*." I couldn't manage to say Worth's name.

"He's been a devil to deal with since you've been gone," Clem said. "Almost like he was punishing you but, I don't know, missing you at the same time?"

"Eeew." Worth's face popped into my head, the way he'd leered as he grabbed me during our private rehearsal.

"My thoughts exactly."

Clem had stopped crying but couldn't dry her eyes because I was holding her hands. She pulled away gently to withdraw a handkerchief from her sleeve.

"I don't think there's anything to be done," she said after she blew her nose. "We started rehearsals today."

"I know, but I'll have my say with him anyway. Is he here?"

"Haven't seen him. The rehearsal for *Cymbeline* is this afternoon, so he'll be in for that." Clem's lips tightened. "If I were in your shoes—"

"Well, you're not." It was too snappish, and I regretted it the minute I said it. "Sorry. I'm in a foul mood."

"I was just going to say that maybe there's a better way to handle him," Clem continued. "Did you read Miss Cushman's letter, by any chance?"

The mention of the letter brought me to a happier mood. "I've read it ten times at least!"

"Did she—did she offer any advice? I just wondered, you know, because, well, you'd asked her for it, and—well, it was awfully kind of her to write back."

I withdrew the folded vellum from my pocket. "I like to

keep it close," I explained. I read Clem the bit about playing a breeches role.

"She's given you smart advice. I particularly like the part about Worth being a businessman. Read that again?"

"'He is a businessman first and foremost and may see the benefit of the novelty to his ticket sales.'"

"Maybe when you see Worth, you could say you've had a letter from Charlotte Cushman herself suggesting you play a breeches role. A small one, to start. And most important, she says it would be good for the theater."

I saw the beauty of it, but what if he didn't like Miss Cushman? Worth struck me as the type of man who wouldn't take to a lady as successful as she was, likely earning much more than he did.

Clem seemed to read my thoughts. "Start the conversation with something just slightly groveling, whatever you can stand—you know, you've learned your lesson type of thing. Then launch into the idea. It's worth a try, George. It can't hurt any more than what he's already done to you."

"You don't know the half of it," I mumbled.

Her head tilted. "But I *want* to know. What happened that night? It wasn't like you to lose your lines. You knew Juliet front to back."

I kept my eyes down so she couldn't guess the truth. I was determined to put the whole thing with Worth behind me and move on, not let anyone, even Clem, know what I'd endured.

"Bad case of stage fright, I guess," I said. "I'm sorry you had to witness it."

Clem placed a finger under my chin and lifted it. "George."

My name had never sounded so tender. I wanted to tell her the truth, but not in Worth's space or anywhere nearby.

"I'll tell you, Clem, I promise. Later."

I grabbed her hand again for no reason and stood there holding it like a fool. Finally, I gave it an embarrassed squeeze.

Then Clem did something I never expected and didn't know what to make of. She lifted my hand and touched my fingertips to her lips. Hardly a kiss, really, more like being brushed by velvet, but my knees wobbled just the same.

"See you soon, George," she said.

Chapter 16

That night, I busied myself preparing a contrite speech for Worth. The thought of having to deliver it to him face to face took my appetite away, so I skipped another meal with Mama and Maude and struggled over the wording at my writing desk.

The soft rap at my door sounded like Aggie's touch, and I assumed she had brought me a light meal.

Mama was the last person I expected to see standing in the doorframe. She held a tray with a plate of cold chicken and a thick slice of buttered bread, which she set down on the bed.

"You've lost weight."

In the time since I'd played Juliet, my frocks did fit more loosely. If I ever had to borrow one of Mary Louise's costumes again, it wouldn't be a struggle.

"You've got such a big frame it doesn't seem healthy."

It was an odd sort of compliment, but I smiled and said I would eat the chicken later, thrilled that she was no longer shunning me.

"I go back to the theater tomorrow," I pointed out.

"Yes, I know. It will be good to have your salary again and not have to scrimp."

I glanced away. I didn't need to be reminded how my debacle had affected my family. If we could get through the next few minutes without her bringing up Maude—

"I told Maude she must find a way to replace your figurine."

I sniffed. "Pa gave it to me."

"I know that. But if we can find another, it will be yours. Your uncle will look into it when he's in London."

I glanced over at Miss Cushman's severed head on the mantle, resting on a pillow I'd fashioned for it out of one of my handkerchiefs. A replacement wouldn't be the same. Pa's gift was one more indication that he'd recognized my ambition and supported it.

"I also wanted you to know that this weekend's promenade went much better than the week before."

I hadn't wanted to think about the promenade ever again.

"Your uncle introduced us to a young man named Mr. MacReady whom he met through a business loan. Seems his father owns a group of warehouses downtown, and young Mr. MacReady has just become general manager of two of them."

I wondered where this was going. The fear shot through me that she was about to suggest I walk with them the following Saturday and meet the man.

"Your sister came home all aflutter," Mama continued with a funny smile. "She seems to have taken a fancy to him in a way she didn't to Mr. Templeton. He's younger than the other gentleman, that's for certain, no more than twenty-two. And very pleasant looking." Perhaps Mama had noticed Mr. Templeton's unfortunate nose, too.

I held back a laugh. Just days earlier, Maude had whined about dying a spinster because of me and broken my cherished statue in a fit of pique. Now, miraculously, she had met the man of her dreams. If I hadn't ruined the outing with the Templetons, Barnaby would have begun courting her and she'd be shackled to a middle-aged man with a bulbous nose. The irony was rich.

"You might say I saved the day," I blurted out. "And all because I couldn't hold down my peas."

Mama scowled at the memory. "None of your sass, Georgiana. Your behavior was abysmal."

"Sorry." I wasn't sorry, but the contrition slipped out unbidden. "Still, I think I've paid my dues."

"You have. For that and for your suspension. You're free to see your friends again and to come and go as you like," my mother said.

"Thank you, Mama."

"Well, then."

As far as I was concerned, there wasn't anything else to say, but Mama had an additional announcement she found difficult to get out.

"One last thing—"

I waited.

"I appreciate your contribution to the family. I'm proud of you and the way you stepped up when your father abandoned us. I'm sorry if I've been hard on you. When you had your . . . problem on stage, it reminded me of your father. You're so like him sometimes."

"I won't let you down like Pa did."

"I know. I meant you're full of passion and talent, like him. Now if your sister makes this match with Mr. MacReady, our circumstances will be even better, and I won't have to worry about either of you." What remained unsaid was that she also wouldn't have to worry about herself because her daughters would be in a position to take care of her.

Mama reached out and patted my cheek as she left. "Happy dreams, Georgie. I'll see you at breakfast."

The next morning, I woke before dawn on sheets damp with sweat, strands of hair sticking to my cheeks and forehead. I remembered a vague dream about being trapped in the bowels of the Prince with a villain chasing me, doors that wouldn't open, menacing faces popping out in the dark. I lingered in bed, my mind darting to all the scenarios that could happen between me and Worth when I appeared for work. Finally, the housemaid arrived with water for bathing and offered to help with my hair. She didn't call it a rat's nest, but the mirror told me it was.

All the resolve I'd felt the day before had evaporated, and I wondered what the consequences would be if I didn't report to the theater. The big thing that would happen, of course, was that Mama would come upstairs, dress me herself, and shove me out the door. She'd made it too clear how she felt about my salary.

Still, I dawdled, getting to breakfast late, lingering over my soft egg and toast, and helping myself to a second cup of coffee while Maude prattled on about Mr. MacReady, whom she was already calling Archie. All the while, Mama's eyes kept traveling to the mantel clock, aware that if I didn't leave soon, I'd be late my first day back.

Mama stirred cream into her coffee, her spoon clinking in the cup. "Maude, don't you have something to say to Georgie before she heads off to the theater?"

My sister's cheeks flushed, and she sighed with the effort of acknowledging her bad behavior. "It was wrong to break your figurine." Another heavy sigh. "I'm sorry, Georgie. It was beastly of me."

I opened my mouth to agree, but I caught Mama's eye and instead offered my sister a tepid thanks. My mother's spoon clinked a bit louder.

"Georgie, don't you get your new prompt books today?"

The minutes ticked away as I drained my cup, but Mama persisted.

"And won't you forfeit some of your salary if you're late?" She likely remembered the company's rules and regulations from Pa: *For making the Prompter wait, fifty cents.*

Mama threw a glance out the dining room window, which faced Bond Street. "Look at that, Louis is here. It's so kind of your uncle to send his carriage for you today."

There was nothing left to do but make my reluctant good-byes.

At the theater, I hoped to see Clem or Ned before anyone

else so I could boost my confidence, but Frances Muller was the first person I ran into. Literally. She was trying to juggle several thick prompt books, the result of her promotion to second leading lady, and she bumped into me as I entered the wings.

"Oh, Georgie. Welcome back," she said, her tone flat. She was such a bad actress that she couldn't even feign camaraderie. "You look . . . thinner."

Harry appeared out of nowhere, heading straight toward me with a frantic look. "There you are!" he said, as if I'd simply been in the green room on a break between scenes. "You're filling in for Miss Lafarge in the matinee. Her voice seems to be gone. Here's the book. Better go study up."

I choked back a laugh at the prompt book cover—*All My Sisters*. In two weeks, Harry had apparently forgotten I'd originated the role of Abigail, which Miss Lafarge had taken over during my suspension.

"Hmm, right," Harry said when he realized his mistake. "Well, then, go refresh your memory."

The unexpected casting meant there'd be no time to talk to Worth until later, and that relaxed the knot in my stomach. I descended to the dressing rooms to see what state my Abigail costume was in. Victoria Lafarge, a twig-like creature a good wind could snap in two, wouldn't have worn it, so I assumed my frock would be where I left it in the wardrobe or trunk marked with my name.

It wasn't. The wardrobe held nothing of mine but the cape Sallie had helped me rig up to play Lady MacDuff. My trunk contained a sparse assortment, too—the maid's apron for Pert, some extra drawers and chemises, hosiery, the veil I'd worn as Juliet. Other costumes had been sent out for laundering.

I knew I'd hung Abigail's day dress in the wardrobe. I'd planned to wear it again in a scene in the new play for continuity. Because *All My Sisters* was a contemporary piece, the frock was one of my own day dresses, a simple violet with purple velvet trim that didn't scratch or itch or pinch in any way.

Frances came into the dressing room as I was rummaging

through the wardrobe in an obsessive way, as if my dress were hiding from me.

"Has someone been in my things? I'm missing my violet dress."

"I wouldn't know. But a few other people have complained about missing costumes." She clicked her tongue. "If you ask me, someone needs to look in *Sallie's* room."

The way she said it grated on me. "No one asked you," I snapped.

Still, her accusation jogged the memory of catching the young man in Sallie's room wearing something that resembled Worth's shirt. And I recalled the first day I'd met Sallie, loaded down with an armful of clothes. Nothing unusual there, I reminded myself—she was a dresser, after all. She removed items for cleaning and pressing, and maybe she had forgot to bring them back in a timely manner. That was likely the fate of my violet dress.

Around the bend of the narrow hallway leading to Sallie's room, I heard low, insistent women's voices, one with Sallie's soft cadence. Her door stood ajar, and I peered through the opening into the space, barely lit with a few flickering candles as the gas lighting didn't extend back that far. Sallie was deep in earnest conversation with another woman. With their matching head wraps and high cheekbones, the two appeared to be related.

From their whispers, I made out a few solitary words: "Maryland" and "children." I would have waited for them to finish, but if my dress had disappeared altogether, I had precious little time to send home for another.

I did the only thing I could think of and coughed, bringing their attention to the doorway.

"Miss Georgie!" Sallie said. "You're back!"

"I am." In the pause that followed, I glanced awkwardly from one to the other.

"This my sister, Cassie. She's been . . . helping out."

Cassie and I nodded to each other. Her skin tone was a tint darker than Sallie's, but the resemblance between them was even stronger close up.

"Cass taught me everything I know about sewing," Sallie said. "You ever need something special."

"I could use something, but it isn't special," I said. "I'm missing the dress for today's matinee. The violet? It was in the wardrobe—"

"Oh, I got that, miss," Sallie said, and my chest loosened with relief. "Had a stain on the skirt, and I thought it might be spoiled, but I got it out for you. Free of charge."

That grabbed my attention. Pesky stains like lip pigment cost a nickel, and for some reason Sallie was being accommodating. I was prepared to thank her, ask for the dress, and be gone, but she cut in before I could.

"I'll bring it to the dressing room in a minute. Cassie's just headed out."

"But—" Cassie began, and Sallie gave her a little poke in the arm.

"Well, thank you. Good to meet you, Cassie."

"Miss," Cassie said as I turned to leave.

The matinee went without a hitch, my lines flowing out of me like I'd been born saying them. When I exited Abigail's final scene in Act Three, Clem was waiting in the wings, a huge grin on her face. She hopped up and down as if she couldn't contain her excitement, and that made me hop, too. Clem hugged me close, and for a girl whose eyes came only to my chin, her embrace knocked the breath out of me.

"So proud of you!"

With a jerk of his head, Harry signaled that we should stop hopping and hugging and leave the wings as soon as possible. Then he pointed down with a sharp jerk of his index finger, which in his language meant only one thing.

My throat tightened. Worth wanted to see me.

Clem understood Harry's code, too. "You want me to come along?"

I'd rehearsed my speech, and I had brought Miss Cushman's letter to the theater with me. "I have to do this by myself," I said.

I stopped to retrieve the letter and to wipe the pigment off my lips and cheeks before knocking at Worth's door. In the seconds before he responded, my stomach flipped and flopped and flipped again.

"Yes," he said finally.

Worth stood with a prompt book in front of him, while the men's dresser, Joe, sat to his right. They appeared to be running lines.

"Yes?"—as if he hadn't summoned me.

"Harry said you wanted to see me." I remained just inside the door, close enough to make a quick escape. Seeing Joe calmed my jumpy stomach. Worth wouldn't try anything untoward in front of the dresser. But then—

"I did. Joe, give us a moment."

Joe retreated and clicked the door behind him.

"I caught part of Act Two," Worth began. I steeled myself for criticism, but his tone was unusually warm and smooth. "Nice work. You picked up Abigail right where you left her."

"Thank you." I bit back what I was thinking: If I'd done such nice work, why couldn't I play the role again in Clem's new melodrama?

As if he read my thoughts, Worth continued, "Unfortunately, I can't give you Abigail's role for *My Youngest Sister*. We've started rehearsals already, and Frances has been working hard at it."

"I heard her."

He squinted at my snide tone. "If you have any notes about the role to share with her, it would be appreciated."

My fists curled into the folds of my dress. Worth surveyed me curiously, just my face, nothing below my neck. Maybe he had moved on to another actress, someone more willing to indulge his roaming hands and lips.

"There will be other roles for you, Georgie. I don't often judge incorrectly, but in your case, I did. I've reassessed, and I don't see you as a leading lady." He paused as if to gauge my reaction, then added, "Not now, for certain, but possibly not ever. That doesn't mean you can't have a fine career in supporting roles."

I was unaware I'd been clenching my jaw until a dull ache throbbed in my left cheek.

"I understand, sir," I said in the meekest voice I could dredge up, one that came from some girlish depth of me I wasn't usually in touch with. "I made a mess of Juliet, and I think you're correct in your assessment."

Worth's chin turned up in surprise. "That's very sporting of you, Georgie. I appreciate it." His attention returned to his prompt book. "Find Joe and tell him he can come back in, would you?"

"I do have one idea, though, if I could pass it by you, sir."

His eyes found mine again. "What do you mean?" No one in the company was supposed to have ideas except him.

I withdrew my idol's letter from my pocket. "I've had a letter from Miss Charlotte Cushman," I said.

"You?" he said, staring in wonder at the vellum in my hand. "How could that have happened?"

"Oh, I initiated it, sir. Of course, someone as important as Miss Cushman wouldn't know Georgiana Clifford from a speck of dust. My uncle took me to see her playing Romeo, and I just had to write and let her know how it affected me as a young actress."

He snapped his fingers at me. "Give it here."

I hadn't anticipated that. "I'd rather not share the personal bits," I said. "But if you'd allow it, I would read this paragraph she intended for you."

"For me?" He waved at me impatiently. "Well, go on, girl."

"'I will say that my career benefited enormously when I began to pursue breeches roles,'" I read aloud. "'The opportunity to portray Romeo, Hamlet, and others allowed me to stretch my acting wings. Perhaps Mr. Worth will let you try a smaller role to start. He may see the benefit of the novelty to ticket sales.'"

He rubbed his chin. "Is that all?"

"There are some other things that are more personal, as I said, but this part was in response to my asking for advice." I smiled shyly. "Breeches roles, sir. What do you think?"

He frowned, his eyebrows meeting in one line across his forehead. "I think Miss Cushman has little else in her kit."

His rude dismissal of my idol stung. For a split-second, I thought it was all over, but then he went on, "I also think it's not a half-bad idea. We haven't had anyone capable of handling breeches roles in the company, and they're so very popular these days. Real crowd pleasers with men *and* ladies."

My heart picked up speed as he continued to think aloud.

"It *is* a shame to waste your talents playing maids just because you aren't cut out for Juliet and other leading roles. You might do well as a boy. You have a certain quality about you, don't you? Not to mention your height."

I held my breath, waiting for his next words to burst the bubble of hope rising in me.

"Let me think on it," Worth said. "I will get back to you."

The best words I'd heard in two weeks.

Chapter 17

Miss Lafarge's laryngitis improved slightly, but by the following Wednesday she still wasn't up to performing. Worth let me close out the matinee of *All My Sisters*, playing Abigail one last time.

After, Worth called the company into the green room for a celebration—a champagne toast with cupcakes.

"There aren't enough for us all," I pointed out to Ned and Clem. "We'll have to fight for them."

"I challenge you to a duel for the one with lemon frosting," Ned said.

Worth raised his glass in tribute. "To today's successful closing performance, the best of all," he said. "To the company!"

I joined the chorus of voices that said, "To the company!" I'd never tasted champagne before, and the cold fizz tickled my nose. Clem's face lit up as she tipped back her glass.

"And even better, this play alone has sent our ticket sales through the ceiling. We'll be doing regular matinees from now on. To matinees!"

"To matinees!"

Worth offered several more toasts to various members of the company. Would he never get to Clem?

The bubbles had gone straight to my head and made me brave enough to initiate a toast of my own. "Author, author!" I cried out. "Without Clem, we wouldn't be here."

Clem blushed a bright pink.

"To Clem!" Ned called out, and the company repeated the toast.

Worth stared at me, then added, "Yes, to many more successes by the talented Miss Scarborough."

"Here, here!"

The company broke up and dribbled out of the room, happy and giggly. As I was leaving, Worth took hold of my elbow, managing a near-empty champagne bottle and a glass in his other hand.

"You didn't trust me, Georgie," he said. "I was saving Miss Scarborough for last. She *is* the most important, after all."

He dropped my elbow and poured himself another swallow, then emptied the bottle into my glass. His action stirred a fuzzy memory in me—Pa on some birthday or anniversary or holiday, splashing champagne into crystal for the adults. Over and over again.

"I'm sorry I jumped in like that," I said. It was taking a good deal of effort for me to put one foot in front of the other. I glanced ahead for help from Clem or Ned, but they were already at the green room door.

"Your first hit of the bubbly?" Worth asked.

At that inopportune moment, I hiccupped and smiled sheepishly. "Please don't tell my mother."

"I've not had the pleasure of meeting your dear mother, so your secret's safe with me."

He tossed back his drink, and I fixated on his throat as the liquid traveled down it, his prominent Adam's apple protruding even more than usual. I reached for my own neck and downed the second serving he'd poured for me.

"Someday perhaps Mrs. Clifford will attend a performance and you'll introduce us."

Now completely tipsy, I blurted out the first thing that occurred to me. "Oh, my grandmother rarely leaves Brooklyn, and she'd never come to a *theater*! She's much too proper."

Worth gave me a curious sideways look. "I meant your

mother, of course."

"Oh, Mrs. *Cartwright*," I corrected, loud enough for Ned to turn around with eyes round as carriage wheels.

"Georgie!" Ned said. "Are you coming or not?"

In that instant, reading the horrified look on Ned's face and the blankness on Clem's, I realized what I'd let slip out. My fingers darted to my mouth to push the name back in. The only hope was if Worth was inebriated, too, or wasn't paying attention.

But he was a much more seasoned drinker than I, and my correction didn't pass unnoticed.

"Cartwright, you say." He put down his glass and the empty bottle and took me by the elbow again in case I had thoughts of escape. "Isn't that curious? That's the name of a disgraced actor I gave the sack to, oh, five or six months back. Not long before your uncle brought you to my attention."

Drink, apparently, can also make you weepy. My eyes filled, and a sob escaped my throat.

Ned stepped in and steered me away by my other elbow. "Georgie, we better get you some strong coffee at Groff's," he said with forced merriment. He winked at Worth. "The non-sense girls talk when they're drinking, right, sir?"

Worth nodded, but the question in his eyes suggested he wouldn't let this go.

"Someone's been mighty busy," Clem said as soon as we were on the other side of the stage door in the street.

The days had finally turned cool, and the crisp late October air hit my face in a welcome, sobering blast.

"Must take a lot of energy to hide something as big as who your father is."

In my ears, her voice sounded muffled and distant, like she was standing at the back of the Prince's vast parquet under the tiers.

"Can we discuss this when we're inside Groff's?" Ned said. He continued to grip my arm, likely worried I'd trip over the cobbles as we crossed to the beer cellar.

Clem planted her feet and didn't budge. "You told me your

father died falling from a height. You even sniffled when you told me! I had no reason not to believe you. But then, you *are* a good actress."

"Steady on, Clem," Ned said.

I struggled to recall my words. "I said we lost him," I corrected. "I didn't say 'died,' exactly. You assumed that. And he did fall . . . to his knees, onstage."

"It makes me wonder what else I don't know about you, George, what else you've lied about or withheld."

"Clem, please—"

"Just shut up, Ned, OK?" Clem often used street language, but I'd never heard her tell anyone to shut up. The words came out with a spray of spittle. "I'm talking to George, not you."

My tongue sat heavy in my mouth. "Worth wouldn't have hired me if he'd known, and once I got the job I was scared to let too many people know."

"Too many people? *That's* what I am to you?"

The stage door opened, and two walking gentlemen emerged onto the street, laughing loudly about something.

"See you at Groff's!" one of them called to Ned as they slipped across the street. He looked after them wistfully.

"You go, Ned," I said. "I'm feeling less woozy, and I don't want that dreadful coffee."

Ned glanced toward Groff's, then back at me and Clem. "You sure, Georgie? I should see you home."

"I'm sure."

"So gal*lant*," Clem said.

Ned scowled. "You've never liked me, have you, Clem? Yet I've done nothing to you as far as I can tell except maybe exist. You simply can't stand anyone else getting Georgie's attention. I have to tell you, your jealousy is *not* attractive."

"As if I'd want to attract you," she lobbed back.

An actress or two trickled out of the theater and shot us curious glances. I longed to be anywhere but on Prince Street in the middle of an argument. Plus, I worried that Worth, like the others, would be leaving soon for his dinner break before the evening curtain.

"Ned, please go," I pleaded under my breath. "You're making matters worse."

He released me and bowed dramatically from the waist. "Ladies."

And then Clem and I were facing each other. A dull pain throbbed behind my eyes, and it hurt to look at her.

"I will tell you everything," I said, "but not here in the street. Let's take a hack to my house. We'll talk in my room."

"Unlike some people," she said with a defiant lift to her chin, "I haven't the money for hacks."

"I know you don't, but I do."

She wavered on the brink of refusing. "I can't spare more than thirty minutes," she said. "There are bonnet linings to cut for tomorrow or I'll fall behind. Mrs. Tassie hasn't been happy about all my hours at the theater."

After two weeks without a salary, I had precious little money to spend on a hack, but I was desperate to set things right with my best friend. "How about I pay your return fare so you get home faster?"

Clem's eyes flickered, giving me hope I could win back her trust. I slipped an arm through hers before she could change her mind, and we marched off toward Broadway.

In the foyer of our house, Mama extended a courteous dinner invitation to Clem, but her face wore a mix of emotions: annoyance at me for bringing home a friend without warning, blended with worry that Aggie would have to stretch the evening's meal to serve four instead of three. If we hadn't recently lost forty dollars because of me, it would not have been much of a problem.

Clem's polite refusal made my mother's shoulders fall from their on-guard position.

"There are bonnets to be made," Clem offered as explanation. "Mrs. Tassie is a demanding employer." Her voice held a chirpy lightness I knew she didn't feel.

134

At the reminder that Clem worked for a milliner—and Mrs. Tassie, who ran one of the finest shops in Manhattan—Mama looked peppier. "Tell me something, Clementine." She fingered one of her bonnets, which lay abandoned on the foyer table. "I love this bonnet, but it's several years old and it makes me feel dowdy. Any suggestions for livening it up?"

"Oh, Mama, you can afford a new one now I'm back to work," I said, anxious to bring Clem up to my room. "Why don't you just go to Genin's and pick one out?"

Clem harrumphed. "Genin's may be the largest hatter in town," she said, "but Mrs. Tassie's bonnets are so much finer quality."

She took the hat gently from Mama's hands, angling it this way and that. "The frame is sturdy. Some fresh ribbons and flowers would perk it right up, maybe even a new lining. Why don't I take it with me today and do it for you?"

"How kind! I'll pay you, of course."

"You've always been so hospitable," Clem said, her tone warm and flattering. "Let me do this for you . . . Mrs. Cartwright."

Mama started when Clem used her correct name instead of Mrs. Clifford, which she'd been cautioned to accept from anyone at the theater. She fired a quizzical look at me, but I averted my eyes.

"Thank you, Clementine," Mama replied. "You'll come for Sunday dinner next week, won't you?"

"And I'll have your hat for you then."

Safely in my room, I clicked the door closed behind us and pointed at the bonnet in Clem's hands. "You didn't have to do that, you know. Mama can afford to go to Mrs. Tassie herself. I don't like her trying to get free labor."

"And I don't like being lied to," Clem said, laying the hat on the bed. She faced me with folded arms. "So."

"So." Clem remained standing as I perched on the edge of the bed. "So, my father is William Cartwright."

She nodded, having figured out as much.

"You may have read how he disgraced himself at the

135

Prince last spring. He was inebriated on stage."

Clem stared at me impassively.

"Worth's very strict about things like that," I went on. "I don't know how many times Pa showed up in his cups, but that night my uncle and I were in the audience and witnessed it. It was my birthday, of all days."

Her expression softened.

"He actually *did* fall, Clem. Not from a horse, it's true, but I thought he'd tumble right off the boards into the pit. The audience was booing and everything. It was awful."

"But he isn't dead," she said.

"No, but he might as well be. He lost his position and disappeared after that, and no one's seen him since."

That wasn't quite accurate, and I backtracked, scared of leading Clem astray again.

"Actually, he disappeared and *I* haven't seen him since," I corrected myself. "I honestly don't know if Mama or Uncle James knows where he is because they won't talk about him to me. It's almost like he *is* dead." I swallowed hard. "He may very well be dead . . . or in prison or something."

Clem's arms loosened and her hands fell to her sides. "And that's why you became an actress."

"No . . . well, yes, in part. I've wanted to act since I was a little girl. That and the whole part about my admiring Miss Cushman is the God's honest truth. But it turned out when Pa left us, acting was also the best path forward for a girl like me, the only way to earn a decent living and not be forced to marry. I had to keep my real name a secret to get the job at the Prince."

"Except Ned knew." She sniffed her disapproval.

"I met Ned at acting lessons, before I took the stage name," I explained. "Look, Clem, I agree with Ned. I don't know why you're so jealous of him. You needn't be. I love you both."

The word *love* slipped out effortlessly and floated between us like a dandelion puff. As the room warmed with expectation, I hurried to fill the awkward pause.

"Anyway, you see why I had to change my name. I needed

the job, I needed to succeed at it. Until very recently, Mama was making elaborate plans to get me married to anyone who'd have me." I sniggered at the thought. "As if anyone *would* have me."

Clem sat down next to me on the bed, reached over, and took my hand in hers. I was conscious of my slick palm, but Clem didn't seem to notice or mind.

"I'd have you, George," she said. "I would have had you from the first day we met, when you tried to go into the theater through the whores' door. You were so *cute*."

My cheeks and ears got hot, and I was sure I'd bloomed a deep pink. Clem's right hand went up to my cheek and brushed it. Then she coaxed my head toward hers, her eyes closing as she leaned in to kiss me.

On the lips.

It wasn't that the kiss didn't make sense. We'd been slowly moving toward more intimacy, and being with her energized me. Kissing Clem, my best friend in the world, made more sense than kissing a man like Worth, which had been a violation.

But as her lips reached mine, I drew back. She wasn't a man, and didn't she need to be for this to happen? Could girls really kiss each other as more than friends? I was pretty sure Ned and Richard Pomeroy kissed, but what if no women had ever done it before? I didn't want to hurt Clem, but I couldn't take the leap forward either.

"Oh," she said, her eyes widening.

"I'm sorry, I just don't think I can."

Clem looked stricken as she stood up abruptly.

"I misread things," she said, her face now as red as mine must have been a moment earlier. "It can be hard to know with girls."

Her statement hit like a splash of cold water. Clem had been keeping secrets of her own.

"You mean you've done this before?"

She sighed. "There was a girl at Bellport Academy. Arabella." The name came out soft and wistful, almost like a cloud.

"We planned to live together. But when the time came to go through with it, she changed her mind."

My throat closed up, but I wasn't sure why. I didn't want to kiss Clem, but I didn't want to *not* kiss her, either. I especially didn't want to imagine her kissing someone named Arabella, a girl she'd known at school, long before we ever met. I'd naively thought Clem and I were experiencing the same feelings as new and confusing.

"And where is this Arabella now?"

"She's engaged to a fella who was a year ahead of us at school. They're getting married in the spring."

"So, *you* lied, too."

"I did not! I mentioned Arabella to you several times, I know I did, that she was the one who learned millinery first and taught me the basics. Remember? She made the connection with Mrs. Tassie, and she found Miss Bottoms's boardinghouse, too. I wouldn't even be here without her."

The girl's name still didn't ring a bell, but I did recall hearing that a school friend had helped Clem start out in the trade.

"I just left a few details out, that's all. I always thought we'd get around to talking more about her someday. Further down the road."

I couldn't think of anything else to say, and Clem was fresh out of words, too. She picked up Mama's bonnet and turned it round and round in her hands in a dizzying way. I took a satchel out of my wardrobe and gave it to her to keep the hat clean on her trip back to her gritty neighborhood.

"I guess I should go."

I didn't mean what I said next, but the harsh words tripped out of me. "I guess you should."

I didn't see her out. Emotions tangled inside me, a mix of arrogance, dejection, and deep confusion about who I was and what I wanted from Clem. At my bedroom door, I listened to her soft footfall on the stairs and to Aggie wishing her a pleasant evening. Then I flung myself onto the bed, buried my head in my pillow, and wept as quietly as I could.

Chapter 18

My first Saturday back on the boards, I played yet another lady's maid with ten lines in a forgettable melodrama that Worth hoped would catch fire like Clem's had. The dramatist—a fellow named Fredrick Price—never made an appearance at the theater, not even for the performance, and a rumor circled through the company that Worth had written the piece himself under a pseudonym.

"Price . . . Worth . . . get it?" Ned said.

The audience greeted the curtain's fall with tepid, confused applause, and none of the dailies stooped to review it.

The snub angered Worth in a way that seemed extreme even for him, and I wondered if there was truth to the gossip about the play's author. The company sometimes experienced flops, and Worth might yell and fuss about them for an hour before moving on to the next play on the bill. The pace of the theater didn't allow for prolonged rumination, but this particular failure made Worth brood like Hamlet.

On a day that Sallie and I were hunched over my trunk, trying to assemble a costume for my next role—Lucetta, a waiting woman (another maid, but a sixteenth-century one) in *Two Gentlemen of Verona*—the door to the walking ladies' dressing room snapped open, and we both jumped. Even though I was dressed, I instinctively grabbed the cape in Sallie's hands to cover myself.

Worth swept in, a prompt book tucked under his arm.

"Sir, you should knock," Sallie piped up. "Ladies might be dressing."

He glanced around. "Well, they aren't. What are you doing?"

I handed the cape back to Sallie, who folded it tidily. "We're putting together Lucetta's costume," I explained.

"I'm pulling you from that."

My spirits sank. Lucetta wasn't a role to shine in, but it was a role nonetheless.

Worth extended the prompt book he was holding toward me, and it was much fatter than Lucetta's. "You will now be playing Tranio in the *Shrew*."

The room stilled. Everything about the moment was baffling and unreal. First of all, Worth never deigned to assign roles or hand out books, even though we all knew the decisions came from him and not Harry. Second, the role of Tranio, servant to Lucentio, had great possibilities and could be a scene-stealer. It was a larger role than my recent suspension warranted.

And third, if a woman played it, it would be a breeches role.

"Tranio?"

"You're not deaf."

I had not yet taken the script from him, so he shoved it into my hands.

"You seem well-suited to the part. You're quite the deceitful thing, much like him, aren't you?" Worth smirked, gauging my response. I lowered my eyes to avoid his, but his next words undid me. "And, since your father never played the role, no one will compare you to him."

I was overcome with a sudden coughing fit.

"Sallie, a glass of water for your mistress. Quick, girl." Worth watched her do his bidding, then continued, "I'm not as gullible as you think. And this . . . fit or whatever it is, plus the sheepish look on your face, confirm what you let slip the other day. You are in fact Georgiana Cartwright, William's daughter."

Sallie's hand jerked in mid-pour, and a few drops of water splashed onto the floorboards between us. We both stared down at them dumbly.

"Unless Georgiana isn't your name either," Worth added.

My throat still tickled badly, and I downed the water Sallie handed to me. After, I managed to answer, "It *is* my name. And please, sir, I didn't think you gullible."

"Yet, you and your uncle assumed you could fool me. If he even *is* your uncle." One eyebrow shot up in a rakish way. "Or is he your *uncle?*"

The lewd suggestion shouldn't have shocked me, but it did. Worth's impropriety apparently knew no bounds.

"He really *is* my uncle," I replied as steadily as I could. "I'm sorry, truly. Don't blame Uncle James. I needed the job when Pa abandoned us, or we would have been ruined. I took my mother's maiden name and pressured her and Uncle James to go along with the charade. Please don't be cross."

And then Worth did the most surprising thing of all. Instead of chastising me further, as I fully expected, his face erupted in clownish glee.

"I'm not cross! Far from it. It's actually quite delicious. You playing Tranio is part of a new plan I've come up with."

Never mind that Miss Cushman had come up with the plan and I'd laid it out for him. I glanced at the book in my hands, reeling from the possibility of playing such a plum role.

"I've notified the dailies," he went on. "You and I will do an interview tomorrow morning in the green room."

"I'm to talk to the papers?"

"You don't think I'd hide this under a basket, do you? 'Cartwright Daughter Unmasked—Talented Actress in Own Right.'" He framed each word with his hands, imagining the headline in bold type. "And playing a breeches role to boot? Pure gold. We'll fill the house to overflowing."

I opened my mouth to ask him what exactly I'd be expected to talk about, but he held up a hand to silence me.

"The press will want to know where the great Cartwright is, of course. Bumby used to lock him in his dressing room so

141

he wouldn't drink before a performance. Did you know that, Georgie? I'm sure Sallie remembers that happening, don't you, girl?"

Sallie's forehead wrinkled at the memory. "Maybe once or twice, sir."

"More frequently than that, is what I heard. If only I'd thought to do that, your illustrious father would still be with us. Wait—you and Sallie aren't hiding him somewhere down here, are you?" His eyes darted around the dressing room with amusement.

Sallie's hands clenched, and my breath caught for her. She had asked me not to tell anyone about the man I'd seen in her room. "I ain't hiding nobody or nothing, Mr. Worth."

"No, I reckon not," Worth said. "Well, Georgie, have an answer ready about his whereabouts. God knows I've got nothing."

After he left, Sallie began stuffing costumes back in the trunk without a word.

"I'm sorry you put in time on my Lucetta costume for nothing," I said as she packed.

She didn't respond. When everything was neatly squirreled away, she dropped the lid with a thunk. Before she could go, I reached in my pocket and fished out a dime.

"Thank you, miss. Anything else?"

If learning my true identity affected her, I couldn't tell from the impassive look on her face. I both wanted to hear more about Bumby locking Pa in his dressing room and was scared of the details. "Not now, Sallie. I know you're a ladies' dresser, but if you get any ideas about Tranio, please let me know."

Sallie nodded and considered me thoughtfully. "I'd have never guessed your secret. You don't look nothing like him."

I rubbed my chin with a laugh. "I got his jaw, unfortunately, and his height, but not his nice wavy hair. I hope I picked up a bit of his talent and not any of his . . . bad habits."

"He had good habits, too." She left me with that mysterious assessment and the promise that she'd think about my breeches costume.

How was I to discover Pa's whereabouts—if he even *had* whereabouts?

Mama and Uncle James would never give me a straightforward answer. If something unsavory had befallen Pa—say, he was holed up in a tenement or locked away with the lunatics on Blackwell's Island—neither would want me divulging it to the papers. Negative publicity would toss the Cartwright shame back into the open and possibly threaten Maude's prospects with Mr. MacReady.

And I knew my mother and uncle wouldn't trust Granny Clifford with the sensitive information of where my errant father had gone. My grandfather Clifford had cast Mama out for marrying an actor, and Granny had acquiesced with the shunning until her husband died and she let Mama back into the family. Whenever she saw Pa at family gatherings, though, Granny's sour expression had made her feelings clear.

The only other person I could think of turning to was Lily Templeton, who was just weeks shy of officially becoming my aunt. The engraved wedding invitation had arrived in the post that week. I wondered if, in an amorous moment, Uncle James had divulged something to her about Pa.

One of the city's finer families, the Templetons had lately relocated to fashionable Gramercy Park, to a rosy sandstone house with all the latest amenities that made our fine brick dwelling seem like a dowdy spinster. Months before Pa's debacle, I'd been there for tea with Mama and Maude. After Pa disappeared, I knew from listening at doors that the Templetons wanted Lily to break off her engagement to my uncle, but she persisted and love won out.

The Templeton residence was not the kind of place to go uninvited, and it was too late in the afternoon for visitors. Yet, in desperation I went anyway. For my birthday, Mama had ordered calling cards for me—a black swirl of my name embossed on thick stock. Although I found them too bothersome and silly to carry, that day I brought one with me.

Sure enough, the Templetons' butler held out an engraved silver plate for my card. I'd obviously left no impression on him the other time I'd visited.

"I'll see if she's in." He wouldn't have been much of a butler if he didn't know the location of everyone in the household, but he pretended anyway.

When I'd come to tea with Mama, I hadn't spent time in the grand foyer but had been ushered to a seat in the parlor almost immediately. Now, as an interloper, I stood . . . waiting. My eyes traveled from the delicate molding decorating the walls to the mahogany banister with its elaborately carved newel posts to the etched globes of the gas chandelier. After I'd counted the globes twice, my attention returned to the newel posts and I counted them, too.

Lily appeared, finally, on the staircase, her bright smile suggesting she wasn't horrified by my intrusion. Two long lengths of lace were draped over her arm.

"Just the person I wanted to see!"

Lily led me into the parlor as if I'd been invited after all. She whirled toward me and held out the lace, which turned out to be two wedding veils. Her voice was a bit higher-pitched than usual, almost frantic-sounding. "Which would you choose for a veil?"

As I glanced from one to the other, I had no opinion. They both looked like lace to me, but Mama and Maude would have been able to distinguish between them.

"My mother had this one made for me in Brussels, but she didn't consult me. It *is* pretty and so fashionable, don't you think?" She didn't wait for an answer. "This one, my grandmother wore at her own wedding. It's dated, but it holds meaning for me."

"It would be nice to wear your grandmother's veil," I replied. Correctly, it turned out.

"Yes, I think so, too." She abandoned the veils on a chair and lowered herself onto the settee, patting the space next to her. Unlike the elaborately gilded pieces in Mrs. Stansbury's parlor, the Templetons' furnishings were darker and more modern-looking, covered in rich green damask.

"But you didn't come here to help a hysterical bride."

"You don't seem hysterical at all," I said. "Just awfully busy." Guilt at adding to her busyness washed over me.

"Exactly! There are too many decisions!" Her curls bobbed in a dizzying way. "Tell me, though, what I can do for you, dear Georgie. You aren't backing out of being bridesmaid, are you?"

"Oh, no, never! You were so kind to ask me."

Maude had been jealous, but the truth was, I wished Lily had chosen my sister instead. Because pink was apparently the current color for bridesmaids, my dress was a frothy concoction that required a strong hoop and layers of petticoats to stand out properly, giving the impression of a fruity meringue. I despised it.

"And your dress has been properly fitted? My seamstress was to your liking?"

"Oh, absolutely. Sylvie's doing Mama's dress, too."

"Excellent!"

Her shoulders relaxed but stiffened again as soon as my next words came out.

"I'm here to ask you about my father. Specifically, if you know where he is."

She smoothed her skirt although it looked as if it had been meticulously ironed. "Oh, that's a question for your uncle. I barely knew your father."

The word *knew* jumped out of the sentence.

"Uncle James seems to think I'm still too young to handle the information, and neither he nor my mother want me to worry," I said. "But I'm an adult now, supporting my family, and I deserve to know what happened to him. I don't know if he's even alive! Mama doesn't wear mourning, so that makes me think he's still out there somewhere."

She nibbled delicately at the corner of a nail.

"Is he? Alive?" I pursued.

Lily took a breath and let it out slowly. "I shouldn't say, but—"

My pulse picked up speed.

"Your father *is* alive. James told my father that he's working with a small theater company. Not in New York. He was trying to assure Papa that Mr. Cartwright wouldn't come back to haunt us."

"It doesn't make sense," I objected. "Surely someone would have found out that he joined another company. It would be in the papers."

"Not if he changed his name and moved to Charleston."

"Oh."

Lily's information was at least something. Not much, but if asked, I could confirm that Pa lived on.

And I could continue to hope that, someday, he'd recognize the harm he'd inflicted on us—on *me*—and come home.

Before the most important shows at the Prince, Worth filled the green room with reviewers, laying out a lush spread of cheeses, cakes, wine, and ale in an attempt to sway their opinions. The better, more reputable papers never showed up, seeing it as a bald-faced effort to buy good notices, so I was counting on my interview occurring with just a couple of fellows from the shady flash press.

But when I arrived at the theater the next morning, Ned pulled me aside and told me the green room was full to bursting.

"They couldn't close the door if they tried. Everyone's here, Georgie," Ned said. "Harry said he spotted Jessup from the *Sun!* He wouldn't be caught dead at Worth's puff events."

The minute Ned pointed it out, I heard a deep rumble from the direction of the green room, like the first cannonballs dropping into the trough of the thunder roll. But this wasn't thunder; it was a mingling of voices. My instinct was to head back out the stage door. Worth hadn't told me if he wanted me to follow a certain script for this event. "I'll do most of the talking" was all he had said as instruction. Yet wouldn't these reporters want to hear from the party in question—me? Hadn't Worth set me up as the story?

A sudden, sharp memory hit me. Pa had a theatrical persona he trotted out for strangers, and I'd witnessed it on different occasions when he was with our family in public. He might be silent and brooding with us, but when approached for an autograph, he'd become animated, bow deeply, and say, "You honor me, madam" or "The pleasure is mine, my good fellow."

Once, on a Sunday stroll our family took along the Battery promenade, a chap from a penny paper recognized him and lobbed him a question about playing Lear. Pa halted, with a pitch-perfect response at the ready. "Sir, that role is a mountain whose summit I have yet to reach. Like every other actor who attempts Lear, I pray my shattered body won't be added to the pile already strewn along the climb."

Where had that come from? Was it extemporaneous, or did he write his own gems so he'd always have a reply when called on?

And what was *I* to do? I'd never faced fawning audience members on the street or at the stage door, and I counted on Clem, Shakespeare, and others to write my lines.

"I don't know what to say to them," I told Ned, panic flooding my chest. "They're going to ask about Pa!"

"You need your own script," Ned said. "When you get a question you don't want to answer, pivot and answer a different one."

"Like what?"

"Like that charming story of running lines with your father. Concentrate on what you learned from him about the craft of acting. Ignore his disappearance. Seize control."

Worth's voice boomed into the wings, rising above the cacophony from the press. "Gentlemen, let us begin!"

"But where is Miss Cartwright?" someone called out.

Worth chuckled. "You know how women are, always keeping us waiting. We'd all be younger men if we hadn't spent so many years waiting for women. Isn't that right, fellas?"

The room exploded with laughter. That sound, combined with Ned's advice, had a funny effect on me, making my fear dissipate like a wisp of smoke. I handed Ned the script I'd been carrying.

"Go get 'em," Ned said with a grin.

Harry hovered at the green room door, waving at me. With a stagehand's help, he shoved a few men aside to usher me in, but the effort wasn't needed. When it was clear the star of this particular show had arrived, the sea of men parted.

"And here she is now!" Worth called out. "Gentlemen, Miss Georgiana Cartwright!"

Although I hadn't done a single thing or uttered a word, applause greeted me as I passed to the front of the room and took a spot next to Worth, who gave me a shallow bow.

"Thank you for joining us, Miss Cartwright."

Worth's tone started as peevish but quickly changed. He offered a brief rundown of my tenure with the company, but omitted the fact I'd hidden my true identity from him. In fact, he made it sound as if my deception had been his brilliant idea.

The press was not a well-mannered bunch. Shouting out questions even as Worth introduced me, they reminded me of what Aggie said audiences at the Bowery Theatre were like—clamorous and insistent.

"But why keep her identity a secret?"

Worth had an answer for everything. "Miss Cartwright needed to establish herself as a credible actress in her own right. Which she has now done."

"What about that turn as Juliet?" another reporter asked.

"It makes more sense now we know who her father is!" someone else shouted out. "Maybe she likes the bottle as much as her old man."

Laughter rippled through the room again, but this time it was tinged with nervousness. The comment about drink crossed a line of propriety. Plus, I didn't fancy being addressed as "she" and "her" when I was standing right next to Worth.

Seize control, Ned had said, and I could see him now in

the doorway next to Harry. He may have winked at me, or it might have been my imagination.

"Gentlemen," I began, as loud as if projecting to the back rows of the theater. "Your attention, please." When Worth repeated my request, the men's voices quieted to a hum. With my audience's attention secured, there was nothing to do but proceed and hope the right words came out when I needed them.

"I think we can all agree that my father, William Cartwright, is among the greatest actors of his generation. He has been compared to everyone from Edmund Kean to Junius Brutus Booth."

Is, I'd stressed and watched heads bob in agreement.

"Today, if you wish, I'd like to share the very personal story of learning the craft of acting at this great man's coattails."

Cries of "Go on!" and "Tell us!" filled the space.

I could see Worth's head bobbing from the corner of my eye. And so, I devised my own script.

It seemed like hours before they let me go, but after, Harry's pocket watch told the truth: the interview had lasted under fifteen minutes. Instead of relating the story the papers expected to hear, I had offered another, more compelling one. The questions they lobbed at me became specific to my memories of helping with Pa's many roles. I embellished my own part with a dramatic flair that Pa would have approved of. Not only had I run lines with my father, but I'd copied his notes into his prompt books in my neat schoolgirl handwriting. I transformed into prompter and scribe rolled into one.

When the queries came to an end, Worth pronounced the interview over and encouraged the press in attendance to return for my performance as Tranio. That set off a fresh round of interrogations about whether Pa had prepared me to tackle a breeches role, and if I thought myself better suited to men's roles because of my height. Worth cut them off.

"Miss Cartwright must return to her preparations," he said. "Please enjoy the refreshments."

I wended my way back through the maze of indistin-

149

guishable male faces. Near the door, one jowly man leaned toward me, blocking my way, his breath a foul mixture of eggs and pickles.

"You've not told us where he is," he said.

Pulling the words out of thin air, I replied, "After performing almost daily for more than twenty years and assuming hundreds of roles, my father is taking a much-needed sabbatical."

I thought that would end it, but the stinky-breath man pushed on.

"And when will he be back?"

"When he is," I snapped, but smiled sweetly at the same time. Harry stepped forward and escorted me out of the room.

Chapter 19

Mama never read the papers or she would have seen that my next role would be played in trousers. Still, I knew the interview I gave would have satisfied her. In every paper that covered the story, Pa appeared in a flattering light, the doting father priming his daughter for the stage, the dedicated actor who simply needed time away from a demanding schedule. The months between his disappearance and my resurrection of him proved ample time for reporters to forgive his disgraceful behavior. I wanted to send notice to him that it was safe to return.

The press elevated me as the eager heir to the Cartwright theatrical dynasty. As Worth had anticipated, the papers clamored for my next performance.

"With her foray into breeches roles, will Miss Cartwright prove the Charlotte Cushman of her generation?" the *Spirit* boldly asked.

That translated to ticket sales, which translated to Worth's joy. My employer strutted backstage for a full day after the stories appeared with a grin plastered across his face, as if hearing the clink of coins into the cash drawer.

Members of the company, too, lavished me with new respect and compliments, even Frances Muller. "Well, that explains your talent," she allowed. "You come by it naturally instead of having to struggle like the rest of us."

151

I should have been triumphant, but instead the blues got me. Clem was absent from the theater, even during rehearsals for her play. Every time the stage door creaked open my heart picked up a beat. I expected her to sweep in carrying pages she'd revised overnight.

I'd been a fool, dismissing her from my room, miffed that I hadn't known about her and Arabella and confused that I both wanted to kiss her and wouldn't dare. I twisted between wishing she were a boy and knowing a boy wasn't who I wanted at all.

I didn't know if Clem would come to Sunday dinner as invited and bring back my mother's bonnet. Maybe she'd just drop it off at the Prince.

There was no one to confide in, but Ned noticed my mood. "What's with you?" he asked when we met in the green room to run lines for the *Shrew*. He was slated to play Tranio's master, Lucentio, so we had numerous key scenes together. "You're destined for second leading lady in no time!"

I was about to demur out of modesty when my friend followed up with a biting remark: "Or maybe second leading *gentleman* would be more fitting."

His rudeness jolted me. Ned was usually tender and sweet, and his coaching before the press interview had saved me. Now he seemed to display his envious side, the one all actors and actresses had, including me.

I let the comment go with a forced smile. Maybe he meant it in sport, I reasoned. I was counting on his advice about walking and talking like a young man. Among the male members of the company, I trusted only him and Harry for counsel.

Ned had also committed to helping me devise a costume. As we were roughly the same height, he had offered me something from his own trunk—"as long as I don't need it," he hurried to add. Thanks to his promotion, Ned's costume collection had burgeoned, and he kept the men's dresser busy with special tailoring requests.

We ran our lines for Act One, Scene One without any

trouble on my part, but Ned was more on-book than off. He cursed under his breath several times and asked to start over. I questioned if he was feeling all right, but his reply was mumbled and swallowed up.

"What is it?"

He closed his prompt book with a slap. "I don't learn my roles as easily as some of the other fellas, and it's hard competing with them," he said. "Now I have to compete with a girl, too."

The way he said *girl*, as if it constituted an inferior species, rattled me again. Clearly, he wasn't joking.

"I didn't know the company was a competition," I said.

That wasn't exactly true. Although company members might help each other with costumes and running lines, acting was a cutthroat profession, and I'd been as competitive as the next person.

Still, Ned and I had shared something different, a unique bond of unconditional support. Now our exchange opened a chasm between us, and a wave of loneliness coursed through me. Within a short span, I'd had rifts with my two best friends, and I couldn't remember when I'd felt so unbalanced and on edge—except when Pa left.

Ned didn't reply to my statement, begging off and explaining it was "a bad day." I didn't have the nerve to follow up with him about costumes, so I turned instead to Pa's trunk and wardrobe.

Unfortunately, Pa's study was locked.

"Missus told Nora not to clean it anymore," Aggie said when I asked her on the staircase. "It's likely gotten pretty dusty since summer."

"I need to look at his costumes."

"What for?"

I hesitated, not wanting Mama to get wind of my role before it was under my belt.

153

"You mustn't tell a soul," I whispered. "I'm to play a breeches role in *The Taming of the Shrew*."

"Oh, Miss Georgie!" Aggie said, clapping her hands together. Although Aggie was skeptical of Miss Cushman's independent life, she was as enamored of her talent at playing men as I was. "How daring! Which part?"

Before I could reply, Maude's bedroom door flew open. She stared at us with suspicion. "What's daring?"

I fumbled to make something up. "I'm in line for an important role."

"What's daring about that?"

I knew Maude wouldn't suspect if I concocted a play title out of thin air. "It's a new play everyone's been talking about." I paused as if for dramatic effect, but really because I needed to come up with a title. "*The Locked Room.*"

She cocked her head to the side. "A mystery?"

"Exactly."

"Archie—Mr. MacReady—loves mysteries. He's read *The Murders in the Rue Morgue* twice!"

"This one's probably not as good as that. You needn't mention it to him." I added quickly, "Or to Mama. I don't want to disappoint her if I don't get the role."

Maude raised a skeptical eyebrow but then headed back into her room, no doubt to dream about her next rendezvous with her beau.

My mother was out calling on a friend, so Aggie led me to a box in the kitchen that held an assortment of keys. Different sizes of iron keys, some on rings, some loose; delicate brass keys with a cloverleaf design at the top; winged keys for winding clocks—I didn't know which locks any of them matched, but Aggie did.

"Here it is," she said, fishing a key from the pile.

"How did you know that?"

She ignored the question, shushing me into silence until we were safely inside the study with the door closed behind us.

The room was tucked away in the rear of the house on the ground floor. I'd been there so many times with Pa I knew the layout in the dark. Aggie drew back the wine-red curtains Mama had chosen for the room because they resembled the theater's, and the afternoon light poured in. Dust motes danced in front of us before landing on the carved mahogany desk, still strewn with Pa's prompt books. On top was *Othello*, the cover bearing an ink stain. I remembered that Pa had been scratching notes to himself in the script as I entered on that last day we ran lines together.

Pa was everywhere in this space, including in a portrait on the wall, and a sob escaped me. His eyes in the painting followed me about. The room still smelled of him, too—a mix of the sandalwood fragrance he bought abroad, the peppermints he kept for lubricating his throat, and the expensive cigars he smoked for relaxation.

"We should hurry," Aggie said. "Your mother could be home any minute."

The mention of Mama snapped me out of it. I rubbed my tears away with the back of my hand and followed Aggie to Pa's wood and leather trunk, sitting under the window where I'd last seen it. I lifted the brass latch easily.

I'd rifled through Pa's costumes before. I'd even had the audacity to try on some of his capes and hats, strutting across the room as I recited lines from this tragedy or that. Men's clothes offered so much more comfort and freedom of movement than the feminine wear I was forced into.

From his trunk I chose black tights and a soft emerald velvet tunic with purple trim that was folded under a stack of crisp white muslin shirts. I didn't recall ever seeing Pa wear it; in fact, it looked too small for his broad chest. He rarely played in comedies, yet it befitted a jester or fool, and I wondered if it dated from his early career at Niblo's Garden. When I held the tunic up to the light, I spotted an ancient grease stain on the front, which I expected Sallie would be able to get out.

Pa's wardrobe yielded an elegant black doublet and gold cape I could change into when Tranio portrayed his master, Lucentio, and a soft black velvet cap that would be big enough to cover my hair when tucked up. Among Pa's shoes were slippers that I could stuff cotton batting into to correct for my size. Pa had small feet for a man, not much larger than my own.

"That everything you need?" Aggie's voice wobbled with anxiety. We wouldn't hear the front door open this far back in the house.

My priority was getting the costume pieces safely to my room, where I could deal with fitting later. Choosing from Pa's clothes had brought a rush of comfort and relief that dispelled my sadness at his absence. "I'm ready," I said.

Aggie began to draw the curtains, but as she did, my eye caught a gleam of metal next to Pa's desk. I could just make out the brass closures of Pa's black leather tunic-vest, standing up on its own like a soldier.

"Aggie, wait."

Pa had only one leather vest that I knew of. He had gone to great expense to purchase it in London. The intricate tooled leather was a marvel of craftsmanship, but how he moved across the stage in such heavy wear had mystified me.

"This sets me above Forrest and Booth," he had explained when Mama balked at the extravagance. When she continued to protest, he snapped, "It's my money to spend, Rebecca."

"Miss Georgie, come on," I heard Aggie hiss, but my eyes continued to roam. On the floor next to the abandoned vest was Pa's saber. It had been presented to him by a group of wealthy theatergoers after a memorable performance as Macbeth. Inscribed on the blade were Pa's name and the date of the presentation, just a few months after Maude's birth. It was probably his dearest possession, so greatly loved he'd posed for his portrait wearing it. Everyone referred to it as "the Scottish sword."

As I leaned down to run my fingers over the sword's engraving, the room's curtains closed, pitching me into blackness.

"Aggie, I wasn't finished," I said, but I could see in the dim light that she had already scurried to the door.

"We have to *go*."

Begrudgingly, I grabbed the costume pieces I'd chosen and followed her into the hallway.

"It's a blessing your ma isn't home yet," she whispered, relocking the door behind us.

My heart had beat its way up into my throat. Not from fear of being caught by my mother, but because Pa had worn the vest and used the sword every time he played his signature role of Othello . . . including on the night of his disgrace.

Which meant he'd been in our house since then.

Which meant no one had told me.

Aggie was already bolting toward the front staircase when I called out, "When was he here, Aggie?"

She halted with her back to me.

Which meant Aggie had been among those who hadn't told me.

"I know you heard me."

Aggie did a slow 180-degree pivot. "I'm sorry," she said. "Your uncle said not to say anything, that it would only upset you."

My uncle. I let the betrayal sink in.

"And Mr. Cartwright was here and gone so fast!"

That explained how she had recognized the study's key so quickly.

"When?"

"The night after the . . . incident," she said. "You and Miss Maude were in bed, and I was clearing up in the kitchen when your uncle knocked at the back door with Mr. Cartwright in tow. Sure, your da looked like something the cat drug in, all dirty with his shirt in tatters. Your uncle was carrying his costume. He told me go pack up a bag quick-like, and then they were gone again. That's all I know, I swear!"

Her eyes clouded with anguish, and a few tears gathered at the corners. I'd only seen Aggie cry when she was reading a letter from her mother that made her homesick.

I couldn't afford to be on Aggie's wrong side when she was the one guarding Pa's study. Besides, it was my uncle who had kept the information from me, when I'd asked him countless times if he knew what had happened to my father. My complaint was with him.

"Never mind now," I said, and Aggie's facial muscles loosened. "But maybe you can make it up to me."

Chapter 20

The next day, my hopes of seeing Clem for Sunday dinner were dashed when my mother's bonnet was waiting on the table in my dressing room at the Prince, reborn with mahogany ribbons, an apricot-colored lining, and fall-toned silk flowers. The color combination would complement the undertones of red in my mother's honey-brown hair. Clem clearly excelled at her millinery trade as she did at playwriting, and Mama would be thrilled.

The note tucked into the satchel with the bonnet for Mama was brief.

> *My dear Mrs. Cartwright,*
>
> *I am sorry I cannot join you for dinner this Sunday. My birthday is this week, and I will be traveling home to Williamsburg for a family celebration. Thank you again for the invitation, and please accept my sincere regrets. I hope your refashioned bonnet will make up for my absence.*
>
> *Yours, Clementine*

Clem's birthday! I had a vague memory of her saying it was in November, but then I'd somehow forgotten it. She was turning twenty, a momentous occasion, and I wouldn't be with her.

I fished through all the tissue protecting the bonnet, hoping for more, and indeed Clem had placed a note for me at the bottom of the bag.

> *George, I took the liberty of sending Miss Cushman a reply to her kind letter. I hope that wasn't too forward, but I knew you would struggle with the words and would want to reply, and it took me no time at all. I've enclosed a copy of what I sent. I also thought a brief poem might be in order. Perhaps this will help you forgive me about Arabella.—CS.*

Mama got a warm "Yours," but I got "CS"?

As in the first letter to Miss Cushman, Clem chose the perfect tone.

Dear Miss Cushman,

> *How thrilling to receive your response to my letter! I am humbled that you took the time from your busy schedule to reply . . . and to offer such sound advice to a fledgling actress. I took your counsel to heart and am pleased to report that Mr. Worth agreed to let me play my first breeches role! I will appear as Tranio in the Prince's November production of "Taming of the Shrew," and I have only you to thank.*

Clem and I hadn't spoken since I was assigned the role of Tranio, so how did she know? Maybe she'd read my interview in one of the dailies and was following my progress—a thought that made something quiver in my chest. But then I realized she probably just heard it at the theater.

> *As a thank-you, and in lieu of flowers, I have enclosed*

a poem penned especially for you. It was meant to be playful, and I hope you'll accept it with grateful admiration.

Most humbly yours,
*Georgiana Cartwright (formerly Clifford)**

**Since receiving your letter, I have found the courage to reveal publicly my true identity as the daughter of tragedian William Cartwright and will henceforth be listed in playbills using my father's surname. I bear no shame in being his offspring—I learned much at the feet of my father—but I have learned an equal amount by following your illustrious career.*

The sudden reveal of my identity to Miss Cushman made me gasp, but then thrilled me. The great actress likely read theater news and gossip and, if nothing else, perhaps the stories that compared me to a young *her* might have caught her eye. Would she put my name together with the correspondence she'd exchanged with an admiring young girl? It was vain to think she'd notice me, but all theater people are vain—so why should I be spared the flaw?

When I came to the end of the letter, I turned the sheet over expectantly for the poem:

"Our Charlotte"

What's all this haste? Why rush so, good woman?
Don't you know? I've the chance to encounter Miss Cushman!
A figure appears crossing swords, giving speeches,
Not Forrest or Booth, but Our Charlotte in breeches!
What wondrous performance: That strut on the stage,
Miraculous rendering of words from the page,
Her voice and her stance showing power and poise.
She outshines each actor, displaces the boys!

The verse radiated enough innocent charm to make anyone smile. Clem must have popped off the trifle quickly, which made it more realistic that I was the author.

As I was rereading the letter and poem a third time, Sallie entered the dressing room with my father's velvet tunic over her arm. Not only had she removed the stain without a trace—"Baking soda does the trick, miss"—but she'd given the tunic a brushing that made it look almost new.

Sallie was happy to pocket the nickel I offered as a bonus. I now tipped her as a matter of course, but she stared at the coin as if it was a new occurrence before tucking it into her pocket.

"Sallie, did you see Miss Clementine bring this satchel by?"

"Yes, miss. She came knocking early this morning before Mr. Pendergast opened up. Nobody here but me and Falstaff. There was a banging at the alley door, and I thought—" Sallie stopped short, a hint of worry crossing her face. She hung the tunic in the wardrobe and gave it several pats, then turned back to me, fully composed again. "She asked would I put it on your dressing table."

"Was that all she said?"

She tilted her head to the side. "You expecting more?"

I don't know what I had expected, but I found myself clinging to every word of Sallie's brief account. She'd seen and talked to Clem, and I hadn't.

"No, no, that's fine, Sallie. And thank you again for the lovely work on the tunic."

"You'll be handsome in it for sure." Her appraisal brought heat to my cheeks. No one had ever used the word *handsome* for me, but reviewers called Miss Cushman "a handsome figure" when she played male roles.

Sallie hesitated at the door, and I asked if she had another message for me. Maybe, I hoped, she'd forgotten something Clem had said.

"No, just thinking about Mr. William." After that first day she'd found out I was Pa's daughter, Sallie hadn't brought him up.

"Is there something I should know about him?"

She bit her lip. "He used to tip me, too, even though I done nothing for him. I seen his wicked side, for sure, everybody did. When he was drinking and had to be locked up." Her eyebrows lifted at the memory. "But nobody ever tipped me for nothing except him."

My eyes watered at the thought of my father rising above the drink that had brought an end to his career at the Prince.

"What else?" I asked with a catch in my throat.

"What else what?"

"Well, you mentioned once that he had good habits as well as bad. Were there others, besides the tipping?"

Sallie paused, as if assessing what she could reveal. "He helped me sometimes," she said. "Not sure I can say any more than that."

I pondered how little I knew about Sallie, about the folks I'd seen in her bleak room at the end of the hall—the young man she said Harry knew about, the quiet sister she whispered with. "You sure have a lot of secrets," I said with a smile. "I'm good with secrets."

"I reckon you are," she said.

Voices of actresses returning downstairs from the green room made us both start, and Sallie's dark eyes fixed on the door. She had no reason to trust me, but for some reason she decided to that day. She grabbed my sleeve and pulled me along with her.

When we entered her room, Sallie's sister, Cassie, popped up from the mat like a jack-in-the-box and dropped a shirt she was in the middle of stitching. Strewn across the quilt was an assortment of clothes—a woman's muslin frock, a cape and bonnet, smaller apparel for children. On Sallie's single chair rested miscellaneous foodstuffs—a loaf of bread, a handful of bruised apples.

"What you bring her for?" Cassie said, a tartness in her voice that hadn't been there when we met.

"Miss Georgie's Mr. William's child." Sallie closed the door behind us. "We can trust her."

I nodded in agreement as I pieced together what had been going on in Sallie's room. Pa had told me about a network of people who helped Negroes flee slavery by providing safe houses, clothes, and food. "They do God's work," he said—one of the few times I ever heard him mention God when he wasn't taking the Almighty's name in vain.

I never questioned how Pa knew so much about abolition work. After all, he read voraciously, and just last spring I'd come upon him in his study shaking his head with sadness over a book. When I asked the title and what upset him about it, he stared at me for a long moment before answering. "*Uncle Tom's Cabin*," he said, "by a lady named Mrs. Stowe. You'll read it, too, George, and we'll discuss it." But he'd fallen into disgrace before he could pass it along to me.

I'd reasoned that the people who helped fugitive slaves were white, but now signs pointed toward Sallie and Cassie, too. It made sense. Although theaters saw a lot of foot traffic, the below-stage warren of hallways at the Prince could provide hiding spots for runaways when everything went dark after a performance. Embarrassment washed over me as I recalled taking Sallie to task weeks back for harboring the young man in her room. The sisters' scheme must work because Harry was privy to it and condoned what she and Cassie were doing. Maybe Mr. Bumby, the previous manager, had, too.

"Oh," I said in a whisper, glancing over my shoulder to make sure the door was firmly closed. "I shouldn't be here. I don't want to compromise anything."

The sisters exchanged a look.

"We could use some help," Cassie said after a pause, "now Mr. William's gone." Her words suggested Pa had done more than give Sallie extra coins "for nothing."

"What can I do?"

Abetting fugitive slaves was a federal crime, and I'd never imagined myself as that level of brave. The moment I volunteered my services, I feared I was signing up for a job I couldn't handle.

"Unless you think it's too risky," I hastened to add.

Sallie held my eyes. "We're expecting a family with two children tomorrow. Cass and me are sewing outfits for the woman and young ones, but there ain't nothing for the man." I followed her glance toward the pile of clothes on her bed.

"Oh! Pa bought clothes for you?" I assumed his pocket money went for drink and maybe the horse races, but maybe he'd spent it in more useful ways, too.

"Sometimes," Sallie said. "Sometimes he said he ... found them."

Cassie silenced her with a sharp jab of the elbow. This might explain why some of the company's costumes had gone missing, why the shirt on the young man I'd seen in Sallie's room looked familiar. Annoyance flashed in me at Pa's reck-lessness. No one in the company would have suspected the great actor of stealing clothes, so he probably thought pinch-ing costumes a clever idea. He might even have had fun doing it. But Frances, for one, had no trouble thinking the worst of Sallie. Pa's actions had put Sallie at risk, and it was miraculous that she had not been confronted yet.

"I can get you men's clothes," I asserted. "Some more sub-stantial food, too."

Sallie fished in her pocket for the coin I'd given her. "Take this back, miss, in case you need it."

"That's yours," I said. "You will have everything tomorrow morning. Will that give you enough time to alter the clothes if you need to?"

The muscles in both their faces relaxed, and Cassie nod-ded excitedly. "You seem like Mr. William's child all right," she said, and pride rushed through me.

Mama was so tickled with her refurbished bonnet she donned it immediately and wore it to the dinner table. She couldn't say enough good things about Clem.

"Clementine *must* come to dinner," Mama said, rereading her note. "I'll send her word that I won't take no for an answer.

165

Lily and James will be here, too, and I'm sure Lily would love to see Clementine's work. She could get her commissions among the best families."

My stomach did a happy flip at the thought of seeing Clem, whose absence I'd felt almost as acutely as Pa's.

Mama didn't notice me leaving dinner food on my plate, but in the kitchen Aggie gave me a curious look when I asked if she'd wrap up my chicken for me to eat later in my room.

"You never eat in your room. Unless it's cake."

"Come to think of it, I'll take some cake for later, too. Two or three slices." When she raised her eyebrows, I added, "I have to stay up till all hours studying my part, and I need the energy. I wouldn't want to flub my lines."

"Promise you'll actually eat it then and won't leave the meat to spoil," Aggie said as she did my bidding. "I wouldn't like Nora to find it when she's cleaning your room."

That night, I packed the leftover food in a big square of muslin. After Mama retired to her room to read, I sneaked back into Pa's study. Pa's everyday clothes were still in his dressing room upstairs, and there was no way to pinch them without Mama finding out.

I grabbed anything that might resemble regular men's traveling clothes, settling on breeches, a shirt, and a weskit that looked too large for me to ever use for a costume. The outerwear consisted of flowing, Elizabethan-style capes that didn't really suit a runaway's needs, but I pinched one anyway; it would be better than being cold. Although clean-smelling, the cape sported stains that I figured would make it look more authentic. Excited by my achievement, I stuffed everything into an oversized satchel Pa kept for transporting costumes, but before I could make my exit a light flickered behind me.

"Aggie! You scared me."

"You need *more* costumes?" she asked. The impertinence of her tone caught me off guard, and my temper flared.

"It's none of your business what I need," I said. "Don't forget who pays your salary. Here, replace the key, please."

Reprimanding Aggie was up to Mama, the lady of the

house, and my harsh rebuke flustered both of us. I brushed past Aggie into the hallway, wondering if it was too late to apologize. I half-turned with my mouth open, prepared to smooth things over, when she said, "Sure and I stepped out of line, miss. Won't happen again." Her soft voice wobbled.

"Look here, Aggie," I said, "I don't know why I said that. It was ghastly of me."

"You said the truth, miss. You're my boss, right enough."

My throat tightened with fear that I'd ruined everything between us, that I could no longer linger in the kitchen, chatting amiably with her over her dailies. Despite the difference in our backgrounds, despite the fact that she worked for my family and was bound to call me "Miss Georgie," we'd been friends—or so I'd imagined.

In the morning I waited until Aggie was upstairs giving instructions to Nora, the housemaid, then sorted through the larder and added slices of cooked bacon, hard-boiled eggs, and a wedge of cheese to my stash. If Aggie missed anything, she wouldn't raise the issue. As my scolding had made clear, it was food I had paid for.

Instead of leaving home early and taking the food to Sallie's room immediately upon arriving at the theater, I brought the satchel into the walking ladies' dressing room so I could remove my cape and gloves first.

I shared the cramped space with three other walking ladies, and that morning, because Harry had called a final dress rehearsal for 10:00 a.m., two of them were already at their mirrors, primping and applying makeup.

"Well, if it isn't Tranio," Paulette said. "Shouldn't you be using the *gentlemen's* dressing room?"

They both tittered at the silly joke, and I threw off my cape. "Very funny."

"What is that smell?" Jane asked, her nose upturned. "Bacon?"

"Bacon?" Paulette added. "Did you bring bacon in here, Georgie?"

I flushed with embarrassment. "It's for Ned," I said. "He loves bacon, and it's . . . his birthday soon." I had no idea if Ned liked or loathed bacon, and he'd never told me when his birthday was.

"Ah, someone's sweet on Ned," Jane teased. "He *is* cute, I'll grant you. But bacon's an odd present."

Paulette's facial muscles twitched. "Oh, for heaven's sake, Georgie, get it out of here," she said. "The last thing I need is to reek of *eau de bacon* when I'm playing next to Mr. Worth." Her role of the widow required a scene in Act Five with Petruchio, performed by our employer.

I obliged, scurrying down the hall to Sallie's room. My *tap, tap, tap* went unanswered, so I deposited the satchel inside along with a note: "Clothes and food, as promised!"

To my disappointment, when I saw Sallie soon after, she didn't acknowledge my donations to her effort. In fact, she barely looked at me as she helped me into my tunic and tights, then shifted to assisting with Paulette's costume. The lack of recognition for the trouble I'd gone to left me pouty, but I shrugged it off and went to rehearsal.

Chapter 21

At the conclusion of the full company rehearsal, Worth unexpectedly praised my Tranio in front of everyone.

"Your scene impersonating Lucentio is especially strong," he pointed out. "I kept waiting for you to stumble over his lines, but then I near spat with pride when you came out with 'He'll have a lusty widow now, that shall be woo'd and wedded in a day.' Good God, girl, you even swaggered."

Worth's smirk brought a flash of heat to my neck. Some of Tranio's lines, like the one he had quoted, were indeed embarrassing to say, but I'd run them over and over in front of a mirror until I could imagine myself as a man speaking them.

"Your costumes are also excellent. Did one of our gentlemen lend them to you?" Although he addressed everyone, Worth glanced directly at Ned. "If so, he's to be thanked."

"No, they're from my father's collection," I said. "I'm glad you think they suit."

Worth turned away from Ned, offering me a generous smile. "Oh, yes, they more than suit. You're likely to steal every scene tomorrow and be the talk of the town. I see more breeches roles in your future."

The *Shrew* performance was even stronger than the rehearsal. We played to a full house that chortled in all the right places, and had to pause several times for spontaneous applause. At the final curtain, a few audience members threw white camellias onto the stage. In the language of flowers, camellias meant something positive, but I couldn't recall what.

"They're to show admiration for an actor," Harry explained.

"Mr. Worth's Petruchio was very fine," I allowed.

The prompter grinned. "No, Georgie, listen."

From the wings, I could hear voices calling, "Brava! Miss Cartwright! Brava!" I stayed rooted in place, shocked and thrilled at the same time. There was nothing I could do to answer their calls. Members of the company were forbidden to take a separate bow unless the manager approved it. Plus, an actress could only appear in front of the curtain if escorted by a fellow actor, and she couldn't speak for herself.

To my surprise, Worth stepped forward and held out his hand for mine. "Shall we?"

In the glare of the footlights, I made out a few pleased faces in the front rows. I took off Pa's cap, revealing my tucked-up hair to appreciative murmurs. Then I curtseyed, gracefully and without toppling forward.

"Miss Cartwright is deeply honored," Worth said in his best leading-gentleman voice. He bent to gather together a bouquet, which he presented to me with a gallant flourish. I raised the flowers to my nose and was startled to detect no scent at all, so I fanned them out to my side, as if the gesture of smelling flowers that lacked fragrance had only been more fine acting.

"Ladies and gentlemen, you will be seeing much more of Miss Georgiana Cartwright soon!" Worth said as we departed for the wings.

Backstage, Worth continued to hold my hand longer than he needed to. I tried to release it, but he retained his grip.

"Find me Monday at two, Miss Cartwright," he said, raising my fingers to his lips in front of Harry and members of the company. "That is, if you want to discuss your future." He dropped my hand abruptly and trod off with one of the second gentlemen.

I basked in warm congratulations from Harry before proceeding downstairs to change. Jane and Paulette had already shed their costumes with Sallie's help.

"Well, here's the triumphant Miss Cartwright!" Jane said, with a pinch of envy. "I'd so love to get called out myself someday."

Sallie yawned into her hand as she turned to assist me. "You need me, miss?" she asked, her eyes heavy. It was unlike her not to congratulate me for my victory appearance in front of the curtain.

"Did you see it, Sallie?" I whispered. She helped me out of the tunic and brushed it off thoughtfully. "My first curtain call!"

"I didn't, miss," she said, as she hung up the costume in the wardrobe. Her affect remained flat. "I'm sure you'll have more. I'll be going now."

Peeved, I threw on my wrapper and followed her into the hallway. At my footsteps, Sallie turned around with a horrified look.

"Anybody could see you in that wrapper!"

"What's wrong with you?" I kept my voice low. "You never even acknowledged the clothes and food I brought you or thanked me. Did the shirt and trousers fit the fellow?"

Sallie's eyes brimmed with tears. "A slave catcher picked them up near the Pennsylvania line." She swiped at her cheeks roughly.

The information made my breath catch, and words failed me. I'd been congratulating myself for the minor part I played in the escape plan while the family was being dragged back to enslavement.

"I'll bring your things 'round, miss. Sorry I didn't say thanks."

I flushed with embarrassment. "Please keep them, Sallie. The clothes might fit the next man. If I can do anything else—" I let my offer trail off, unsure what more I could do.

The thrill of the curtain call diminished as Sallie hunched her shoulders and retreated around the corner.

Ned usually saw me home after an evening performance, but that night when I looked for him after changing into street clothes, Harry told me he had already left. "Seemed in a hurry."

Still shaken by Sallie's news about the slave family, I asked the prompter if he could help me secure a hack.

As it turned out, I didn't need Harry's help. Uncle James was waiting at the stage door in the chill November air, his brougham at the ready, a wide grin splitting his face. My first emotion was a flash of worry he would tell my mother about my breeches role. But my second was betrayal that he had insisted he didn't know Pa's whereabouts.

"Funny to see you here," I said.

Lily peeked from the window of the brougham. "Brava, Georgie!" she called out. "Such a performance. And your first curtain call!"

I took the seat next to her and my uncle leapt in after me. Lily grasped both my hands. "What a thrilling evening. Had I not known it was you up there, I'd have thought it was a young man in the role."

"I'm honored you both came," I said, with a sideways glance toward my uncle.

"Why was it funny to see me?" he asked.

With Lily's enthusiasm brimming over, it was the wrong time to broach the darker subject of Pa. "Oh, because I didn't tell anyone about it."

"You think I wouldn't read about my own niece in the papers?"

"Mama didn't," I pointed out. "She wouldn't be happy if she knew I played a man."

"True, she's not keen on breeches roles." My uncle pressed his fingers to his lips. "Your secret's safe with me, but it's a pity to keep her in the dark. She's missing the true launch of your career, the moment we'll all look back on when we're old and gray and say, 'That's when Georgie made her name!' Why, I'd be shocked if Worth doesn't promote you immediately."

I too hoped Worth planned to elevate me to second leading lady, but to avoid jinxes I said, "Probably too soon for that."

Lily continued to hold one of my hands as we rumbled up Broadway. "You know, I agree with James," she said. "Your mother should know about your triumph. There's only glory in playing a role well, and so many fine actresses have gone before you. It's a venerable tradition."

"And a lucrative one, too," my uncle added. "You'll be earning more than your father before you know it."

Uncle James had provided the perfect segue into talking about my father. "Speaking of Pa," I began. Lily tucked her hands into her lap as if she knew what would follow. "I was wearing one of his costumes tonight, uncle. Did you recognize it?"

Uncle James's face clouded. "I didn't."

For a few seconds, only the clacking of horses' hooves sounded in the brougham.

"Pa's study has been locked, but I was able to get in."

My uncle shifted in his seat and glanced out the window.

"Funny what I found . . . Pa's leather vest, the one he uses for playing the Moor? It was there, like someone left it in a hurry."

Lily gasped.

"And the Scottish sword, too. He was always so proud of it, I was startled to see it abandoned like that. What do you know about it, Uncle?"

My uncle continued to focus his attention out the window, inclining toward it as if something fascinating was taking place on Broadway.

"James, you must answer her."

I'd never heard Lily's tone so sharp-edged. With the direction put to him by his bride-to-be, my uncle had no choice but to meet her eyes, then reluctantly mine. His cheeks reddened.

"Tell her what happened. I heard you trying to reassure my father that he wouldn't be back to disgrace us further. Now Georgie deserves to know the whole story."

My uncle doled out his explanation in short bursts. "I put him on the boat south myself. I have a . . . business connection. In Charleston. A gentleman the bank made loans to. He owed me . . . a favor. He got Will on. Managing a small company."

"But why would any theater accept him?" I blurted out. "He was so utterly disgraced—"

"The gentleman's a theater investor. He insisted Will hide his identity, so your father is posing as my brother, William Clifford. The investor knows who he is, but no one else in the company does."

I couldn't find my voice over the clatter of the carriage wheels. After the longest brief carriage ride of my life, the brougham pulled up to the curb at Number 4 Bond Street. The three of us remained rooted in place.

"Do you have contact with him?" I asked.

My uncle leaned forward and took both my hands gently in his. I'd always admired his hands, long and graceful like a pianist's, and I fastened my gaze on them. Feelings of betrayal by my uncle made way for sadness as I thought of my poor father fleeing to a city he didn't know, hiding his identity, living among strangers.

"I do, but we've not been in touch in several weeks. He seems to be avoiding the drink, which is good news."

I waited expectantly.

"I need to check in with him again. Business and the wedding . . . I've been so busy." He tossed a sheepish smile toward his fiancée. "He didn't answer the last letter I sent to him, but he may have just overlooked it."

My mood crept toward anger—this time, at Pa. He had left us all in the lurch, even the brother-in-law who'd saved him.

Louis opened the carriage door and Uncle James alit stiffly. He held out his hand to me, but I had one more question.

"Mama knows where he is, too?"

His eyes darkened. "She said she didn't want to. Every now and then she checks with me to see if he's still alive, but that seems to be the extent of her curiosity."

Maybe she simply wanted to know if she should start wearing mourning.

"I'm sorry, Georgie. I weighed telling you, but you were doing so well at the theater without him, I thought . . ." He shrugged and let the sentence dangle between us.

"You should get Georgie inside now," Lily said. "It's been a long night, and she's looking pale. Can you walk, dear? James, maybe you should carry her—"

My uncle moved to scoop me out of the brougham, but I gathered my skirts and sprang from the carriage step to the sidewalk on my own.

"Thank you for the ride," I said, a bit more tartly than I intended.

The weight of the slave family's capture, combined with my new knowledge about Pa, sat on my shoulders like a heavy mantle. Mama was waiting up for me, but I merely said goodnight and went straight up to bed.

Chapter 22

Worth wasn't in his dressing room at the time he requested I find him. I checked the wings, the green room, the lobby, and the parquet itself, with no luck. Harry, who was talking earnestly to a stagehand about a malfunction with the gas table that controlled all the lighting, told me our manager was lunching at Groff's.

"Do you know when he'll be back?"

"I don't keep his appointment book, Georgie," Harry said. "It's bad enough how much I'm responsible for around here!"

I slunk away. I rarely saw Harry angry and didn't want to stir up his wrath.

I knew a girl shouldn't go to Groff's on her own, but Worth had told me to find him at two o'clock if I wanted to discuss my future, and it was now after two. Reasoning that Mr. Groff knew me as Ned's friend and would watch out for me, I took the risk.

Indeed, when the proprietor found out why I was there on my own, he steered me quickly to Worth. The theater manager sat facing the back of the room, joined at his table by Ned and another second gentleman, Julius. The three bent over empty plates and coffee cups and didn't notice my arrival. Worth gesticulated with his hands, concluding a bawdy story: ". . . and that, gentlemen, is how you bed Lola Montez."

Both of Worth's companions thumped the table with

pleasure. Ned had no desire to bed any woman, even a famous actress, so I knew his enthusiasm was feigned. When he spotted me over Worth's shoulder, his cheeks flushed at being caught. He cleared his throat, nodded in my direction without greeting me, and said, "Sir, it's Georgie."

Worth swiveled on his stool. I feared a tongue-lashing for cutting in on his gentlemen's time, but instead he hopped down and bowed.

"Miss Cartwright! I didn't expect to see you here, of all places."

"You told me to find you at two o'clock. To discuss" —I lowered my voice, although Groff's persistent din almost necessitated shouting— "my future."

Worth smiled politely, but his face registered a blank look. He had clearly forgotten his precise direction to me from the other evening. "So I did, so I did. And you bravely found me where other ladies fear to go."

"I hope I'm not interrupting—"

"Nonsense." He turned to the table and instructed Ned and Julius to leave us. "It's time for you to be back at work anyway," he told them. Julius grinned at me suggestively in leaving.

I didn't like being alone with Worth, but a crowded saloon was a better choice of setting than his dressing room. I perched on the stool next to him and declined his offer of coffee or ale.

"Your reviews were stellar," he began. "You've read them, of course?"

"Yes, sir."

In fact, I'd read the notices so many times I had committed them to memory. I'd been avoiding Aggie's company in the kitchen, so I purchased the dailies myself, reveling in the laudatory words for my performance: "beguiling," "arresting," "transformed." Critics even marveled at Tranio's small flourishes, like the way I delivered a cheeky aside about Lucentio that garnered guffaws from the audience: "Nay then 'tis time to stir him from his trance." The *Herald* critic concluded my performance was "the most compelling depiction of the sly servant in the past five seasons. Miss Cartwright not so much impersonated Tranio as vanished into him."

Now Worth continued his own assessment, snapping me out of my reverie. "You've had your ups and downs. When you're up, like Saturday evening, you're in top form. You have a future in breeches roles."

"Thank you, sir. I did enjoy it so much. It felt like I may have been born for these roles."

He reached over and lightly raised my chin with his index finger. A shiver of fear traveled through me as he examined every inch of my face. Worth must have felt me tremble but didn't remark on it and simply dropped his hand to his side.

"Yes, I should have seen it earlier. You're quite the boyish thing. That would explain a lot, wouldn't it?"

My face caught fire. Leave it to Worth to ruin a congratulatory moment by undercutting me—calling me a "thing" and then implying my lack of conventional femininity accounted for why I had not responded positively to his attentions.

His next words made up for the previous ones. "I'm promoting you to second lady with a fifteen dollar a week raise. You won't see that kind of money for girls anywhere . . . outside of the brothels."

If he meant to unnerve me with the mention of brothels, I refused to let him. "Thank you, sir. That's most generous." I suspected a second gentleman made more than thirty-five dollars, but I was willing to settle, for the moment.

"Harry will be assigning your new scripts shortly. We'll be doing a special holiday matinee with dancing and singing and scenes from important plays, like a new drama by Mr. Price called *The Great Fire*. Lots of spectacle to please the crowds."

I smiled, remembering the company gossip that the playwright "Mr. Price" and Worth were one and the same.

"We'll do crucial scenes from some of the public's favorite tragedies, like *Hamlet* and *Romeo and Juliet*. For that, you'll take one of the leads."

I cringed at the memory of playing Juliet opposite him. "Sir, I don't see—"

"Not Juliet, girl!" he said. "By God, I learned my lesson there. And not Romeo either—that's too closely tied to Miss Cushman and might invite negative comparison. I'm thinking of a role no woman has ever done." He paused for effect, as if trying to read my face. "I'm thinking . . . Mercutio."

My mouth went dry. "That's Ned's role, sir. He's quite proud of his good notices."

Worth slammed his fist against the table, making other customers' cups rattle. "Do you think I don't know my own company? Yes, it *was* Ned's role. Yes, his notices were good. But for this performance it's yours." He eyed me curiously. "If you don't want it, I'll give it to Ned and you can play . . . I don't know, whatever's left over."

In my view, Mercutio was one of the best roles in the tragedy. Playing Mercutio as a breeches part could allow me to establish my reputation firmly, maybe even thrust me into company with Miss Cushman. Depending on the scene we'd be performing, it would likely require me to learn stage combat. Further, turning it down would be a slap in the face to Worth's authority, for which he could fine or suspend me again.

Still, accepting it meant competing outright with Ned, straining our relationship further. My friend had already expressed alarm that I was taking roles from men in the company, and now I'd be taking *his*.

To play or not to play Mercutio, that was the question.

It took only a second or two for me to make up my mind. "Thank you, sir. I most definitely want the role."

I kept the news of my promotion from Mama for a week. I had secret plans for the extra fifteen dollars.

Harry begrudgingly advanced me the raise from the cash drawer. "Don't make this a habit. And don't tell any of the others. I'm not running a bank." He counted the fresh bills twice before surrendering them to my outstretched palm. "You've not started playing the horses, have you? Horses and the drink are the downfall of many a young actor with too much money in his pocket. I wouldn't like to see a young lady going the same direction."

"Mr. Pendergast! What an idea." I smiled sweetly, summoning up feminine wiles I'd seen other girls use. "Besides, the ladies of the company are far more likely to spend their income on dresses, gloves, and chocolates."

With the money tucked in my pocket, I took a hack to Stewart's emporium. And there was what I'd come for: the leather and brass traveling inkwell I'd admired and wanted for Clem.

"A smart choice," the clerk said as he wrapped it carefully in layers of tissue. "For your father or brother?"

My eyes fell shyly, and he added, "Ah, I see. Your sweetheart's a lucky fella."

I didn't correct him. It was not a lady's inkwell but designed with a gentleman's taste in mind, and there was no easy explanation for why I was purchasing it. He offered to have it delivered that day, but I stammered something to bide time while I pondered the enormity of the inkwell as a gift. Was I acknowledging that my affection for Clem was what other women felt for men? Was I deciding that two women *could* be sweethearts—even if there was no precise name for it? The thought made my cheeks catch fire.

I pushed on before I could change my mind. "I don't need delivery today. What I need is an engraving to the inside top cover," and the clerk took my dictation: *To Clem, with deepest affection. G.*

I wanted to address it to Clem from George, but there was no explaining that to the clerk. More than anything, I wanted to say *I've missed you terribly and I've been a complete ninny and you mean more to me than anyone ever could*—but that wasn't something you could engrave on the lid of an inkwell.

"I am certain your young man will cherish this," the clerk said.

The delivery instructions, though—Miss Clementine Scarborough at Miss Bottoms' Boardinghouse for Ladies on Pearl Street—gave me away. As the clerk scribbled down the name and address, his look fell somewhere between surprise and disapproval.

"You're certain Miss Scarborough wouldn't like something more . . . ladylike?" he asked gingerly. "We have an exquisite porcelain and gilt piece with delightful cherubs on it. Perfect for a lady's writing table."

I pictured Clem seated at her rickety desk, ink smudges on her hand and face as she toiled over another play. She would no doubt poke fun at a fussy lady's inkwell that could easily fall and shatter. "No, I don't see her liking cherubs. This is the one."

He must have figured a sale was a sale, because he finished the transaction quickly.

"And when will it be delivered?"

"We can finish the engraving next week and have it out by, say, Tuesday."

"Any way to rush it?"

It cost more, but I paid.

Chapter 23

The news of my promotion spread quickly through the company, partly because of the commotion downstairs when the stagehands transported my costume trunk to one of the two much more spacious dressing rooms designated for second ladies. Mary Louise Burton had moved up to leading lady, so I'd be taking over her space and sharing with Frances Muller.

Frances showed the stagehands where to set my trunk and pointed me to the available vanity and mirror. The lighting was so much brighter than in the other dressing room it took a while for my eyes to adjust.

"Together again," Frances said.

"You know you missed me."

"Well, I'm glad we're not in competition anymore. There's no way I could *ever* play a convincing man."

The casting for the holiday matinee had also filtered down through the players. There would be two scenes from *Romeo and Juliet*, including a choice one for Mercutio—the fight scene at the start of Act Three. Worth would play Romeo, and Julius was assigned Tybalt, while Ned took the smaller role of Benvolio. I overheard him complaining to Julius as I passed the green room.

"I've performed Mercutio to acclaim," he said. "It's unfair to take it away from me."

"Well, old man, what say I take a stab at her for you?" Julius said.

The two chortled at my expense, but Ned's laugh sounded forced. I couldn't help lobbing my own quip from the doorway.

"And then Mr. Worth will get to take a stab at *you*."

Both heads jerked toward me. "Just having some fun, Georgie," Ned hurried to explain.

"You must learn to take a joke," Julius added. "You won't make it in theater without that." He winked at his companion. "If you want to play a boy, you got to play with the boys. Right, Ned?"

The twisted adage could serve as an apt complement to Harry's "What happens between men and women, that's just what happens." With a firm nod, Ned added, "That's for sure."

My stomach sank at the thought that Ned had turned on me. My first instinct was to scream at him. I was the one with whom he had shared his deepest secret and who had vowed to hold onto it forever. I had even pretended to be his sweetheart for his mother's sake! Would Julius be as chummy if he knew Ned fancied men?

But maybe Ned's response wasn't so clear-cut. Maybe he had agreed with Julius because *he* had to play with the boys to get ahead, too—which meant acting the part of a man who liked women.

So instead of berating him, I took a different tack. "I've been 'making it in theater' quite well, I'd say. Let's compare our notices someday, shall we, Julius?"

Julius snickered and poked Ned in the ribs. "Wrong time of the month for somebody, looks like."

"Let it go, Jules," Ned said, sounding almost like his old self.

Julius fastened his belt and scabbard around his waist. "Let's run through the fight scene, old man."

"Benvolio doesn't fight," Ned said with a grimace.

"Of course, but be a sport and take Romeo's part to help me out. Worth hates to practice the fights, and I want it to be perfect."

"You'll want Mercutio for that scene," I pointed out. "I could run through it with you."

It was common for actors to help each other learn and practice stage combat, but after the bickering we had just engaged in and the gauntlet I'd thrown down about reviews, Julius had no reason to include me. Ned opened his mouth as if he were about to agree with me, but his companion said, "Are you still here?" and I retreated to the wings to find Harry.

"Never did any combat myself," Harry said when I broached the topic of lessons. "In my day, I played the fool on stage."

"You were an actor, Mr. Pendergast?"

Harry frowned at the memory. "Those days are best forgotten." He pondered my options. "You know, Julius is quite a swordsman. Studied fencing with Mr. Roland in London. He's teaching Ned."

"Yes, they're at it in the green room. But Julius made it clear he wanted to practice *without* Mercutio."

Harry studied my face. "Too bad they didn't teach fencing at that proper girls' school you went to."

I chuckled at the thought of Miss Haines or Mademoiselle brandishing a sword, but Harry's face looked serious.

"My education was expensive and useless," I said. "I know which fork to use at table and I can speak a little French."

"Lost opportunity if you ask me. Fencing's healthful, and the skill would come in handy should a lady find herself"—he paused—"in a compromised situation. Out on her own, don't you know. Not that ladies like you are out on their own . . ." His face reddened.

"Oh, of course."

My thoughts, though, flew to Clem, who was often out on her own and who did not seem troubled by it in the least. She'd gone to a school with boys and received an unusual education for a girl, and I wondered if fencing had been part of her instruction.

"And there's always Mr. Worth," Harry said after a considerable pause. "He likes the fights to be spontaneous, but he'll want your Mercutio to be convincing."

I sighed. Rehearsing alone again with Worth was not going to happen if I could avoid it.

If I were to play breeches roles on a regular basis, I needed unfettered access to Pa's costume collection. And for that, I needed more than the key to his study so I could sneak in. I had to tell my mother the truth.

I found her in her bedroom on the morning of her final fitting for the brown silk brocade she planned to wear to my uncle's wedding. She was also wearing the completely refurbished bonnet that Clem had made, and the colors suited the ensemble as if designed with it in mind. Mama's skirt swished back and forth as she assessed herself in the cheval mirror.

"What do you think? It's not too young for me, is it?" Although her question expressed worry, I caught a mischievous twinkle in her eyes.

Sylvie, the seamstress, replied before I could. "Why, madam, you could be a bride yourself!"

My mother's face lit up, although the seamstress was clearly flattering her. Mama was a few years on the wrong side of forty, but I hurried to add to the compliments and reassure her.

"You look stunning, Mama. The dress shows off your coloring to perfection."

"Yes, Sylvie's outdone herself, I think," my mother said, as if the seamstress wasn't kneeling on the floor beside her. Mama cast a final glance at herself in the mirror before vanishing behind the dressing screen with Sylvie.

"Did you want something, dear?" Mama called out.

"Yes, there's good news."

"Just a moment, then."

Sylvie emerged holding the gown in her arms like a precious child, and my mother reappeared in her wrapper.

"Would you press it yourself, Sylvie? It would be too delicate a job for our housemaid."

"Yes, madam," Sylvie said.

Mama watched the seamstress go before adding, "It's an extravagance, I know. But my brother's wedding—"

"Oh, the expense is completely justified," I hastened to say. "Besides, now—"

Mama took a seat at her vanity, and our eyes met in the mirror. With her hair down and a beguiling blush to her cheeks, she did, all of a sudden, look younger than her years— the girl waiting for Pa at the stage door. I'd wondered how Pa could abandon his family, but now I puzzled over how he had set aside such a lovely wife.

"Besides now what? You said you had good news."

"Mr. Worth's promoted me to second leading lady! At thirty-five dollars a week!"

"Oh, my dear girl!" Mama turned from the vanity and clapped her hands together. "You said you would do it by the end of the year, and just look." She popped off her vanity bench and took both my hands. "I should have trusted you. You have saved this family, Georgie."

Mama crushed me to her bosom, and as my arms wrapped around her back, I took in her delicate, familiar scent of violet water. She stroked my hair in a way she hadn't since I was much younger. I wanted to hold on forever, like a puppy, but after a few precious moments she disengaged.

"I couldn't be happier," she said.

With that, the time seemed right to bring up the issue on my mind.

"I'm so glad I've made you happy," I began. "Now here's the thing, Mama. I've not been completely honest with you."

Her face clouded with worry, as if her elder daughter might suddenly announce she'd embarked on a more unsavory career than acting.

"But then," I continued, "you've not been completely honest with me, either."

My mother straightened her back.

"I found out about Pa," I said. "That Uncle James helped

him leave and has stayed in touch with him. Which explains why you don't wear mourning."

Mama frowned. "Your uncle shouldn't have told you that."

"He didn't offer it. I pried it out of him." I sucked in a deep breath. "I've been in Pa's study, Mama. I saw his Moor costume and his sword. I knew he'd been here after . . . that night. I confronted Uncle James about it."

"Aggie shouldn't have let you in. I will speak to her!"

"I take full responsibility. She unlocked it for me against her better judgment." As I plowed forward, Mama's facial expression went from annoyed to something like fretting. "I needed access to Pa's costumes because . . . Mama, I'm playing breeches roles now. I've already played Tranio to grand reviews, and now I've been cast as Mercutio. Mercutio, Mama! Who knows where I'll go from there? I knew you wouldn't approve, so I wasn't honest with you. But I'm being completely honest now. You should know that Mr. Worth thinks I could be the next Charlotte Cushman."

Worth hadn't said that outright, of course, but he'd implied it. If my statement wasn't completely honest, it was close enough.

Mama's mouth flopped open in surprise, as if I'd grown a second nose. She shut it, and her face went blank.

"I'll need access to Pa's costumes all the time now. And the Scottish sword, too." She didn't flinch, and her expression stayed flat. "And I need your support. In return, I promise I will do as well as I can in my career so I can take care of you always . . . and Maude, too, if things don't work out as she hopes with her beau."

My mother reached out and, for an awful second, I feared she might slap me. Instead, she tucked away a strand of hair that must have slipped out of my braid.

"It's time to air out that musty old room anyway," she said at last. "He isn't coming home."

My eyes watered. "I guess he might not want to."

"I don't know if he wants to or not," Mama corrected, "but I know *I* don't want him to."

My stomach twisted into a tight knot. "But Mama—"

"I won't divorce him because that would cause a scandal for you and your sister. I won't pretend he's dead by wearing mourning, and I won't have him back. Those are my terms."

I nodded, but I knew it was going to take many more conversations before I could let go of Pa for good—if I could even do that.

"I'll instruct Nora to tidy up the study and give it a good dusting. We'll get some new curtains, something brighter and less brooding, and a more feminine-looking desk. I've never liked that big, hulking thing your father chose. The wardrobe has seen better days, too." She paused. "From now on, Georgie, you're to consider that room yours."

My heart pulsed like a hummingbird's wings at the news. I gave my mother a grateful, gentlemanly bow, which she initially scowled at, then dismissed with an amused wave of her hand.

Chapter 24

Saturday morning, the household fluttered with activity as we dressed for Uncle James's wedding. I'd been excused from performances that day because Worth himself was attending the nuptials. There was also an understanding that I would pick up additional roles during the week to earn my salary.

I shunned the fussy side curls that Mama and Maude liked so much and that I'd been forced to wear as Juliet. Now that I was earning almost twice as much as before and Mama had designated Pa's study as my own, I figured I could do pretty much what I liked. And I liked a more streamlined look, my hair coiled into a bun at the base of my head. Neither Mama nor Maude said a word against my choice.

I was the first one dressed. My voluminous petticoats made sitting difficult, so I stood in the foyer, casting side glances at myself in the mirror, wondering why the dress had to be so very pink. I readjusted the spray of silk roses in my hair, trying to be comfortable even though the hairpins pricked me and would likely prick more once I donned my silk bonnet.

I was the one closest to the front door when the knock came. I imagined it might be the driver of my grandmother's carriage, which would take us to Calvary Church on Gramercy Park.

"I'll answer it!" I called, because Aggie and Nora were busy assisting the others.

I thought I heard Mama's voice protesting, but it was ridiculous to keep someone waiting.

In the doorframe was the most welcome sight—Clem, dressed in a plain wool cape I hadn't seen before, her blue velvet bonnet askew. Her cheeks bloomed cherry red.

"George!" she said, as if I were the last person she expected to see in my own house. She took in my outfit from top to toe. "Oh, you're going out! I'm sorry to intrude, but they told me at the theater that you wouldn't be in today. I got worried so I thought I'd run up here."

Her appearance suggested she had literally run the three blocks from the Prince. I reached out and took her icy hand, making a mental note to buy the girl a muff for Christmas. Inside the warm foyer, I hugged her tight, breathing in the cold air that emanated from her. The flowers in my hair got tangled with her bonnet ribbon, and we giggled as we pried ourselves free.

"You are the best thing I've ever seen." I rubbed her hands to warm them.

Her eyes crinkled as she took in my flouncy dress. "And you look . . . pretty," she said, with a smirk.

"You needn't humor me." I sighed. "I know I look ridiculous. But it's Uncle James and Lily's wedding day."

She stopped surveying me and shyly withdrew her hands from mine. "I'm sorry."

"It's not your fault I'm being forced to look like a confection at Taylor's."

"I mean for barging in uninvited. I couldn't wait to thank you for the inkwell, it was so—oh, I can't even say."

"Clem Scarborough without words?" I teased.

"It just—it was the most thoughtful and handsome present I've ever gotten, so absolutely perfect for me, George, it was like it was *made* for me. And the inscription! However did you manage it all?"

I shot a nervous glance up the staircase, in case my sister had finished dressing and decided to listen in. "I've gotten a promotion," I said. "There will be more presents to come!"

"Oh, George, that's wonderful! I mean, the promotion, not the presents. Although presents are wonderful, too, of course."

"Speaking of presents, Mama's wearing the bonnet you made her today. It matches her gown to perfection."

"She sent me a note saying how much she liked it."

We paused shyly, as if out of words, but I knew that was impossible because we always had so much to say to each other. I longed to tell her how I'd missed her . . . how if she tried to kiss me again, I wouldn't shrink away. But in the foyer, where anyone might see us, what I carried in my heart wouldn't come out.

"Let's go to my room," I said with a glance at the hall clock. "We won't be leaving for church for at least twenty minutes, probably thirty if Mama's hair hasn't turned out to her liking."

We tiptoed up the stairs so we wouldn't attract attention, but my mother called out, "Who was at the door, Georgie?"

"Wrong house," I said. "They wanted the Jacksons."

"How silly," I heard her mutter before she lost interest and instructed Nora to "try that curl again."

I drew Clem into my bedroom and clicked the door closed behind us. I pressed myself against her, so forcefully she gasped, and I yanked at her bonnet ribbons. She finished untying them herself and slipped the hat from her head to the floor.

"George, are you . . . sure?"

I leaned in. Clem's lips were as satiny as lips could be. I'd never willingly kissed anyone, yet our lips met as if by instinct, sending a shiver through my core. Clem's hands held my waist and pulled me in close, her tongue exploring my mouth. A soft moan rose up from my toes. This was what kissing was supposed to be.

I'm not sure how long we stood like that, mouths joined until I felt lightheaded with the thrill of it. Clem was the first to pull back, but gently. We both breathed as if with exertion.

"I should leave before they finish dressing," she said.

"Or you could stay here and wait for me to get back." I

191

was only half-joking when the next idea flew out of me: "You could spend the night."

She smiled, a new kind of smile, as if she almost considered accepting the offer.

"I can't," she said. "But meet me tomorrow at my boardinghouse after your family dinner, and we'll pick up where we left off."

We stole back to the front door as my mother's voice rang out: "Is everyone ready to go?" Clem gave me a second, quicker kiss before she dashed out onto the street, leaving me in a fog of bliss, my hand on the knob of the wide-open door as I tried to memorize every moment of her visit.

"Why in the world are you letting all that cold air in?" Mama asked from the top of the stairs.

I snapped out of my reverie in time to see my grandmother's carriage pull up to the curb and provide me with a perfect excuse.

"Granny's here," I replied.

On the endless walk down the church aisle behind the three other bridesmaids and the maid of honor, it took a lot of concentration for me to put one foot in front of the other as we'd rehearsed. At the altar, the bride's attendants were charged with spreading out Lily's veil, but I shirked my duty and stood off to the side, still floating from Clem's kiss and the promise of more to come.

During the service, I should have focused on the solemn words and the exchange of vows, but instead I struggled to stifle giggles of excitement at my new love. My mind kept straying back to Clem's hands on my waist, pulling me in—especially when the priest pronounced that my uncle could "kiss the bride."

Afterward, the guests and wedding party congregated on the stone steps of Calvary Church to cheer the couple's departure in my uncle's carriage. The vehicle was adorned with gold and green velvet swags, like an early Christmas package.

Worth emerged from behind and took me by surprise. "What are you so happy about? You were positively beaming throughout the service."

"Well, it's a happy occasion, isn't it?" I said, ruffled that he'd been watching me without my knowledge. "And I'm still celebrating my promotion, sir."

Worth's lips curled. "No, it's more than that. It's almost as if you—" The church bells began pealing, and all I heard of the rest of his muttered comment was "up to tonight." The whispered exchange caught me off guard. He'd been so well-behaved around me since assigning me breeches roles that I assumed he'd made a silly comment at my or my uncle's expense.

I smiled as if I'd heard him clearly. "That's for certain," I replied, and it was Worth's turn to be startled.

"Why, you vixen," he said. His hand found the small of my back, and I wondered what I'd agreed to with such certainty. "You know, Georgie, I'm very good to the girls I form attachments with. You could go far at the theater."

I wanted to go far, but not as his "attachment." With a weak smile, I descended two steps to put distance between me and his hand, but Worth followed.

"Sadly, it's back to the theater I go. No rest for the wicked," he said with a jaunty tap of his topper. "We will run through your fight scene soon."

I gulped. "Of course, sir. I'll tell Julius."

"Julius knows what he's about. It's you who needs to practice." He peered at me sharply. "Unless you already have a great deal of stage combat experience."

"No, I—"

"Of course, you don't. Have you a sword at least?"

That made me lift my chin with pride. "My father's," I said. "The Scottish sword. I've been practicing with it." Which wasn't exactly true—I'd only practiced lifting it—but I had hatched a plan to enlist Clem's help with the fight.

"The Scottish sword! Well, then, find me in my dressing

room and show me how you wield it," he instructed. "And then I'll show you how it's really done." The "it's" was so vague, my stomach dropped. I was never happier to see someone leave.

From the church, the wedding party and guests took carriages to Delmonico's, the elegant restaurant I'd read about in Aggie's papers. Mama, Maude, and I traveled with Granny Clifford again. I hadn't seen my grandmother since the summer, and she gripped my hand as if she meant to keep me with her always. On the ride to church, she'd professed that I'd grown taller since I'd visited her, and now she peppered our ride with questions about what I'd been up to. When I opened my mouth to tell her, my mother cut in.

"Georgie's been learning so much about running a household, Mother," she said. "You'd be proud of the progress both she and Maude have made."

When Granny squeezed my hand, the showy sapphire and diamond ring that Mama and then I would inherit bit into my palm. "That is good news. The last time I saw you, you couldn't stop talking about"—she shook her head in distaste—"*acting*. I'd say this family has had quite enough of acting and actors to last several lifetimes!"

My eyes met Mama's across the carriage, and she raised her brows in a signal I read as *keep quiet*.

"I told your mother years ago that the theater was no place for a lady. And certainly not one from a family with our lineage." Granny Clifford prided herself on descending from the city's early Dutch settlers, back when it was called New Amsterdam. "Luckily, your mother's fascination with joining your father on the stage ended quickly."

Mama's face drained of color.

"You wanted to be an actress?" Maude and I blurted out at once.

"Oh, not seriously," Mama said with a toss of her head. "It was a whim of your father's when we were courting."

Granny harrumphed. "Whoever had the idea, *you* presented it as your heart's desire. That and your sudden marriage helped send your father to an early grave. Thank heavens you found your senses and started a family."

I knew the "starting a family" part had not been easy. Mama had suffered one miscarriage after another until she finally carried me and Maude to term. After that, there was another failed pregnancy that Pa said had almost killed her and that she found too delicate to talk about with her daughters.

I continued to stare at Mama, who had focused her attention out the window.

"I wish James had not chosen Delmonico's," she said as the coach drew up before the building's Roman columns, which I'd read had been imported all the way from the ruins of Pompeii. "He knows I associate this place with your father."

Mr. Templeton, Lily's father, had selected the venue, but I didn't correct Mama. Instead, I freed myself from Granny's grip and reached across the carriage to slip my hand into my mother's. Taking my cue, Maude laced a protective arm around her shoulders.

The wedding luncheon surpassed anything a girl in stays could possibly eat, starting with oysters and progressing through two soups, stuffed lamb, and filet mignon—an absurd amount of food, most of which would likely go to waste. I had one oyster and a forkful or two of the other courses, but even that small amount made me full to bursting. Why did women imprison themselves in stays when it prevented eating as much delicious food as they wanted?

By the time Uncle James and Lily left for their honeymoon in London and Paris, their guests were straggling out with their boxes of cake. I shook my head when offered a box, but Maude jabbed me in the back with her finger.

"You *have* to take cake, Georgie," she said.

On any other day, the multitiered confection would have tempted me, decorated as it was with swirls of sugar blossoms tinted to match the bridesmaids' dresses. When Lily had rapturously described the cake weeks earlier to my mother, she had explained that, at her request, the flowers would be flavored with strawberry cordial. "The baker said he's not had the request before!"

Now, Maude continued to insist, "It's impolite to refuse it."

"It's worse to regurgitate my lunch," I replied, picturing the awful time I'd thrown up my dinner in front of everyone on Broadway.

"Don't be disgusting," my sister said with a sour look. "Just take a box. If you don't want it, give it to Aggie or Nora."

That sparked an idea, and despite the fullness of my belly, I accepted a box. I would take it to my assignation with Clem the next day when I was pretty sure I wouldn't be wearing stays—or much of anything. Maybe Clem would let me pop bits of the confection into her mouth without a fork, a thought that sent a tremor down to my toes.

Chapter 25

As instructed by Clem, I arrived at her boarding house after our midday meal. Bella the spaniel greeted me with a jolly yip and a vigorous wag of her behind, once again sniffing the fragrant cake I carried.

"My, aren't you the bearer of treats!" Miss Bottoms declared.

She wore the exact same severe gray dress I remembered from my earlier visit, and this time her complexion matched her frock. If she was unwell, I didn't have the heart to tell her I'd only brought one slice and it was meant for Clem.

"My uncle's wedding cake," I explained as I handed it to her. "I hear the frosting is flavored with strawberry cordial."

"I don't know as I've ever had strawberry cordial cake. What do you think of that, Bella?" The spaniel spun 'round in a circle, as Miss Bottoms held the cake like a precious gift of gold or silver. "How about a slice of oyster pie in exchange?"

The memory of Clem's description of stomach upset from her landlady's oyster pie made me a bit queasy myself, and I declined the offer. Miss Bottoms opened her mouth to present a choice of something else when Clem appeared on the staircase, calling out, "George! I thought I heard you!"

The landlady cocked her head to one side. "You go by George?" she asked. There was no disapproval in her tone, just curiosity.

"It's Georgiana. But my father always called me George."

"Isn't that a coincidence? *My* father called me Eddie."

Clem made a face on the staircase to try to distract me, and I barely contained a giggle.

"For Edwina?" I asked to stifle my amusement.

"No," Miss Bottoms said. Her story came to an abrupt end, and she retreated to the other room with her treasure, Bella padding eagerly behind her.

"What was all that Eddie business about?" I asked once we were safely behind Clem's closed door.

Her hands found their way to the buttons of my cloak and I watched, fascinated, as she began undoing them one by one. The simple gesture made me quiver with excitement.

"She's got secrets, Miss Bottoms does," Clem said, intent on her task. "You know, I'm not sure she always lived as a woman."

"How is that possible?" How could a gentlewoman running a boarding house for ladies live as anything *but* a woman? I continued to watch Clem's hands, busy at my undressing.

My cloak fell in a puddle of crimson to the wooden floor.

"How is anything possible?" she replied, planting her hands firmly on my waist. "Say, this." Her lips covered mine, as soft and sure as I remembered them from the previous morning. Clem pulled away slightly and let her hands travel to my bodice, where they cupped my little bosoms. "Or this."

I gasped. Who knew girls could make each other feel this way? My arms flew around Clem and drew her in. Forget Miss Bottoms—I wanted more of Clem's kisses, and whatever else she could dream up.

"You're not keeping anything else from me, Clem, are you?"

We lay facing each other on her narrow bed, chemises bunched up above our waists. One of Clem's legs draped lazily over mine as she twisted one of my locks between her fingers. Her upper lip glistened with our recent exertion.

"The good thing about ladies' drawers is they don't let you keep much to yourself, do they," she said with a lascivious grin. Her hand wandered again to the place between my legs. Indeed, the split in our undergarments had made access to each other's most private parts effortless.

"I didn't mean it *that* way," I said as her fingertips drew light circles on my inner thigh.

"Well, I may have kept two or three things back," she allowed. "I don't want you to learn all my tricks at once and tire of me."

"I didn't mean that either," I said, placing my hand over hers to still it. I didn't want the distraction during this serious turn in the conversation. "Now that we've come this far . . . given ourselves in this very intimate way, well, I don't want any more surprises. You know all my secrets, who I am and what I'm about, and I hope I know yours."

She propped herself up on an elbow and reached to the nightstand for her specs. She took her time to adjust the wires over her ears before she gave me a long look.

"You mean about Arabella?"

"No, I don't want details," I said. The idea of learning more about their relationship seemed like an invasion. "I meant . . . was there anyone else you've forgotten to mention?"

Her face and body relaxed. "Oh no, George, I'm not *that* experienced! There was just the one, and she's out of the picture forever. And no boys at all." Her lips tightened, and I feared what came next. "Arabella *did* send me a note, inviting me to her wedding next May, but I won't go."

Relief washed over me. "If you want, we could go together."

"Wouldn't that be fun? Showing off my beautiful, talented lady!"

"No one thinks I'm beautiful but you," I said, running a finger over her lips. "I haven't the kind of looks that get a girl noticed."

"I disagree! You're so tall and elegant, you're almost regal. Like Miss Cushman."

A look of panic filled her eyes suddenly, making them

round as orbs. Clem jumped off the bed, pacing the small room like a trapped animal.

"What is it, sweetheart?"

"Where is my wrapper?" she asked in a panic.

"Why are you up? Come back to bed."

"You'll have to be home soon, won't you? It's getting to be dusk."

I stood and took her gently by both arms. "Clem, what's the matter? I'm so sorry I asked about Arabella, but everything's fine now. I trust you."

Fat tears glistened at the corners of her eyes, and I could feel her trembling under my touch. "There. Is. One. More. Thing." The words were separated with little gulps.

My hands dropped to my sides. With my eyes, I located my dress on the floor in case heartbreak was on its way and I needed to leave in a hurry.

Clem sucked in a deep breath. "I wrote the Charlotte Cushman letter," she said.

I sputtered with laughter. "Well, of course you did. I was sitting with you when you wrote the first one, remember? And the second one was just as wonderful! Exactly what I wanted to say, and that poem was—"

"No, no, no. Oh, you'll hate me!" Clem glanced down at the scuffed floorboards. "I mean—oh, George, I wrote the letter *from* her, too. I convinced my brother to write it down. He has a fine, strong hand."

At first, I couldn't quite take in her meaning, but slowly, pieces of the puzzle slipped into place. Charlotte Cushman had never written to encourage me; it had been Clem impersonating my idol. I'd reveled in a fake letter and even had the audacity to read bits of it to my employer.

"Please don't hate me, George. I mailed the first letter I wrote, I swear, but there was no reply from her and when you were suspended on account of the Juliet thing, you needed encouragement so I took matters into my own hands."

"Don't I feel foolish," I said, but in fact a mix of emotions swirled in me. I'd been ridiculously vain to believe someone as important as Charlotte Cushman would correspond with me, so that brought me shame. Then again, the letter I thought she'd written had emboldened me to go to Worth with the idea of playing a breeches role, and that had given me satisfaction. "What would you have done if she *had* written back and there'd been *two* different letters from Miss Cushman?"

Tears trickled down Clem's cheeks. "I'm not sure she even got your first letter," she said. "You know, she's been moving around so much on her tour, who can keep up? And I just . . . George, I just loved you so! I mean, I *love* you so."

I went to her and folded her in an embrace until her shaking stopped. "I love you, too, Clem," I said, pushing away damp strands of hair so I could kiss her salty cheeks.

She sniffed. "So, do you think less of me now, like I'm someone you can't trust?"

"I think *more* of you. You're the dearest person in the world. You did me a loving favor. Because of that letter I'm better positioned at the theater." But that wasn't the whole of it. "Oh, Clem, don't you see? I've claimed what I'm meant to do as an actress—because of you."

We had just a little time left before I had to leave, but we made good use of it.

Chapter 26

As I had hoped, Clem had a knowledge of fencing from her days at Bellport Academy. "Headmaster considered it good exercise for girls as well as boys," she told me. "I found it great fun."

I breathed more easily at the thought of not being trapped with Worth in his dressing room while he "instructed" me and detailed what sort of "attachment" he expected from me.

"Can you help me fight convincingly?" I thought back to Miss Cushman's appearance as Romeo. "When Miss Cushman played her brilliant fight scene, she took a couple of quick lunges that made the most convincing illusion. It really looked like Romeo had struck down Tybalt."

"Mercutio won't be striking anyone down, though," Clem said, rubbing her chin. "You need to take a few lunges and then succumb to Tybalt's fatal blow. But the short answer is, yes, I think we can work that out nicely."

I had Pa's sword, but we had no weapon for Clem to practice with.

"Check the properties room," Harry told us. "Mr. Culpepper left some things behind."

The properties room was a below-stage space tucked away behind a tattered velvet curtain. I'd never been inside, and when Clem drew back the curtain, I thought about abandoning the endeavor. Someone had stacked chairs and tables and carpets on top of each other in a mound as if to start a bonfire, and I wondered how the stagehands found anything they needed. Falstaff had apparently claimed the small amount of available floor space as his second home, littering it with a trail of dried droppings.

"By gum, this is magnificent!" Clem exclaimed. I was startled that the girl I'd given myself to, my true love, had a completely different reaction to the same space.

Clem led the way as we stepped around the furniture heap and dodged a half-eaten mouse carcass to arrive at a mahogany sideboard laden with table settings, vases, and mismatched candlesticks. No swords, but among the rubble we discovered a dagger and a brass fireplace poker.

"The poker might work," Clem said. "It's the right length."

Clem didn't stop with the poker, though. She dug in the sideboard's drawers for "treasures" that intrigued her.

"Would you look at this!" she said of a handsome pistol, small enough to fit in a pocket or boot.

She wanted to stay and root around for other goodies, but I reminded her we had precious little time before she was due to deliver her linings to Mrs. Tassie's shop.

We chose the empty downstairs hallway for our lesson. Most members of the company, including Ned and Julius, had congregated in the green room for practice. "Plus, if I'm really bad at it, I won't poke a hole in anything," I said.

"Except maybe me," Clem said with a worried smile.

"Pa's sword isn't sharp." But when I touched a finger to the tip to demonstrate, I drew a bead of blood.

"Now I'm really scared," Clem said.

We positioned ourselves at the distance of our weapons. "There are three basic moves that I recall," Clem began.

"That you recall? You mean there are more you *don't* recall?"

"Don't interrupt, George, or we'll never get through this." She went on to explain the lunge, the attack move that Miss Cushman had done so well; the parry, a defensive motion that blocked the lunge; and the riposte, a counterattack by the fencer who had parried.

When I said I didn't see the difference between a riposte and a lunge, Clem retraced her steps and said, "Best to stick with the lunge and parry."

I pushed Pa's sword forward in what I thought might approximate a lunge, but Clem dropped her poker and came to my assistance.

"Feet apart like this," she said. Her hands on my thighs sent a shiver right up my back. "Now bend your knees slightly."

"Clem," I said with a small moan.

"George, we're dueling, not making love."

"Fooled me."

She planted a quick peck on my neck. "First things first. Now the arm wielding the sword should bend, like so. Let's give it a try."

When her hands left my body, I missed them. "Show me a second time?" I cajoled her. "How my feet should go."

Her arms went around me again, and I turned my face toward hers. Our lips came together, but Clem pulled back. "Focus, George. As you reminded me, we don't have a lot of time."

She resumed her place, knees bent as she had demonstrated, poker extended. "Get into position. Hold up your sword as I showed you." She slid toward me and we tapped blades gently. "Good! I'm going to lunge slowly, and you fend off my sword with yours. Think of it as a dance."

Thwack!

"Brava! Now you lunge, and I'll parry."

Thwack!

"Excellent! Let's put it all together for four counts back and forth, and then I'll stab under your arm."

"Clem!"

"I don't mean I'll really stab you, love. I'll make a motion to stab you, and then you fall to your knees, mortally wounded."

Thwack! Thwack! Thwack!

"Let's keep going, Clem! I'm just getting the hang of this. I'm not ready to die."

Thwack! Thwack! Thwack! Thwack!

"Well, isn't this a pretty scene?" came an all-too-recognizable voice from the end of the hallway. Clem and I jumped back from our combat and found ourselves facing Worth who was in full costume for Hamlet.

"I've had dreams about women dueling over me."

"Sir," I said—a meaningless response, but the only thing that came to mind when caught off guard. I wondered how long he'd been watching us in the shadows and if he'd seen our kiss.

"Most enjoyable, ladies," he said, with a slow, exaggerated clap. "Miss Scarborough, you might consider breeches roles yourself."

"I prefer to be in the wings, sir," Clem replied. "I studied fencing at school and was just giving George a hand with Mercutio's fight scene."

"That your father's sword, Georgie?" He stepped forward and took it from me to admire it.

"Yes, sir."

"A handsome instrument. I saw him wear it but never examined it up close." Worth returned the blade to me. "I'd say you've made a good start at the fight. From the third tier or the back of the parquet, it might even look convincing. But from the front rows and the boxes—I told you I'd teach you what you needed to know."

Worth squinted as he grabbed Clem's poker next. "Where'd you get this ridiculous thing?"

"Properties room," I managed to get out.

"Oh, Lord. Wait here a moment." He handed it back to Clem with disgust, then strode back down the hallway to his dressing room.

Clem and I exchanged sheepish looks. *Do you think . . .?* she mouthed, then put her fingers to her lips to mimic blowing a kiss. I shrugged. If he *had* witnessed our intimate moment, it was unlike him not to have made it into a vulgar joke. I was banking on him having arrived for the swordplay only.

Worth re-emerged from his dressing room seconds later with his own rapier in hand.

"Here's a blade worthy of a match with William Cartwright's," he said, aiming it toward me dramatically and taking several swipes at the air between us. "I'll be Tybalt this time. Stand back, Clementine. Let's try again. Georgie, take it from 'Good king of cats, nothing but one of your nine lives.'"

Luckily, I recited my speech perfectly, yet with a fast-beating heart that had worked its way into my throat.

"I am for you," Worth as Tybalt said, drawing out his sword. Then as Romeo, he continued, "Gentle Mercutio, put thy rapier away."

"Come, sir, your *passado*," I said, in character.

"And . . . go!" Worth called—not part of the script, but we were off.

Thwack! Thwack! Thwack! Thwack! Thwack! Thwack!

Having already engaged with Clem and unaccustomed to so much physical exertion, my arm grew tired quickly, each new strike depleting my energy. But I was afraid to stop. Worth had such a fierce glint in his eyes, I worried he might accidentally forget we were play-fighting and stab me for real.

Clem urged me on from the sidelines. "That's it, George!"

But on our very next exchange, with my wrist weakened, Worth knocked my sword to the floor. He took advantage of my fumble to lunge forward and back me up against the wall, his rapier tip hovering close to my collar. He smiled like the devil, just inches from my face.

"You'll need more stamina for Mercutio to be believable," he said. "I know a thing or two about stamina."

A drop of sweat trickled into my eye. Worth's face filled up the space in front of me. I could hear Clem breathing heavily, but I couldn't see her.

"You're clearly spending too much time on other . . . pursuits. Isn't that right, Clementine?" he said from the side of his mouth. His sneer suggested he had, in fact, seen our kiss.

"Mr. Worth, stop!" Clem cried out, but he ignored her.

"You're going to need a lot more practice, Georgie," he continued, though he didn't specify at what. "Let's take this to my dressing room."

"I'm awfully winded, sir. And my wrist—"

It didn't seem possible for him to lean in even closer, but he did, like he intended to kiss me himself. A hard bulge pressed against my leg.

"We'll strengthen it in private. You do remember what you said to me at your uncle's wedding?"

I had hoped whatever I'd agreed to or suggested at the church wouldn't come back to haunt me, but now it had.

"I don't remember saying much of anything, sir."

"Don't play coy. Enough." Worth grabbed my weakened wrist. "Clementine, you're dismissed."

I felt like I might black out from the way he twisted my wrist. But then I heard a shuffle behind us and Clem calling out, "Mr. Worth! See here!"

"I said you can go!"

He shot a peeved look at Clem, and I took advantage of the moment to jam my heel down on his instep. Worth yelped, released me, and stumbled backward.

That's when I swiveled my head to the left and saw Clem aiming the pistol directly at his head.

"The lady says she's tired." Here, apparently, was another of Clem's secrets: She knew how to handle a pistol—or how to make it appear that she did. To my relief, she cocked the thing she'd stolen from the prop room. "Sir."

Worth held up a hand in truce. I doubted the pistol was loaded, but Worth had no way of knowing that.

"That's good, sir, take it nice and easy. No sudden moves. Why, you might frighten silly me, and this thing could go off. I keep it in my boot for protection, but I've never had call to use it." Still brandishing the pistol, she shifted it this way and that as if to examine it. "How's it work anyway?"

"The police are but a few blocks away. I could have you carted off to the Tombs," Worth said. He controlled his voice, trying to keep it even, but I detected a tremor in it. He was always the tormentor, the bully, and I'd never seen him scared. I savored the moment.

"They're so busy these days with the riffraff from Five

Points, why would they come here for a girl like me?"

"Put that away before someone gets hurt. You might shoot off your own foot—or mine."

"I'll be happy to put it away, as soon as you say you'll leave George alone when she tells you to," Clem said.

"I can do what I want with her, and with you, for that matter. You both belong to me. Why, I should fire you for being such ... blackguards." The insult reserved for men made me smile in spite of the serious situation. "Don't you laugh at me, Miss Cartwright. I'll see the two of you never work in theater again."

"Speaking of firing—" Clem said. She aimed the pistol at the wall just to the left of Worth and pulled the trigger. Worth's whole body clenched in anticipation of the shot, but the only sound in the hallway was an empty click.

"Just poking fun, sir. I found this beauty in the prop room. Lots of wonderful stuff in there." Clem ran her fingers appreciatively over the short barrel. "But then, you were joking around with Georgie just now, too, I imagine. When you put the sword so close to her throat and grabbed her wrist like that? It was damned impressive. Looked like you were really threatening her."

"You and Clementine need to develop a sense of humor," he said in my direction. "Why would I harm one of my best assets?"

The word stung, like I was a building he owned and wouldn't dream of tearing down. But all I said was, "Well, now you've had a joke for a joke."

"*You* knew it was a prop?"

I nodded, and Worth forced a laugh that echoed off the walls. "Well, you two had me going, didn't you? Well played."

Worth made a little bow toward Clem. "I trust you'll return that to the prop room," he said, nodding at the pistol. "We don't want to add thievery to your crimes."

Then he turned back to me with teeth gritted, his face as taut as stretched leather.

"You'll be fine in the scene," he said. "Why don't you two

just carry on as you were. We needn't mention this imbroglio to anyone in the company." *Of course not,* I thought. *He wouldn't want the gents knowing he was scared of a girl with an empty pistol.*

"I'll see you at rehearsal." Worth slinked off down the hallway without another mention of meeting in his dressing room.

Clem's face showed a mix of relief and amusement. I curtseyed low, as if my friend were the Queen of England.

"Brava," I said when I rose. "I think you should consider the boards after all. We could have our own swordplay act at the Bowery—George and Clem, the Blackguard Girls."

Clem chuckled. "Only if it could be Clem and George." She lifted her skirt hem provocatively and tucked the pistol into her boot.

"You're keeping it? But it's got no bullets."

She shrugged. "Such a small drawback."

Chapter 27

By the week of the holiday matinee, tickets in the parquet and boxes were sold out. Worth had performed his promotional magic, placing advertisements in several of the dailies. Bills plastered on fences and posts listed all the players and acts but drew attention to one in particular:

GREAT BLAZE OF 1845!
LIVE! ON STAGE!

The great New York City fire of my childhood was fresh enough in people's minds that a simulation was guaranteed to pique interest—possibly more than the sword fights Worth's ads and posters promised. The conflagration that had started in a warehouse in the summer of that year, destroying most of the wooden structures of lower Manhattan, hadn't extended far enough north to endanger my family's home, but a blanket of smoke had choked us just the same. Mama had not allowed me or Maude out of the house for over a week.

A few in our theater company, especially the senior members, grumbled about Worth's use of bigger and more dangerous spectacles on stage.

"People want beautiful acting, not all these illusions and artifice," Mrs. Reynolds protested. "I resent playing second fiddle to a fire."

"What is acting itself if not artifice?" Harry said. "And I reckon nobody here resents their salary"—a quip that quelled further objections.

Like all the other supporting actors and actresses, I had three scenes to play for the matinee, peppered throughout the afternoon along with dances by the ballet girls, duets by sopranos and baritones, and monologues by leading gentlemen and ladies. Multiple scenes meant costume changes, and Sallie was kept busy darting back and forth through the hallway from the second ladies' dressing room to that of the walking ladies. For the beautiful tailoring she'd done to Pa's velvet doublet so that it would fit me, I tipped her a hefty twenty-five cents.

"Holiday shows and benefits!" she muttered under her breath. "He'd never think to bring in another girl to help."

I was not important enough yet to warrant a benefit, a performance that showcased an actor or actress's best roles in brief scenes. Benefits paid handsomely, with players taking home better than half of the cash proceeds. If I did well as Mercutio, I might get a chance to reprise the role in a benefit of my own in the coming year, and then I'd be on my way to securing the fortune that would support my family.

My fight scene, of course, was foremost in my mind. I practiced all week with Clem, when she wasn't working for Mrs. Tassie or we weren't stealing kisses or slipping hands into each other's skirts. Finally, Julius deigned to run through it with me before the full rehearsal so we could get accustomed to each other's moves.

"I don't want you tripping me up when it's you who's supposed to die," was the way he put it. Like Worth, Julius's preferred fighting was *thwack!*-ing away more times than I could handle, like pirates aboard a ship. I tried to convince him the brief, slowed-down combat I'd seen Miss Cushman engage in had made the audience gasp.

"Three lunges and parries," I said, proud to have remembered the proper names of the moves, "and that was it. It was the most amazing thing."

Julius didn't believe me until we tried it out ourselves

with Ned watching.

"She's right, Jules," Ned said, when we'd completed the sequence. "It almost looks like a dance, and the audience doesn't expect the fatal blow so soon. You'll stun them for sure." His concession to my idea allowed me to hope that he and I might mend our tattered friendship.

Accompanied to the matinee by Mr. MacReady, my mother and sister took over my uncle's box at the Prince and generously invited Clem to join them. From their European honeymoon, Uncle James and Lily sent flowers to the theater for me, a spray of red and white camellias with a note that read simply, "We are certain Mercutio has never looked so fine!"

When Maude wished me well, I cautioned her that she couldn't *actually* wish me well or it could bring bad luck.

"Hope it goes badly?" she said.

In Acts One and Two of the matinee, my scenes amounted to encores—Pert in *London Assurance* and Tranio in *the Shrew*. Both drew vigorous applause. Indeed, the audience seemed to be thrilled with just about everything that happened on stage, even the ballet girls' cabrioles and pirouettes.

Our fight scene was scheduled late in the final act, before Mrs. Reynolds's monologue, another ensemble in front of the curtain by the corps de ballet, and the much-anticipated Great Fire.

By mid-act, I was dressed and pacing the wings in a way that annoyed Harry. "You're making me nervous. Go wait in the green room," he commanded. "Roddy'll come for you in plenty of time."

The green room buzzed with actors and actresses running their lines one last time and checking their costumes in front of the full-length glass. Julius was practicing his slow lunges in front of Ned, but he stopped when he saw me.

"Ready?" he said, as if I were the one who'd been caught going through the paces.

I suggested we mime our moves without our swords for good measure, which we did several times.

"I like it," Julius finally admitted. "It feels right."

Before long, the company call-boy yelled into the room, "Mr. Worth! Mr. Marshall! Miss Cartwright! Mr. Murtagh! Five minutes!" and it was time for our scene.

Worth had not been in the green room with us; he was already in place next to Harry, reading the prompt book and tapping his foot when the three of us arrived in the wings.

On stage, I could tell that we were hitting everything perfectly even before the audience made any audible response. An actor knows when a scene works and when it's either dragging or accelerating, and our pacing was impeccable. The audience sucked in a collective breath as Mercutio called Tybalt a "rat-catcher" and egged him into a fight. Then, as desired, the lunge that struck Mercutio down brought exclamations from the parquet. I even heard cries from the boxes (Mama? Clem?) as I recited my near-death lines: "A plague o' both your houses! They have made worms' meat of me: I have it, and soundly too: your houses!"

In the wings, a smile split Harry's face. Ned, who as Benvolio had led Mercutio offstage, gently squeezed my shoulders without a word. When he reentered the scene, Ned never faltered in his final monologue, a long speech that might have once stymied him. "And, as he fell, did Romeo turn and fly. This is the truth, or let Benvolio die," he pronounced before exiting to vigorous applause.

With no more scenes to play, I remained in the wings for Mrs. Reynolds's speech as Lady Macbeth, a star turn not to be missed, and I even caught a bit of the ballet girls' final dance. I decided not to watch the Great Fire unfold, instead taking to my dressing room to change into street clothes so I'd be ready to meet Clem the moment the spectacle ended.

Once in the dressing room, eyeing myself in the mirror in Pa's handsome doublet, I realized I didn't want to don my confining stays and dress again. There was something so appealing about the costume that I left it on, no matter how odd I might look on the street or how much attention I might draw, and I merely removed my makeup. When finished, I sat comparing my reflection in the glass to the penny plains I'd arranged on the dressing table to inspire me—Miss Cushman as Romeo, Mrs. Drew as Mark Antony, Madame Vestris as Don Giovanni. Pa had always said I'd be on a card one day myself, memorialized in my most famous roles; would Mercutio be among them?

The boisterous fire scene interrupted my musing. Through the ceiling, I could hear the screams of ladies playing victims and the shouted commands of Worth, who took the role of head fireman. The clapping and whooping that followed told me the scene had drawn to a thunderous close.

I made my way back up to the wings, where the company was in fine form, the fellows slapping each other's backs, the actresses chattering about the matinee's success. If anyone thought it strange that I was still in costume, they didn't remark on it.

Julius pumped my hand as if he'd forgotten I was a breeches player and not a chap. "Well done, Georgie. That scene was one for the ages."

Even Worth congratulated me. "You proved me right. From now on, you're our Mercutio."

I watched Worth's eyes dart from mine and fasten on something just past my head. "Well, well, to what do we owe this honor?" he said. "I thought you were on that endless tour of yours."

I heard a sonorous, amused voice behind me, and my heart picked up a beat. "Matilda and I are in the city for a few days, and I just had to see the actress everyone is calling a young me."

My head pivoted slowly as an owl's until I stood eye to eye with a buxom woman in a form-fitting ladies' suit, a silk tie at her throat, a coat flung over her arm, a gentleman's topper in hand. Beside her was another, younger lady, similarly dressed, but sporting a vest with her suit.

Worth did the introductions: "Miss Georgiana Cartwright—Miss Charlotte Cushman and Miss Matilda Hays."

How many ways could I say how happy I was to meet my idol? I remember blurting out "thrilled," "humbled," "honored," and "ecstatic." The tributes gushed out of me while Miss Cushman nodded and tried to insert a few words of her own. When I stopped babbling, there was such a ringing in my ears, I didn't catch much of what she said, although I could tell from the women's matching smiles that it was positive. The most important part sounded something like, "Mercutio will never be the same for me."

"Jolly memorable," Miss Hays added in her crisp British accent.

"I look forward to following your career, Miss Cartwright," Miss Cushman said. "I had the pleasure of performing with your father twice, once in the Scottish play and once in *Lear*. He was unmatched, and I believe you will be, too."

"If you ever stop in Rome, please do look us up," Miss Hays said, but without telling me how I might do that.

I wanted to fly downstairs and get my penny plain for her to sign, but before I could ask it, the great lady and her companion murmured their farewells and moved on to congratulate other members of the company. Mrs. Reynolds warranted a hug that I envied. After a few words with Worth, the two women donned their coats and hats and made their way out the stage door.

At that moment, my mother, Maude, Mr. MacReady, and Clem appeared in the wings to congratulate me. Clem's mouth formed an *O* of surprise.

"George, was that—?"

"It was!"

"Blame me! So, she *did* get your letter?"

"If she did, I was too much in heaven to hear it. Clem, it doesn't matter! She came to see *me*! She said so, to Worth himself! And Miss Hays told me to look them up when I'm in Rome!"

Worry tinged Clem's voice. "You're going to Rome?"

"Not now. But someday I hope we'll go together."

Clem kissed each of my hands in turn. If my mother and sister saw and thought it odd or unusual, at that moment I didn't care. Still holding hands, Clem and I skipped playfully around the call-boy, then spun the lad in a circle until Harry shooed us out.

My mother didn't approve of me wearing my Mercutio costume into the street, and she insisted I wrap my cape firmly around myself to hide most of it. She also clicked her tongue when I said Clem and I would be joining members of the company at Groff's instead of going home with her and Maude. But she must have remembered who was supporting the family and quickly stepped back her objections.

"Just don't be out late, Georgie."

"My resemblance to Pa stops at the stage door, Mama," I assured her. "I had champagne once and didn't care for how the stuff made me feel. I won't drink anything but water, I promise."

At first, Mama looked startled at my admission about the champagne, but then her face relaxed. "Be sure you take a cab home."

"I'll pay for it to take Clem home, too," I said, and my mother nodded her approval.

In the dusk, Clem and I resembled a courting couple, which we technically were. Our heads leaned in close as we traded thoughts about the matinee and about Miss Cushman. Clem boldly took my arm as we crossed the street toward Groff's.

"We'll be like those ladies someday, George," she said with a sigh. "People will talk about Miss Cartwright and Miss Scarborough."

"Where will we live? London? Maybe Rome, like them. Me acting, you writing—"

It all sounded dreamy, but I stopped short when, ahead of us, I spotted a shadowy group of men in front of the stairs to the beer cellar. Instinct told me I should pry Clem's fingers from my arm. Clem hadn't yet noticed the group, so the sudden detachment confused her. I nodded with my chin in the direction of the trouble.

One fellow appeared to be down on the cobbles, and at first I thought he'd simply fallen. But unmistakably, two others were taking turns kicking him in the ribs. We weren't close enough to hear what they were saying, but the mutters sounded menacing. When a fourth figure attempted to push the others away, he, too, was shoved onto the ground.

"Let's go, George," Clem whispered. "Let's get Harry or the stagehands."

The voices grew louder, the kicking fiercer. One man spat on the fallen figure and called him "Miss Nancy." Another voice, one I knew well, screamed, "Stop, man, I beg you! You'll kill him!"

That voice belonged to Ned.

Because I hadn't trusted leaving Pa's sword at the theater where anyone might pinch it, I'd worn it in the scabbard under my cape, although Clem had poked fun at me for walking out with it on. "In case you haven't noticed, gentlemen don't walk about wearing swords, George." I'd admitted that, yes, maybe I wanted to show it off at Groff's, strut my stuff a bit to celebrate my triumph.

Now, when I reached under my cloak, Clem realized what I was doing and extended a hand to stop me. "George, no," she pleaded. "We need help."

Say it was the costume that gave me bravado or the hard coldness of the blade against my leg. Or maybe it was a rush of pure fear. Something made me surge forward with the Scottish sword drawn, shouting at the top of my lungs, "Who now the price of his dear blood doth owe?!"—as if these rascals would recognize Shakespeare.

I'd hoped that a drawn sword pointed toward them would cause them to scatter back to whatever holes they'd crawled out of, but it didn't. It only temporarily stopped the villains from beating the fellow on the ground to a pulp. But even as I rushed them with the sword, one scoffed, "Well, what've we here, another Nancy Boy? That theater must be crawling with 'em!"

Ned called out, "Georgie, don't! Get Mr. Groff!"

"'Georgie'? Ain't that a sweet name for a fella?" The uglier of the two assailants laughed. "And he's brought his fake blade, too. Oh, I'm scared! Ain't you scared, Kit?"

"This is no fake," I said in the deepest voice I could summon. "Go on your way now before I fetch the police."

"I'm scared, too!" chimed in the second brute. Up close, the thuggish dolts were bigger than they'd looked at a safe distance down the block, with barrel chests and thick necks that disappeared into frayed jacket collars. I wondered if they'd wandered up from Five Points for sport, looking to rob some swells. At first glance, it looked as if they didn't have any weapons but their fists—or at least, they hadn't yet resorted to them.

Then the uglier one withdrew a knife blade, shiny and sharp, from his jacket. "Look at the soft face on this Nancy Boy, Kit. I'm thinking this here's a cherry in boy's clothing!"

"Nah," Kit said, spitting into the street. "Just a pretty boy, is all, Abie."

"We could find out, couldn't we?" Abie said. "What say we have a blade fight right here. I could slice those breeches right off you and see what we've got."

Ned had picked himself up and was edging toward the stairs of Groff's when Abie stopped him and pushed him down hard. "Not so fast."

I'd heard soft footfalls from Clem's direction, which I hoped meant she was returning to the theater for help. But I couldn't count on it, and I couldn't count on Kit not having a dagger, too. With Abie's attention distracted from me for a split-second, I extended my sword and made a jagged slice down the side of his jacket, exposing a dirty shirt underneath.

"What the blazes—" Abie stared down with dismay, and I took advantage of his confusion to carve a matching cut on the other side. Then I took a swipe at his shin, which made him drop his knife with a bellow. He bent over in pain, wailing over his bloody wound, and I stepped forward and kicked the knife in Ned's direction. He scooped it up and got to his feet, brandishing it.

"Goddamn soddies!"

"Let's leave 'em to their filthy ways, Abie," Kit said. "We got their eagles, ain't we?"

I couldn't see a way to retrieve the stolen money without trying to cut Abie again or take a slice out of Kit, too—trouble I wasn't keen to compound. Besides, saving the necks of Ned and his companion seemed more important than getting back their gold coins. With my sword still poised for attack, I called out, "Go, and don't come up here from your sewer again!"

From behind me, a shot went off, clear as a bell in the street. All eyes turned toward Clem, who stood with Harry to her right. The pistol she'd confiscated from the theater was pointed up to the sky.

"Give back the money," she directed the rascals. When they didn't budge, she cocked the pistol a second time. "Don't make me shoot it out of your pocket. I might miss and hit something you value more."

Kit tossed two gold eagles onto the street, where they clinked against the cobblestones and rolled into a crack. With Abie limping on his wounded leg, the two criminals scurried off into the shadows.

"You two come prepared, don't you?" Harry said. He gave Clem's pistol the once-over. "That looks an awful lot like one Mr. Culpepper used."

Clem didn't flinch. "Common make," she said, slipping it into her pocket.

With great care, Harry and Ned helped the stricken man to his feet. His face was as bruised as raw meat from where he'd fallen, and his clothes were muddied and torn from being kicked, but there was no mistaking who he was—Richard Pomeroy, Ned's young man.

"Thank you," Richard said to me through a bloody mouth that looked as if it might be missing a tooth. With difficulty, he added, "I know you from somewhere."

"You waited on me at Stewart's," I said. "Ladies' gloves."

He smiled and then made a bow toward Clem. "And you,

miss. You two saved my life."

Ned had not escaped unharmed, but his injuries appeared much less grave—scraped knuckles from his fall, a torn trouser leg.

"What happened?" I asked, helping Ned brush off Richard's coat.

"We were minding our own business," Ned explained. He lowered his voice so Harry couldn't overhear. "Richard *might* have put an arm around me . . . just for an instant, mind. They robbed us first, and I thought that'd satisfy them, but then they started jostling us for sport, and everything escalated from there."

I thought of how Clem and I had linked arms like a couple, but because I was dressed as a man, it had made us appear ordinary.

"I'm so sorry, Georgie," Ned said, tears rolling down his fair cheeks. He rubbed them away with his coat sleeve.

"Oh, don't be! I'm just glad that we were here and I had Pa's sword on me. *En garde!*" I waved it as a joke before replacing it in its scabbard. I was thinking, too, *And that Clem found bullets for that pistol.*

"No, I mean, sorry for giving you such a hard time—about Mercutio. You were brilliant. I've never played him as well as that and don't think I could. Please forgive me for being so jealous and beastly."

My face warmed with the praise. "No harm done. Now what say we get the two of you a doctor?" I leaned in and whispered, "We don't want Richard's handsome face to be ruined."

On top of his many skills, Harry said he had acquired a bit of medical knowledge along the way and kept bandages, splints, and alcohol at the theater for instances like this. "Actors," was all he said to explain. Richard and Ned agreed to return with him for the needed patching-up.

Clem and I both assumed a tough stance and claimed to be unshaken, but on my part at least, that was a lie. With my work finished for the day, in Groff's I broke my promise to Mama and ordered a stein of ale, which I shared with Clem.

The nasty taste burned the back of my throat, but with more sips, I became accustomed to it.

"You told me you wouldn't keep any more secrets." I breathed the words softly into Clem's ear as she drank.

"I haven't, George! What do you think I kept from you now?"

"You know where to get bullets," I said, "and how to load them."

"Oh, that."

"'Oh, that'?"

"Miss Bottoms owns the same make," she explained. "She lent me some bullets and even showed me how to load the thing. She hides hers in her muff."

I raised my eyebrows.

"Filthy girl! You know what I mean."

I did, but just the same I pushed my thigh up hard against Clem's under the table and we stayed that way until we'd finished our drink.

Chapter 28

Out on the street again, a blast of smoke hit my nostrils. We were too far from Groff's for it to have wafted from the bier cellar. The smell persisted as we headed toward Broadway to engage a hack.

"Clem, wait," I called. "You don't smell that?"

She stopped and sniffed. "Something's burning."

My eyes scanned up and down the street. No sign of smoke billowing from the theater or any other building. "Could it be *The Great Fire* performance?"

"You mean they're using actual fire?" Clem asked.

"Harry told me it's mostly a trick of lighting. They flood the stage with limelight, and that reflects off panes of crimson glass to look like flames. Then they have some kind of powder and bellows in the wings to create fake smoke. All very safe, he said. I'm not sure the smell would travel out here."

Clem looked skeptical. "It's pretty strong," she noted. "I hope the illusion's as safe as Harry says."

"He did mention something about gunpowder," I added, which brought more worry to Clem's face. "I'm not quite sure how that figures in. Maybe he was saying they hadn't tried it yet. My mind might have drifted off. It was so *chemical*."

"Should we look in and make sure everything's OK?"

I considered it briefly. "No. Harry and Worth are up on all the latest effects." No one was on the street with us, so I stole a peck on the lips. "Besides, I just want to get you alone in the hack."

In men's clothes, my ability to hail a cab all on my own made me puff up with pride. As I was helping Clem into the carriage I secured, I spotted a dark figure in a stovepipe hat leaning against a lamp pole across Broadway. The fellow raised a hand to me in a tentative wave.

I blinked a few times. My eyes had deceived me before and dashed my hopes, and I knew for certain that Pa was in Charleston. I dispelled the man as a vision and tucked into the cab beside Clem.

As we rumbled down Broadway, I purposely fell into Clem, pretending it was due to bouncing over the cobblestones. She didn't mind. En route to her boardinghouse, we had precious minutes to ourselves, filled with kissing and groping. Even if someone had spotted us from the street, they'd just see a spooning couple—a gent out on the town with his lady love.

In the morning, I stayed in bed while Mama and Maude headed off to church. I'd have slept most of the day if Aggie hadn't come to wake me—something she never did because Sunday morning was her church day, too. That Sunday, however, she tore open the curtains and let bright, insistent streaks of daylight in.

"Miss Georgie! You must get up! Go on now!" Ever since I'd asserted my position as her employer, Aggie had shown me nothing but deference, so her forceful behavior now was especially startling. She did tack on a contrite "please."

"Why aren't you at Mass?" I asked through a yawn.

"I'll go to the ten o'clock."

The sight of her face, usually so ruddy but now completely white, told me something horrible had happened. My first thoughts went to my father, that we'd had dire news of him overnight. I shivered thinking that the figure I'd seen on Broadway might have been his ghost.

"Is it . . . Pa?"

I tossed off the bed covers. I was wearing only a shirt of Pa's that had been part of my costume, and my bare legs dangled over the edge of the bed.

"It's the Prince!" Aggie said. "Burnt to a shell!"

The news made me lightheaded. I'd never been a fragile, fainting-couch sort of girl, but I could have passed for one at that moment, falling back onto the pillows in a near swoon.

Theater fires were common, and it was nothing short of a miracle that the Prince had never fallen victim. The Bowery Theatre had been rebuilt twice since my childhood, and the majestic Park Theatre, once home to Miss Cushman and Worth, had succumbed to flames not five years earlier. Harry prided himself on the precautions in place at the Prince, the replacing of the gaslights on stage with limelight. And he'd been so precise about the special effects for *The Great Fire*. What could have gone wrong?

"I have to go there," I said, pulling myself up with difficulty.

"It's not safe," Aggie said. "Seems the inside's rubble, and the outside's scarred with black."

My thoughts tumbled in a panic. What about the people? Did Harry get out? Sallie? The company? Ned played a fireman in *The Great Fire*.

"Did anyone get hurt? Or . . . perish?"

"Papers don't say. But the performance was over, thank the blessed Jesus, so the audience'd gone home safe."

The performance was over? That didn't make sense. How would a fire start *after* the effects were shut down?

"I have to go," I repeated. I picked up the rest of the costume I'd dropped the night before at the side of the bed.

Aggie didn't make a move or say a word to stop me, which in the old days she might have done. She simply brought me a pitcher and basin, and I splashed water on my face and pinned up my hair. My eyes were ringed with dusky circles, and my head throbbed from that one shared stein of ale. I managed to stumble downstairs and miss only one step at the very bottom.

But in a throwback to the way she used to treat me, like a little sister rather than her employer's daughter, Aggie barred the door when she saw me planning to go out in the street in Pa's costume. "Your ma would sack me if I let you out like that."

"It'll be safer to go out this way. I'll take responsibility. Now please, Aggie, let me by."

She reached out and tucked a stray lock under my cap in a surprising show of affection. "That's better."

I leaned over and kissed her hand in thanks. She drew it back on instinct but blushed just the same.

I raced to the theater on foot, judging that the fastest and most efficient way to get there. Wearing men's clothes afforded me a freedom of movement I didn't enjoy when I had to negotiate lady's full skirts and heeled slippers, and no one gave a young man in a flowing cape a second look.

Smells from the Prince's fire lingered in the air, reaching me from a block away—sulfur mixed with something sickeningly sweet and charcoal-like. As I neared the corner of Broadway and Prince, the blackened facade of the theater gave me a ping of hope. Her proud marble pillars were still standing! The exterior bones remained! If Aggie was right and the interior was now a shell, Worth might be able to rebuild it to its former glory. Even though he'd treated me badly, I still admired his ingenuity and determination to make the theater the greatest in the city.

A crowd milled around on the Prince Street side of the building. Most appeared to be gawkers, but I recognized a few stagehands under smudged faces. If the hands were here, Harry couldn't be far away, but I didn't spot him in the throng.

The first person I encountered from the company was a welcome sight.

"Sallie!"

She was wearing only the thinnest cotton cape, with no hat or gloves, and she shivered visibly. Without thinking, I threw my arms around her, the intimate gesture surprising me as much as her. Sallie stiffened to a board in my embrace, so I let her out of the hug.

"I'm so glad you're safe!"

"I can't find Falstaff," was the first thing she said. It struck me as odd that the tabby was her top concern, but they *had* been fast companions. "Mr. Harry says he saw him hiding in the alley, but he ain't there now. I been looking for him since dawn."

"Harry is all right, too?" On the cold, overcast day, joy hit me like a burst of sunlight at the news about the prompter, but I backtracked to Sallie's immediate concern. "I'm sure Falstaff will turn up. Cats remember where they live." I knew virtually nothing about cats, but my feigned assurance relaxed the worry on Sallie's face.

"I was terrified you hadn't gotten out," I went on.

"Didn't get back till the fire trucks were there. I was out on a" —she glanced around— "mission."

I nodded. The less I knew about Sallie's missions and the safe house she ran from her room, the better.

Sallie sighed heavily. "We're all out of jobs now."

I stared at her. Obviously, we *were* out of jobs, each and every one of us, but stupidly that hadn't occurred to me until she said it. Gone were my handsome income and budding career. In addition, when the theater burned, so did the costume trunks and wardrobe, my small collection of makeup and wigs, even my cherished penny plain cards from Pa. Thank God I'd taken the Scottish sword with me when I left.

"Oh, Sallie," I said, because the loss was so great it was all I could think of. It hit me then that Sallie'd lost more than I had. Not only was she without employment and possibly her cat, but she also lacked a home and a place from which to run her missions.

"Where will you live?" The thought occurred to me that maybe Sallie could sleep in the tiny attic room next to Aggie's.

"I reckon I'll go home," she said.

"To your sister?"

"Cassie and her man live across the river. Mama's with them, and our brother's not far."

Brooklyn—that explained it. It had been too far for her to travel every day, what with the ferry ride and the wait for one of the Negro omnibuses, which were fewer and further between than those for white people.

"What about your missions?"

"Plenty of folks in the Vigilance Committee I could join. Can't think about that right now. I gotta find the cat." She peeled away from me quickly before I could ask her what the Vigilance Committee was.

I inched closer to the stage door, now just a gaping hole through which I could barely make out the charred remains of backstage. From my stance, I heard the crunch of boots on rubble and saw figures stir inside. As I searched for a familiar face to provide information, Harry emerged from the ruins, his sooty face and clothes rendering him almost unrecognizable, like an actor in blackface.

Julius dashed forward from the crowd and rushed him before I could. "Harry!" He threw himself against the prompter much as I had grabbed Sallie. I had a new glimpse into the second gentleman, who was as moved as I was to see dear Harry unharmed.

"Harry!" I echoed, although I had never called him by his Christian name. I wanted to hug each of them in turn, but they both did a double take at my appearance in men's clothing. Neither commented on it, though, and Harry simply said, "Julius. Georgie. God help us all."

I'd never heard Harry invoke God's name, but I didn't know much about his personal beliefs, and he might have been a devout man. The words seemed to choke him, and he brushed past us to the curb, where he slumped heavily.

I sat down next to Harry, and the cold seeped through my cape and tights. Julius hovered over us like a worried mother.

"Tell us how bad it is," Julius urged.

"Worse than you can see." Harry's head drooped toward his chest. It was hard to make out what he said next, and I might not have if Julius hadn't repeated it.

"That can't be! Tom's gone?"

"Tom" meant only one person: Worth. I gasped.

Harry stifled a sob. "Poor bastard. I told him the show was better 'n fine. The audience loved the way we did the fire, and it was safe as could be. But he wanted something bigger, he said, for the next performance. He wanted a spectacle, he said, wanted to see how quick-match would work." He rubbed his knuckles, which were black with ash.

"What's quick-match?" I asked.

"Gunpowder and naphtha." Harry lifted his head to look me in the eye, only to let it fall forward again. "Dangerous combination. I told him it was too risky, but he insisted it was the best way to get the effect. I tried to tell him, Georgie."

"I know you did," I said. I shot a glance at Julius, who now was on one knee in front of us. "We both know it."

"Old Groff said he heard a boom right after midnight. The stubborn fool must have tried it on his own. Blew himself up and set the whole place afire. And for what? To sell more tickets, when we already had a full house."

Harry retrieved a dirty handkerchief from his trouser pocket and blew his nose noisily. "You'll need new jobs," he said, as practical-minded as Sallie had been. "You'll have no trouble, fine performers like yourselves. You need a reference, you let me know." How I would reach the prompter I had no idea, but maybe someone in the company could tell me.

Harry stood abruptly, and Julius and I rose with him. "You take care now," he said with a solemn nod of his head. "I got to go see Bess." He trudged away with a hunch to his shoulders but was stopped not far from us by Mrs. Reynolds, who fell against him, weeping. He patted her back in quick, half-hearted taps.

Julius and I were left facing each other. My fellow company member seemed eager to leave, but I tugged his coat sleeve to keep him another moment.

"Is Bess Mrs. Pendergast?"

His lips puckered. "No, silly. She's Mrs. *Worth*." But he must have regretted his mocking tone at such a somber time because when he took his leave, he touched my arm gently and said, "Best of luck to you, Georgie. May we all land on our feet."

Afterward, I stood in the middle of Prince Street, not

knowing what to do and trying to absorb the new information that Worth had had a wife.

Chapter 29

My greatest desire was to fall into Clem's arms, but I knew she was already on the ferry to visit her family in Williamsburg for the day, so I headed back home. Mama and Maude had returned from church and heard the news about the theater from Aggie before she headed off to Mass. My mother passed one long, wary look over my clothing but let the matter go without comment. Instead, she and Maude formed a tight circle around me, and we had a family hug that made me less despairing.

Mama brushed away some ashes that had landed on my cape. "Your uncle has so many contacts, I'm sure you'll be fixed in a new position in no time. The Prince was a first-rate establishment, and you did them proud."

My face warmed at her confidence in me, although I also caught a bit of worry on her face. At least she wasn't conveying her fears to me. And at least she didn't seem to be revisiting the idea of finding me a husband.

Maude slid a protective arm around my waist. "You were splendid as Mercutio," she said. "Lots of companies will want you."

"Thank you both," I said. "It means a lot to me. I'll gather all my notices and start looking very soon. Maybe we'll have good news in the new year."

A conspiratorial look passed between Maude and Mama.

"Well, there is some good news right now," my sister said with a shy grin. "There'll be a ring from Mr. MacReady at Christmas!"

My brain was so muddled I didn't take her meaning right away. When Mama went on, all became clear. "Of course, they won't marry till next summer," she explained.

The announcement was meant to be joyful, so I exclaimed my happiness, embraced Maude again, and kissed her once on each cheek. The idea of my younger sister marrying at such a tender age, however, was appalling; next summer, she would barely be eighteen.

But I didn't say anything contrary to ruin the moment. My sister's face beamed, making her lovelier than I'd ever seen her, and I knew she believed Archie was not just a good prospect but the love of her young life. I hoped he proved worthy of her.

A sudden attack of the blue devils hit me as I remembered that Worth had perished in the fire. The man would always be an enigma. On the negative end, he had sacked Pa, pushing our family toward financial ruin. As an employer, he had used his power over me more than once, threatened my virtue and safety, and gotten at least one actress in the family way before deserting her—all while having a wife, apparently, and maybe children.

And yet, he had hired me as an unknown and launched my career. He'd fostered Clem and Ned, too. Fiercely devoted to promoting the theater, his genius had helped the company flourish.

The cascade of opposing feelings overwhelmed me. I made my apologies and went to my room.

I must have slept for a good seven hours, dreaming off and on I was in Pompeii, knee-deep in ashes from the volcano. At the height of the dream, the fragile earth began shaking and tumbling around me, suggesting another eruption, and I screamed out, "Help me!"

I jerked awake with Aggie standing over me again, lightly jostling me out of sleep.

231

"Shh," she said. "You're needed downstairs, and we mustn't disturb Mrs. Cartwright."

Because it was the second time in twenty-four hours that Aggie had woken me, I feared something much worse than the loss of the Prince Theatre. Perhaps some harm had befallen my uncle and aunt on their wedding trip—

"Let's find you a clean nightdress and your wrapper." Pa's shirt, which I'd fallen asleep in again, reeked from two days of wear.

Aggie held out my proper nightclothes in one hand, turning her eyes away as I slipped into them right there at my bedside and not behind the screen. "Stocking feet'll be best," she instructed when I looked around for slippers.

"Exactly where are we going?"

"I can't say."

"You're scaring me."

"Everything's fine, Miss Georgie. Just follow me."

She removed her own shoes, too, and we padded downstairs as quiet as mice.

At the door of Pa's study—*my* study—Aggie stopped and put a finger to her lips as if I didn't already know she wanted me to be quiet. She cracked open the door slowly, so the hinges wouldn't whine, and then hurried off before I could ask another question.

Although technically mine, the study was still outfitted with Pa's things. Luckily, Mama hadn't spent money yet to redecorate with a lady in mind. We'd need all our cash until I got settled in a new position.

In the bright lamplight, I could easily make out the figure perched with one leg up on the desk, one on the carpet. This time he was no ghost or vision.

"Pa!" I said, more loudly than I intended. I lowered my voice self-consciously. "What are you doing here?" I reckoned he had sneaked in through the service entrance with Aggie's help and didn't want Mama or Maude to know of his presence in the house.

He looked much improved from the last time I'd seen him,

when he was staggering across the stage in a drunken stupor. In fact, he looked better than he had in years, his hair neatly combed, no stubble on his chin or trace of whiskey about him. The desk still held his half-empty decanter and glass, but he wasn't imbibing.

My father held out both hands to me in greeting, but I remained a cautious distance away. "What—your father doesn't merit a kiss, George?"

The truth was, I wanted nothing more than to fling myself against him and feel his strength support me, like a father's should. But his leaving had forced me to be an adult before I needed to be, and I held myself back from properly greeting him, even while my feet took tiny steps toward him as if drawn on a wire.

"What do you want, Pa?" I asked with a boldness I didn't feel.

"I read about you," he said. "You're the talk of the theater world."

"I've had good notices."

"That's an understatement! And the interview where you owned up to being my daughter? Astounding." He sighed deeply. "I'm sorry you felt you had to hide who you are, George."

"If Grandfather Cartwright had disgraced himself with the drink and left you and the rest of his family ruined, wouldn't *you* have hidden your identity?"

"Touché," Pa said. He rubbed his hands together as if he didn't know what to do with them. Among the many thoughts that shot through my head was, *He's as scared as I am.*

"I saw you perform last night at the Prince. Your Tranio! Perfection." He blew a kiss into the air.

Pa had been in the audience!

"And you remembered everything I told you about Mercutio and executed him beautifully. That role is yours, now and forever." I bristled at him taking credit for my performance when he'd been nowhere in sight to coach me through it.

"I was so proud, George. Such a thrilling moment. I

wanted to come backstage to congratulate you, but I didn't want to steal your limelight. Later, I saw you on the avenue with another girl. You were still in costume. Such a spirited move, my girl! I waved, and I thought for a second that you recognized me. Did you?"

So my eyes hadn't tricked me. The shadowy figure on Broadway had actually been him. I didn't acknowledge it, though.

"I hoped for a moment of your time to tell you how impressive you were. You have admirers, to be sure, but you need to hear it from family, too. I imagine your mother's had nothing good to say."

The snide mention of Mama chilled whatever warmth his praise had generated.

"Mama is proud of me." I waved my hand around the study. "She's given me your room and plans to get rid of everything and redecorate it."

He clenched the strong, chiseled jaw that had helped propel him to leading parts. "It isn't hers to give or yours to take. My name's on the deed, and everything here belongs to me. Including the costumes you wore yesterday."

His cocky tone was sadly familiar; in it I heard myself chastising Aggie.

"I've been paying to keep the house these past months, not you," I pointed out.

"Still, it's just like your mother to act out of spite."

I stiffened. "You will not say anything against Mama."

He sniffed loudly. "When you're older, George, and married yourself, you'll understand there are two people in every marriage. What happens between them can get complicated. Truth be told, your mother lost interest in me."

Anger spilled out of me. "She lost *babies*, Pa! You told me yourself she almost died."

His lips pursed in a way they did in advance of pouring himself a drink. "That didn't warrant locking me out of her bedroom," he countered. "I don't suppose she ever told you that, did she? No, it's too delicate. But if you're going to lay all the blame on me, do me the courtesy of understanding she played a part, too."

"Maybe if you hadn't forced yourself on her," I said, "she wouldn't have had to lock you out."

The accusation sprang out of fury rather than fact and was likely more about Worth than Pa. But my father looked shaken all the same, like I'd slapped him. "That's enough of that," he said, although he denied nothing. There was a long silence between us then in which my blood coursed fast through my veins.

Finally, Pa offered, "There's nothing to be done about me and your mother now. It's all water under the bridge."

My patience had worn to a nub. "What do you want, Pa?" I said, repeating the earlier question he'd never answered directly.

"Here's the thing, George. I intended to head home"—I winced at his word for Charleston—"without seeing you and leave you in peace, but then I read the news about the Prince in today's papers. And about Worth, poor devil. I didn't like the man, but that's an end I wouldn't wish on my worst enemy. And he probably *was* my worst enemy, come to think of it."

I blinked back a few tears, not for Worth so much as for the incredible loss his death had brought on everyone. Even as enemies, he and Pa were two of a kind, wreaking havoc with their foolhardy actions.

"I've been doing well," Pa went on. "Charleston agrees with me."

"Good for you."

His smile was thin and solicitous. "Your uncle may have told you he helped set me up as manager in a theater company?"

I nodded.

"The receipts have been healthy, and we're in a position to hire some new players. Strong New York actors and actresses to raise our profile even further."

My heart thumped as I waited for the rest of the story.

"I thought—well, I know you might not ever consider

it but—" My heart was beating right out of my chest now. Pa's manner had become uncharacteristically shy. "Would you consider joining my company? I can't offer as much as Worth, I'm sure, but would thirty dollars a week entice you?"

For years, I'd harbored the desire to act alongside my father and share the limelight with him. In a journal I kept when I first started running lines with Pa, I sketched imagined advertisements like, "Cartwright and Cartwright—Together on the Boards!" After he deserted us, I'd ripped out the pages and tossed them onto the fire in my room.

So, despite everything that had happened and the fact that he infuriated me, the idea held a certain appeal—although now we'd be "Clifford and Cartwright," with none the wiser that I was his daughter. Joining him would also provide an immediate solution to our financial dilemma. I could send money home to support Maude and Mama until my sister's marriage.

Even more important, Pa's offer felt like an apology for everything he'd put us through, for the money he hadn't sent home, even for the accusatory things he'd said about Mama. His dark eyes flashed with hope as he said, "What d'you think, George? You don't need to give me an answer now. You can send me word." He reached into his coat pocket for his card. "Will you at least think about it?"

My gut urged me to say yes, but instead I strung the offer out and didn't accept the card. There were so many open-ended questions left hanging, like where I would live. I may have been an accomplished actress already, but I was an eighteen-year-old girl.

"I don't know anyone there," I pointed out. "It could be costly for me to room there *and* send money to Mama. I've promised to support her since no one else does."

He sighed at the jab. I don't think he'd anticipated any negotiation. "I can go to thirty-five, but not a dollar more. After a year, we'll talk about a raise. By then, you might even be a leading lady."

"Still," I pressed, "here I don't pay room and board."

I was angling for an offer to take me in, although I had no idea what his living situation was. For all I knew, he was holed up in a gents-only boardinghouse.

When his silence continued and an offer didn't come, I pushed for it directly. "Any chance I could stay with you? At least at the start."

Pa cleared his throat and glanced with longing at the decanter on the desk.

"Well, *that* would be sticky, George."

"You could introduce me as your talented niece from New York. A niece can live with her uncle"—although I knew very well that "niece" and "uncle" could have unsavory connotations.

"George—" Nothing prepared me for what came next. "I've taken up with a . . . lady." His face colored to crimson, and mine likely went a shade to match. When I lifted a hand to my cheek, it was hot to the touch.

"An actress. We share her rooms, close to the theater and convenient for us both." His look was sheepish, but he didn't apologize.

My hands curled into fists. In the six months since his fall, Pa had not only deserted his wife but already replaced her. Soon, he might even start a new family.

"But I can help you find something inexpensive and suitable, maybe with one of the other ladies in the company. We'll work something out. What d'you say?"

He fished in his pockets. "How about I sweeten the deal and give you traveling expenses? How does twenty dollars sound?"

I stared at the gold eagles in his hand but didn't reach for them, so Pa plunked them carefully onto the desk and dropped his card beside them.

Without a word, I opened the door to the study and stood in the frame, pointing into the hallway. Pa's face registered confusion.

"Get out," I said. "Keep your job and your money. I will never take a cent from you again. I'll support this family on my own, as I've been doing since you saw fit to abandon your responsibility to us."

Pa sighed. "I thought you were smarter than this. You've no income, and I'm trying to help you. Not just now, but into the future. Why, you could take over as manager someday. Think of that!"

Manager! I tried not to waver in my resolve, but my hand trembled slightly as I continued to point the way out.

"The time to help me was six months ago." Then, hoping that just by saying the words I could make them come true, I added, "You think I need you? I'll have a position by week's end. Other theaters have been courting me for *months*. With offers far better than yours."

Pa lifted his coat and hat from the chair where he'd dropped them. He glanced at the eagles on the desk, as if considering whether to pocket them again, but he left them where they were.

"You'll change your mind and come crawling," he muttered as he swept into the hallway and turned left toward the back door. A vague scent of rosemary hung in the air after he was gone, maybe a fragrance his new lady had bought him.

My knees were so shaky I thought I might fall in a heap. I leaned against the desk and with repeated deep breaths was able to steady myself. I wasn't sure whether to be proud of myself for standing up to him or think myself the biggest fool the world had ever known, to give up a good-paying job because my father had disappointed me.

This I knew for sure: I wouldn't tell anyone but Clem. If I'd made a mistake, she was the only person who would not judge me.

I left Pa's coins on the desk, afraid to touch them for fear I'd soil my fingers. Maybe, I thought, I could give the money to charity. His card I ripped clean in half and deposited in the trash can.

Before I went back up to bed, I removed Pa's whiskey decanter from the desk and took it to the back door. He was long gone by then, and except for some movement that might have been a stray mutt, the street was still. A soft snowfall was falling, the tender kind that's the first of the winter. In my stocking feet, I stood on the wet stoop, letting crystal flakes catch on my hair. I removed the stopper of the decanter and poured the amber liquid over the side into the dirt. The cut-glass bottle was likely valuable, so I brought it back inside for Aggie to wash out.

Chapter 30

The note arrived while Mama, Maude, and I lingered at the table after breakfast. It was an unfamiliar way to spend a Monday, with absolutely nowhere to go and nothing to do but consider how to get a new position.

Mama didn't object to me bringing the daily papers to the table to read the theater news while we enjoyed a second round of coffee. The reports focused on Worth's sad demise and his contributions to the world of the theater. They mentioned his wife, Elisabeth Petit Worth, and a stepson. It was hard to imagine Worth as a husband and father of any sort.

Maude popped out of her seat when we heard the door knocker. "I'll get it!" For once, Mama didn't mind that, either. She was busily drawing up some sort of list and didn't take notice of Maude rushing to the door. It was as if someone had tipped a dose of nonchalance into her morning brew.

I heard low voices in the foyer, but Maude returned alone.

"For you, madame," she said, handing me a slim envelope with a bow.

The missive was brief and baffling.

Georgie—

Please meet me at 34 Union Square

at 4 o'clock sharp. The butler will have
your name. I will explain all then.

Yours truly,
Harry Pendergast

Mama looked up from her list-making with mild expectancy, and Maude fished for details. "A little boy brought it 'round. Must be a go-between for you and your paramour." She tittered at her own weak joke.

"What is it, Georgie?" Mama asked. "Not more bad news, I hope. I don't think I could take it."

"It's from the prompter at the Prince," I explained. "It doesn't say why, but I'm to meet him this afternoon in Union Square." I scanned the note again, but a second reading didn't make anything clearer. "Maybe it's about our pay."

My mother crossed a few items off her list before setting it aside. "Let's hope the receipts from the final performances didn't burn, too."

That possibility hadn't occurred to me until she raised it, and my jaw tightened. I thought Harry removed the cash at night, but what if I was wrong about that and Worth did it? Our final pay would be up in smoke, too.

"We'll have to do some belt-tightening again," Mama continued, her fingers brushing the list. "It will be a lean Christmas, for sure, but we've done it before and we'll do it again. I've been putting aside a bit of your pay every week, Georgie, and your uncle's been investing it for us."

Mama's financial judgment made me relax. In a different world, where women were men's equals, she could have been a banker and investor like her brother.

"I've sent word to James and Lily. Hopefully, they haven't left London for Paris yet, and we'll hear from them soon."

"You asked them to come home?" The idea of Lily and my uncle cutting their wedding trip short was upsetting. As comforting as their steady presence would be, I didn't want them to associate me and my career with trouble.

"I simply told them what's what," Mama replied. "They'll draw their own conclusions." She pressed her lips together as if convincing herself of her next words. "I'm sure we'll be fine."

Because Harry hadn't divulged what our meeting was about, I wasn't sure how to dress for it. Would one of my regular day dresses do, or should I wear a Sunday frock? Everything I picked out seemed wrong and ended up in a messy pile on the floor of my bedroom. I'd ambled about in public in men's clothing, and returning to confining women's frocks was unappealing.

I settled on a tailored wool vest and skirt that Mama found plain but that was as close to the suit Miss Cushman had worn to the matinee as my current wardrobe got. Better yet, the skirt didn't require a hoop. When I got another paying position, the first thing I would do was invest in new, more daring clothes and give the frocks I owned to someone less fortunate.

Union Square was a fashionable address, and my destination sat directly across from the park. Of late, fine families had been moving further and further north, as far from Manhattan's growing immigrant population as they could get.

The butler who answered the door at Number 34 knew my name without checking a list. He took my cape and ushered me into a drawing room off the foyer, where to my surprise an assortment of people from the Prince had already convened. Harry stood at the center of the room, while Julius, Ned, Mrs. Reynolds, Mary Louise Burton, and a few other company members occupied all the chairs.

"Ah, Georgie, good! We're all here then."

One chair remained, but because it held a place of honor at the head of the room and looked more like a throne than something I should actually sit in, I stood. Harry coughed and motioned to Julius, who rose and offered me his place until the butler produced another chair.

Who owned this house? Given its opulence, my best guess was Mrs. Reynolds, whose husband came from money, but I ruled that out quickly because she was still wearing her bonnet as if she'd come off the street like I had.

The answer to my question arrived soon enough in the person of a distinguished woman who swept into the room in a mulberry-colored gown that reflected light like a crystal glass of claret. Her ring finger sported a large garnet that complemented her frock, and matching earrings dropped from her lobes. I remembered seeing her backstage with Worth on several occasions; her elegance had made her noteworthy. When Harry addressed her as Bess, I realized I was in the presence of Mrs. Thomas Worth.

"Thank you all for coming," she said.

Bess Worth was far from an ingenue. The strands of gray at her temples suggested she was closer to Mama in age than she had been to her husband. I was surprised she was neither wearing mourning nor visibly shaken by Worth's death.

"I apologize for the short notice about our meeting. I wanted to catch you before you found other employment, which Harry deemed likely to happen soon. I know most of you, and you represent the cream of the crop Tom assembled for his company."

"A shrewd devil, that Tom," Harry said.

Bess looked almost amused. "That he was. In more ways than one." She paused. "His shrewdness cost him his life."

At that, Mrs. Reynolds and Mary Louise started to sniffle, and company members bowed their heads soberly.

"Now, now, no tears for Tom," Bess said. "Let that be our motto. It has a ring to it that he would have liked. Cavendish, would you pour everyone a dram?" She shot a wary look in my direction. "Except for Miss Cartwright here on my left. A spot of apple juice for her, I think."

I glanced over at Ned, who pulled a funny face at me and stuck out his tongue like a kid.

When everyone had refreshments, Bess raised her glass in a toast. "To Tom," she said. "He went out as he would have wanted. May he be at Heaven's gate instead of you-know-where."

Glasses lifted at the odd tribute. "To Tom!"

"And to Bess," Harry cut in. "To the success of her new venture."

"To Bess!"

Instead of taking genteel sips, Bess knocked back her whiskey like a man, then turned to the prompter. "Harry, why don't you begin?"

Harry cleared his throat as if preparing to deliver a monologue. "My pleasure. For those of you who don't know yet, Mrs. Worth intends to rebuild the Prince under her own management."

My heart quickened. The Prince would return! And since I was sitting in Bess's drawing room, she intended for me to return with it.

"However, that will take considerable time."

"Especially because I can't build in the same place," Bess added. "That's too much bad luck for me. I have a scout looking for a suitable location to build from scratch. Someplace further uptown, closer to here."

I sighed. Rebuilding in a new spot might take a year or more. What would I do in the interim? No company would hire me knowing I intended to bolt once the Prince was on its feet again. Even if I kept that bit of information to myself, Bess and Harry would likely announce the plans to the papers. My mind ran through different possibilities. Maybe Clem's millinery shop would hire me as a clerk. Maybe Mrs. Stansbury would take me on as an assistant—

"Now I don't expect you to stay around that long without steady employment," Bess continued, as if reading my mind. "Most of you are in no position to do that. I'm forming a traveling company in the interim called Bess Petit's Variety. We'll tour March through August, and we'll begin rehearsals and preparations next month. I'm hoping that some or all of you will sign on to the tour. Harry and I will begin setting up the bookings soon, to commence in Wilmington and Charleston, and move on to Savannah and New Orleans."

Charleston! I seemed destined to go there, even without Pa's help.

My head spun as company members pitched questions at Bess, and she detailed her ideas for the tour. The Variety would feature a patchwork of scenes from Shakespeare and melodramas mixed with singing, dancing, farce, and dramatic monologues—much like the holiday matinee we'd just done. As she spoke about it with such assurance, I wondered if Bess had been the catalyst for that matinee, not her husband.

"But no explosives," she said firmly. "That was Tom's idea, and he went too far. Harry will oversee the spectacles."

"We can do them safely. We won't squander your money again, Bess."

So, Bess had been behind the Prince financially, too. I knew Uncle James and others were investors, but it sounded as if her own money had been foundational.

The butler passed out sealed envelopes, which we were instructed to open on our own and respond to by week's end. "You'll find your last week's pay and my offer for the new venture," Bess said. "No negotiation. Take it or leave it."

I'd never met a woman so forceful or forthright. Was this how Miss Cushman had navigated her career to great success? Had Mrs. Stansbury been like this when she was young? I could learn so much from Bess Petit that, no matter how little she offered me, I wanted nothing more than to accept it. Mama would have to stretch her budgetary skills and make my salary work.

I'd not spoken a word during the meeting, and suddenly it drew to a close before I'd finished my juice and the butler appeared to collect the glasses. I tossed back the final sip as Bess had done.

As the others were filing from the drawing room, all smiles and happy chatter, Ned hung back to walk me out. Bess raised her chin to me and said, "Miss Cartwright, a word? Alone." Ned muttered that he'd wait for me on the street.

"I'm quite an admirer of yours," Bess said when we were on our own. "Your Mercutio was stunning. I've seen your range, such as Tom allowed you. My husband wasn't putting your talents to good enough use." She sniffed, with what looked like scorn rather than sadness. "I knew your father fairly well a long time ago."

"He—" I almost blurted out that Pa himself was in Charleston, but I caught my words in time. "He taught me a lot."

"I hope you'll accept my offer. I'll see to it you primarily play breeches roles, and leading ones. They really are your forte."

My cheeks warmed at her praise. "I'm so grateful to you, ma'am."

"My husband was a difficult man. I hope you won't hold that against me." She sighed, suggesting she knew about his misconduct. "Things will run differently now."

"That would be wonderful." I realized it sounded as if I'd already accepted the offer, but I didn't care.

"If you have questions, bring them directly to me. Harry's my right hand, but he's not in charge."

A million questions had been shooting through my head, but foremost I needed to know about the people who weren't in the room with us.

"I did wonder, ma'am, and I don't mean to be impudent, but the people who aren't here—"

"—are not getting offers," she finished for me. "There will be certain exceptions, like the stagehands and dressers. I hope they'll come on board."

"Sallie Meeks is first-rate," I said.

"Maybe you'd like her as your private dresser?"

"Golly, yes."

"I'll think on it." Bess eyed me curiously. "Tell me. You don't have a sweetheart or fiancé in the city, do you? Someone you have to consider staying for?"

The question reminded me of her husband, who'd asked if I had a beau when he first hired me. My thoughts turned to Clem, and I hesitated. How to say what we were? If she were a man, she'd be my sweetheart, my intended, my love. What two girls together might call themselves was still something without a word.

246

"No *actual* sweetheart, ma'am."

If she wondered what an "actual sweetheart" was, she didn't ask. "Much better that way. Why, you're the next Charlotte Cushman! And she would be the first to tell you that men will only hold you back. Don't forget that. If you marry, do it later, when you've made your name."

"Yes, ma'am," I said.

"Excellent. We've an understanding." Bess's gaze was piercing, her eyes a shade of deep violet that, like her jewelry, complemented her dress.

But what *about* Clem? I couldn't imagine being gone from her from March through August. The idea made my chest ache, so I ventured one final question.

"Mrs. Worth, you know Miss Clementine Scarborough is . . . was one of the Prince's most successful dramatists. There were no dramatists here today, and I was wondering: will you be hiring any to write some of the scenes we perform?"

"I've not decided what we'll perform." She paused with a curious look. "What is Miss Scarborough to you?"

The question startled me. "We—well, I'd say we're . . . the very best of friends."

Bess must have read something on my face, or maybe it was my stammering, because she put a hand on my arm and said, "You go along now. I have a lot to think about, and so do you."

Ned was waiting for me out on the street. The day had been bright and sunny, all traces of the evening's snow melted, so we crossed to the park and stood in front of the fountain at its center.

"I had no idea Worth was married until yesterday," I blurted out.

"Oh, Georgie," Ned said. "How could you not? Simply *everyone* knew Bess."

"I'd never even heard of her," I admitted. "And she is quite a woman."

"Bess Petit is a force in theater, going back a ways. She's owned several in other cities and managed one in Philadelphia. What she ever saw in Worth is beyond me. He must have been damned good between the sheets."

I blushed at the thought of Worth and Bess in bed. I rushed to change the subject when I spotted the envelope clutched in his hand, already torn open.

"Is your offer good, bad, or middling?"

"Open yours, then we'll talk," he said.

Written in Harry's distinctive scrawl, my offer was more than I could have hoped for. I had to read it twice to make sure my eyes weren't deceiving me.

> *Georgiana Cartwright — Second Leading Lady — $40 weekly*

Five dollars more than my new salary at the Prince! Mama would be over the moon.

At the bottom was a postscript in a second, much neater hand:

> *Miss Cartwright, it is my dearest hope that you will accept this offer. Should you join the Variety, I will make you the star you deserve to be. —EPW*

My hand shot to my mouth, trying to control my smile.

"That good?" Ned said.

I dropped my hand self-consciously. "Pretty much the same as what I had at the Prince," I lied. "I was just shocked she matched it is all."

Ned's eyes welled up. "Well, *I've* been demoted," he said brushing away a tear that escaped down his cheek. "Walking gentleman once again."

"It must be a mistake. Let me see."

I reached for his offer, but Ned stuffed the envelope into an inner coat pocket. "Too embarrassing. She included a note that said I'd move up again 'in time.' But I'm convinced she'll want me to be the farce part of the Variety she mentioned.

Well, I won't play the Irish fool ever again. I've come too far."

"Oh, Ned."

"Don't feel sorry for me," he said, his chest puffing out. "I'll find something else. I'll work at Da's studio while I'm looking for a company that appreciates me. I won't be able to take my own rooms just yet and get Richard out of his board-inghouse, but he'll understand. It's not the end of the world."

I would have been crushed by a demotion, but I couldn't express that to Ned. "Of course, it isn't. You'll get on some-where soon."

We walked back toward Bond Street as dusk fell, saying very little. I'd gotten a wonderful offer, a chance to travel, but it wouldn't be the same without Ned to share it with back-stage and at Groff's. And if Sallie didn't accept Bess's offer *and* Clem stayed in New York, I'd be on my own with a bunch of grown-ups.

Chapter 31

The traveling company took shape over the next few weeks, with some members accepting Bess's offers and others mulling them over before saying yes or no. Clem was among those to take her time and consider what her other options were before agreeing to the one-month stint as a dramatist that Bess presented.

"I can't give up my job with Mrs. Tassie," Clem explained. "There's any number of girls to replace me, and because I can do it fast, it's decent pay."

Clem's dilemma brought me sleepless nights as I tossed about, trying to devise a way for her to say yes. My schemes took on an air of desperation—doing piecework for a milliner in Charleston, helping with the Variety's costumes, even being a dresser—and Clem discarded all of them. In fact, my insistence began to annoy her, so I backed off.

"Let me work on it myself," she said.

As a further disappointment, my hopes that Sallie would be coming with us were dashed. Harry announced that Mrs. Reynolds's longtime personal dresser would make the trip to assist Mary Louise and me. Mrs. Reynolds had declined Bess's offer, saying she didn't want to be so many months away from her husband and children.

At Harry's news, I groaned out loud. "Are you sure Sallie won't come? Does she know there's a raise in it?"

"Says she's not interested at any price." Harry eyed me as if wondering how much I knew about Sallie's activities. "She's got other things up her sleeve, Georgie. Don't go pouting. When you're a leading lady, you can hire any dresser you want."

Unwilling to accept Sallie's refusal without speaking to her, I coaxed Harry into telling me where she had relocated. Luckily, Sallie was not all the way out in Brooklyn with her family but worked at a grocery store just below Canal Street—an odd change of occupation for her, but I reasoned it must pay well or offer lodging, like the Prince.

By cab, I made my way to the venue, a narrow storefront on Lispenard Street with a painted sign announcing it as "Jos. Freeman Groceries." The interior was far less opulent than where Mama shopped, its shelves appearing to need a shipment of goods.

A cheery tinkle announced my entrance. As the only white person in the room, I was immediately out of place. A tall, slender man in an apron lifted his head from conversing with a female customer. The small child with her pointed at me and was reprimanded.

"May I help you, miss?" the man said to me. He towered over the main counter, which along with a basket of eggs and some loaves of bread held a neat stack of books and a magazine or two.

"Excuse me, are you Mr. Freeman?"

"I am."

"I'm looking for Miss Sallie Meeks. I heard she would be here." Mr. Freeman surveyed my face warily, so more explanation seemed warranted. "We were at the Prince Theatre together. Sallie was my dresser. I'm Georgiana Cartwright?" There was absolutely no reason for Mr. Freeman to know who I was, and indeed his face registered no recognition. "I'd love to speak to her if I could. Just for a minute or two."

He nodded but finished the woman's purchase before signaling for me to wait while he slipped into the back of the shop. As I lingered at the counter, I riffled through magazines with names like *Frederick Douglass' Paper* and *The Liberator.*

Other customers entered, and my presence startled them as it had the child, so I moved away from the counter and closer to the door. Sallie emerged from the back after what seemed like an eternity. She was wearing a different dress than I was used to seeing, a cheery blue muslin, and she had pulled her hair back in a tight bun instead of covering it in a wrap. I had thought she might have been happy to see me, but her face wore a strained look.

Without speaking, she motioned for me to move further out of earshot of Mr. Freeman.

"What you doing here, miss? I'm *working.*"

I stammered out an apology for disrupting her day and got quickly to the point of my visit. "Harry said you turned down the offer from Mrs. Worth. I thought maybe you didn't understand—"

"I understood just fine." She lowered her voice. "Y'all are heading south for six months, to Charleston and such."

"What I was going to say was, Mrs. Worth said you could be my personal dresser. That's a good promotion. I don't know what she offered you, but I'm sure it was more than the Prince. And it would be important work!"

Sallie set her lips into a straight line. "It's good pay," she admitted. "Hard to turn down. One thing's not so good." She cast a nervous glance toward the proprietor at the counter.

"Maybe I can intercede somehow?" I suggested.

Sallie crossed her arms across her chest. "*You're* the one don't understand," she said. "It ain't safe for me down South. It's barely safe for me here."

"But you said you were born in Brooklyn," I protested. "You're free."

Sallie wagged her head slowly, as if explaining to a willful child. "Don't have to tell me what free is, miss. Don't make too much difference these days. Slave catchers ain't asking for papers when they snatch folks up and drag them off."

My mouth fell open. I wanted to object, to say she must be mistaken, that this was New York City, but Sallie continued quickly, "My cousin disappeared. Nobody seen them again." Her eyes misted over at the thought.

Mr. Freeman coughed just then, and her attention pivoted briefly to him.

"Besides," she said, "this here's the important work. Those that's free got a responsibility to those that ain't."

A wave of shame rose in me. I hadn't taken into account how vulnerable Sallie was—not just for the dangerous work she was doing but simply for being Black. Even in a Northern city.

Reaching under my cape into the pocket of my dress, I felt for Pa's gold eagles. I forced them into Sallie's clenched hand. "Here, Sallie. For the cause."

"This is a lot of money."

"Mr. William was in the city briefly and left it for me to give you," I said—a blatant lie, but one that no one need be the wiser about.

Her ears perked up. "He ain't dead then."

"He's very much alive and doing well in Charleston. I'll see him when I'm there. If he wants to send more money, is this a good address?" I had no intention of seeing Pa—I had torn up his card and didn't even know how to reach him. But maybe I could scrape together some cash to send Sallie's way.

Sallie's lips turned up in a hesitant smile. "It sure is. You thank your pa for me. Mr. Joseph and the committee will be pleased."

Hearing his name, the shop owner called over, "Everything all right, Sal?"

"Everything's fine, sir." She tucked the offering into her own pocket and nodded once, firmly, as if sealing our relationship.

As Sallie turned and approached the counter, Falstaff the cat edged out from behind it. His body was sleeker than when he'd feasted on mice in the Prince's basement, but he looked none the worse for having lost his old home. Sallie scooped him up, whispered something into his fur, then disappeared into the back room.

Curtain Call

Spring, 1853

My family brought me to the dock to see me off.

Mama petted me like a puppy. "I don't like this one bit," she said with a groan. In fact, she liked the money I'd earn and the fact that Bess had taken a special interest in my career.

What my mother didn't like was the distance my new job put between us, the fact that her daughter would be unsupervised by her for six months. Even though I was leaving her with the daguerreotype of me that Ned's father took, she worried that I would change drastically by the next time she saw me and I was nineteen. "Promise me you'll look just like this when you return," she said, pressing the image against her breast.

My new employer pledged to Mama that she would look out for me. Even though Bess was from a distinguished Southern family, Mama was still skeptical of what kind of attention I'd get on a daily basis. "Best to steer clear of your father," she advised, one of the few times she ever mentioned him. "I expect no fewer than two letters a week, Georgie, or I'll be on the next boat to fetch you back!"

On the dock, Maude was all jittery excitement, but that was her normal state as she planned her wedding nonstop. They had pushed the ceremony back to September so I could serve as maid of honor. Several times an hour, it seemed, my sister stole glances at the gaudy ruby and diamond ring on her left hand whose shine and size made other ladies gasp. I much preferred my own ring, which Clem had given me for Christmas: a simple gold band with an etched floral design that a favorite great-aunt had bequeathed to her. It was a bit too large, so I wore it on my middle finger.

Aggie's work kept her at home on the day of my departure. To everyone's surprise, she had turned in her notice just a week earlier, because her beau had finally asked her to get "hitched," the new slang for marriage. Their dream, Aggie told Mama, was to open a bakery together. "But I don't know as I'm brave enough," she had confided to me. "I'm nothing like *you*, Miss Georgie."

"You traveled all the way from Ireland on your own," I pointed out. "I'd say you're plenty brave."

Uncle James and Aunt Lily came to see me off, too, but my new aunt's face had lost all traces of color. My uncle acted especially solicitous of his wife, his hand supporting the small of her back. He routinely bent toward her and whispered something.

Maude tittered behind her hand. "Want to bet she's expecting already?"

"Write and let me know," I instructed. "I wouldn't want to miss a new cousin."

The person whose appearance at the ship flabbergasted me was Ned. I rubbed my eyes to make sure I was seeing correctly. We'd said our farewells at Groff's earlier that week, when he confessed he couldn't bear to watch the company set sail without him. "Please forgive my absence," he said at the time. "I like to avoid humiliation."

Now here he was on the dock—and with Richard Pomeroy in tow. There was no mistaking the pair of them, even more handsome and well turned-out than my uncle. Mr. Pomeroy's cheek bore one jagged scar below the right eye, a remnant of the night of their attack, but it somehow rendered him more dashing. In their finely tailored suits, one as fair as the other was dark, the two young gentlemen turned ladies' heads—including my own sister's. I wanted to laugh at Maude and say her eyelash-fluttering was lost on them, but I didn't dare.

"You told me you weren't coming!" I reminded Ned.

"Ah, but I'm a good actor after all, aren't I?"

Richard stepped forward shyly to offer me a petite bouquet of pink carnations mixed with sprigs of rosemary. We burst out at the same time with Ophelia's famous line: "'There's rosemary, that's for remembrance.'"

"You know your Shakespeare!" I whispered. "The two of you make a good match."

"Ned coached me a bit," he said, coloring. His voice became choked with emotion. "Georgie, Ned and I will never forget how you saved us."

I was trying hard not to succumb to melancholy at leaving my friends behind, so I pivoted into teasing him. "Well, you are responsible for keeping Ned out of trouble while my saber and I are far away."

As the time to board the ship neared, members of Bess Petit's Variety continued to gather. I spotted Mary Louise, Julius, and several others saying good-bye to their loved ones. Bess Worth scuttled back and forth, giving directions to the actors and actresses, and Harry and one of the stagehands counted and recounted the trunks of costumes being loaded up the ship's ramp.

My eyes darted up and down for the one person who was absent and whom I wanted most to see in the world. Ned and Richard made small talk with me and I tried to listen, but my mind was really on only one thing.

And then she appeared, dressed in her traveling clothes, her glasses slipping down her nose as always, gripping the handle of a battered leather satchel that couldn't possibly hold enough clothes for a month. For Clem, money in her pocket didn't mean new clothes, hats, or slippers, but books, paper, and ink.

"It's a good thing we aren't both show horses," she had told me recently, "or this relationship would never last."

At the sight of her, my hand shot up into the air, and I called out in a loud voice that drew attention, "Clem! Clem! Over here!"

Mama was much more at ease about my tour once she knew Clem would be going, too. In addition to working part-time as dramatist, Clem had secured a second job, penning a series of articles for a women's magazine about the new theater company's lady manager. There was also a promise of more articles when she got back to New York, so she wouldn't have to depend on cutting linings for Mrs. Tassie. Though we would be together for only one delicious month, that was one month more than I had thought we'd have.

Clem's face exploded in smiles when she saw me. I'd arranged for us to share a cabin in the ship and then a room in Charleston. As she put it, "No one need be any the wiser about what goes on behind closed doors." The idea made my toes tingle in my boots.

But as we ascended the ramp to the deck, a pang of remorse hit me. Mama, Maude, and Lily were all crying about my departure. Even Ned's eyes were misty. I fingered something in my pocket for comfort. Clem must have noticed because she reached in to see what I was so intent on. When she withdrew our joined hands, her eyes fastened on Miss Cushman's ceramic head.

Uncle James had brought me an identical Romeo and Juliet figurine all the way from London to replace the one Maude had smashed, but I'd left his gift behind on the mantelpiece in my room. Instead, I carried the broken head with me like a talisman. The remnant of my relationship with Pa tamped down the bad memories and let the good ones resurface, the times he'd urged me on and told me I'd be famous someday, like him. Clem seemed to intuit the token's meaning because she slid my hand back into my pocket without comment, as if she'd interrupted a private moment.

Taking a final look at my family and friends to inscribe their faces in memory, I sniffed back a few tears of my own.

"You're not having second thoughts, George?" Clem said

with some alarm.

"Oh, no." I lifted my free hand to wave good-bye. "Not a chance."

Acknowledgments

For a long time, I've been fascinated by the idea that women and men could live as lesbian and gay when there was no sexual identity as we now understand it. The spark of this novel came from a question: For women who lived as lesbians before the identity existed—such as American actress Charlotte Cushman (1816-1876)—what were their lives like when they were young? When I read that Cushman had young female fans, some of them aspiring actresses, the character Georgie Cartwright was born.

Writing *Dear Miss Cushman* was a joyful experience, primarily because I received a 2019-20 Creative Renewal Fellowship from the Arts and Science Council of Charlotte-Mecklenburg County to write it. The honor was a highlight of my career. By giving me time to try something completely different, the fellowship allowed me to rediscover the happiness I experienced as a child-writer, tapping out stories on my Tom Thumb typewriter.

Huge hugs to my writer-buddies who critiqued the manuscript in various stages of development—Selene dePackh, Rachel Stein, and Lucy Turner (and Lucy's son, Cecil, for his appreciation). And, as always, deep gratitude and love to my smart, generous wife, Katie Hogan, who found time when she wasn't writing herself to comment on the manuscript multiple times.

An enormous amount of research goes into creating historical fiction, especially when a novel is set in a time so unlike our own. Thanks to Tony Rivenbark, executive director of Thalian Hall Center for the Performing Arts in Wilmington, N.C., who took me and my wife on a behind-the-scenes tour of his historic mid-19th-century theater and helped me visualize Georgie Cartwright's experience. Among the historic objects in its collection, Thalian Hall still owns an original painted curtain (or "drop") and a thunder roll, a special effects device that appears in my novel.

I couldn't possibly name every digital and printed source I found valuable, but here are highlights for anyone who would like to read more in any of these areas.

Nineteenth-century New York: Although I lived in New York City for twenty-two years, I would have been lost (literally) without the 1852 "Map of the City of New-York Extending North to Fiftieth Street," available online from the Library of Congress. Also in the LOC's collection, I relied on digitized newspapers from Georgie's era, including the *New York Herald* and *The Sun,* to give me the flavor of 1850s Manhattan. Among secondary sources: the Pulitzer Prize-winning *Gotham: A History of New York City to 1898* by Edwin G. Burrows and Mike Wallace; *Urban Appetites: Food & Culture in Nineteenth-Century New York,* by Cindy R. Lobel; and *The New Metropolis: New York City, 1840-1857,* by Edward K. Spann.

Nineteenth-century theater: On the website of the Billy Rose Theater Division of the New York Public Library, I found the "penny plains" that Georgie collected. *Annals of the New York Stage,* Vol. VI (1850-1857) by George C.D. Odell listed every theater production and cast during that time period; and *Leaves from an Actor's Note-Book* (1860) by George Vandenhoff provided a glimpse into the backstage and onstage world of 19th-century theater people. At Open Source Shakespeare, I was able to hunt for such technicalities as how many lines were spoken by each character in each play. Lehigh University's digitized archive, "The Vault at Pfaff's," chronicles the world of artists in antebellum New York; I based the beer cellar in my novel on Pfaff's. Articles and books: "Bowery B'hoys and Matinee Ladies: The Re-Gendering of Nineteenth-Century Theater Audiences," by Richard Butsch; *Women in the American Theater,* by Faye E. Dudden; "Walking Ladies: Mid-Nineteenth-Century American Actresses' Work, Family and Culture," a dissertation by Nan Mullenneaux; and *Wearing the Breeches: Gender on the Antebellum Stage,* by Elizabeth Reitz Mullenix.

Charlotte Cushman: *When Romeo Was a Woman: Charlotte Cushman and Her Circle of Female Spectators*, by Lisa Merrill; "Hitting Her Mark: Charlotte Cushman Takes the Stage," a master's thesis by Karen Shields; *Charlotte Cushman: Her Letters and Memories of Her Life,* by Emma Stebbins; and *Lady Romeo: The Radical and Revolutionary Life of Charlotte Cushman, America's First Celebrity*, by Tana Wojczuk. The poem that Clem writes for Georgie to send to Cushman is based on one by Gilbert Abbott á Beckett, published in 1846 and quoted in Merrill.

Blacks in New York City and the Underground Railroad: *Passages to Freedom: The Underground Railroad in History and Memory,* edited by David Blight; *A Respectable Woman: The Public Roles of African American Women in 19th-Century New York,* by Jane Dabel; *Gateway to Freedom: The Hidden History of the Underground Railroad,* by Eric Foner; *Streetcar to Justice: How Elizabeth Jennings Won the Right to Ride in New York,* by Amy Hill Hearth; and *Black Gotham: A Family History of African Americans in Nineteenth-Century New York,* by Carla L. Peterson.

Miscellaneous: *The Dictionary of Americanisms: A Glossary of Words and Phrases, Usually Regarded as Peculiar to the United States* (1848), by John Russell Bartlett; "Women and Restaurants in the Nineteenth-Century United States," by Paul Freedman; *The Hand-Book of Millinery* (1847), by Mary J. Howell; and *The Daguerreotype in America,* by Beaumont Newhall.

Last but never least, many thanks to the team at Bywater

Books, including Salem West, for the long hours she dedicates to publishing lesbian literature; Ann McMan, for another stunning cover design; Fay Jacobs, for content edits that helped me add the finishing flourishes; and Marianne K. Martin, Stefani Deoul, Cathy Pegau, Elizabeth Andersen, and Nancy Squires, for the vital roles they play in keeping the company running smoothly.

About the Author

Paula Martinac is the author of a book of short stories and seven novels, most recently *Testimony* (Bywater, 2021). Her debut novel, *Out of Time,* won the Lambda Literary Award for Lesbian Fiction (Seal Press, 1990; e-book Bywater, 2012). Her novel-in-stories, *The Ada Decades* (Bywater, 2017), was short-listed for the 2017 Ferro-Grumley Award for LGBTQ Fiction, the Foreword Indie Award for LGBT Fiction, and the Goldie Award for Historical Fiction; and her novel *Clio Rising* (Bywater, 2019) received the Gold Medal for Best Regional Fiction from the 2020 Independent Book Publishers Awards. She has also published three nonfiction books on LGBTQ themes. She is a lecturer in the creative writing program at UNC Charlotte.

Sign up for the mailing list on Paula's website and be the first to hear about upcoming releases, events, offers, and more: www.paulamartinac.com.

At Bywater, we love good books by and about women, just like you do. And we're committed to bringing the best of contemporary literature to an expanding community of readers. Our editorial team is dedicated to finding and developing outstanding writers who create books you won't want to put down.

For more information about Bywater Books, our authors, and our titles, please visit our website.

www.bywaterbooks.com